Dover Thrift Study Edition

Hamlet

WILLIAM SHAKESPEARE

DOVER PUBLICATIONS, INC.
Mineola, New York

Bibliographical Note

This Dover edition, first published in 2009, contains the unabridged text of *Hamlet,* as published in Volume VII of the second edition of *The Works of William Shakespeare,* Macmillan and Co., London, 1892, plus literary analysis and perspec-tives from *MAXnotes® for Hamlet,* published in 2000 by Research & Education Association, Inc., Piscataway, New Jersey. The explanatory footnotes to the play were prepared specially for the present edition.

Library of Congress Cataloging-in-Publication Data

Shakespeare, William, 1564–1616.
    Hamlet / William Shakespeare.
        p. cm. — (Dover thrift study edition)
    ISBN-13: 978-0-486-47572-1 (alk. paper)
    ISBN-10: 0-486-47572-7 (alk. paper)
    1. Hamlet (Legendary character)—Drama. 2. Kings and rulers—Succes-sion—Drama. 3. Regicides—Drama. 4. Revenge—Drama. 5. Princes—Drama. 6. Denmark—Drama. 7. Shakespeare, William, 1564–1616. Hamlet. I. Title.

PR2807.A2D685 2009
822.3'3—dc22

                                                      2009026172

Manufactured in the United States by Courier Corporation
47572702
www.doverpublications.com

Publisher's Note

Combining the complete text of a classic novel or drama with a comprehensive study guide, Dover Thrift Study Editions are the most effective way to gain a thorough understanding of the major works of world literature.

The study guide features up-to-date and expert analysis of every chapter or section from the source work. Questions and fully explained answers follow, allowing readers to analyze the material critically. Character lists, author bios, and discussions of the work's historical context are also provided.

Each Dover Thrift Study Edition includes everything a student needs to prepare for homework, discussions, reports, and exams.

Contents

Hamlet

WILLIAM SHAKESPEARE

Contents

Dramatis Personae

CLAUDIUS, King of Denmark.
HAMLET, son to the late, and nephew to the present king.
POLONIUS, Lord Chamberlain.
HORATIO, friend to Hamlet.
LAERTES, son to Polonius.
VOLTIMAND,
CORNELIUS,
ROSENCRANTZ,
GUILDENSTERN, } courtiers.
OSRIC,
A Gentleman,
A Priest.
MARCELLUS, } officers.
BERNARDO,
FRANCISCO, a soldier.
REYNALDO, servant to Polonius.
Players.
Two Clowns, grave-diggers.
FORTINBRAS, Prince of Norway.
A Captain.
English Ambassadors.

GERTRUDE, Queen of Denmark, and mother to Hamlet.
OPHELIA, daughter to Polonius.

Lords, Ladies, Officers, Soldiers, Sailors, Messengers,
and other Attendants.

Ghost of Hamlet's Father.

SCENE: *Denmark.*

ACT I.

SCENE I. *Elsinore. A platform before the castle.*

FRANCISCO *at his post. Enter to him* BERNARDO.

BER.	Who's there?
FRAN.	Nay, answer me. Stand and unfold yourself.
BER.	Long live the King!
FRAN.	Bernardo?
BER.	He.
FRAN.	You come most carefully upon your hour.
BER.	'Tis now struck twelve. Get thee to bed, Francisco.
FRAN.	For this relief much thanks. 'Tis bitter cold,
	And I am sick at heart.
BER.	Have you had quiet guard?
FRAN.	Not a mouse stirring.
BER.	Well, good night.
	If you do meet Horatio and Marcellus,
	The rivals[1] of my watch, bid them make haste.
FRAN.	I think I hear them. Stand, ho! Who is there?

Enter HORATIO *and* MARCELLUS.

HOR.	Friends to this ground.
MAR.	And liegemen to the Dane.
FRAN.	Give you good night.
MAR.	O, farewell, honest soldier.
	Who hath relieved you?
FRAN.	Bernardo hath my place.
	Give you good night. [*Exit.*
MAR.	Holla, Bernardo!
BER.	Say,

---

[1] *rivals*] partners.

1

	What, is Horatio there?
Hor.	A piece of him.
Ber.	Welcome, Horatio. Welcome, good Marcellus.
Mar.	What, has this thing appear'd again tonight?
Ber.	I have seen nothing.
Mar.	Horatio says 'tis but our fantasy,
	And will not let belief take hold of him
	Touching this dreaded sight, twice seen of us.
	Therefore I have entreated him along
	With us to watch the minutes of this night,
	That if again this apparition come
	He may approve our eyes[2] and speak to it.
Hor.	Tush, tush, 'twill not appear.
Ber.	Sit down awhile,
	And let us once again assail your ears,
	That are so fortified against our story,
	What we have two nights seen.
Hor.	Well, sit we down,
	And let us hear Bernardo speak of this.
Ber.	Last night of all,
	When yond same star that's westward from the pole[3]
	Had made his course to illume that part of heaven
	Where now it burns, Marcellus and myself,
	The bell then beating one—

Enter Ghost.

Mar.	Peace, break thee off. Look where it comes again.
Ber.	In the same figure like the King that's dead.
Mar.	Thou art a scholar; speak to it, Horatio.
Ber.	Looks it not like the King? Mark it, Horatio.
Hor.	Most like. It harrows me with fear and wonder.
Ber.	It would be spoke to.
Mar.	Question it, Horatio.
Hor.	What art thou that usurp'st this time of night,
	Together with that fair and warlike form
	In which the majesty of buried Denmark
	Did sometimes[4] march? By heaven I charge thee, speak!
Mar.	It is offended.
Ber.	See, it stalks away.

[2] *approve our eyes*] confirm what we have seen.
[3] *pole*] polestar.
[4] *sometimes*] formerly.

HOR.	Stay! speak, speak! I charge thee, speak! [*Exit* GHOST.
MAR.	'Tis gone, and will not answer.
BER.	How now, Horatio? You tremble and look pale.
	Is not this something more than fantasy?
	What think you on't?
HOR.	Before my God, I might not this believe
	Without the sensible and true avouch
	Of mine own eyes.
MAR.	Is it not like the King?
HOR.	As thou art to thyself.
	Such was the very armour he had on
	When he the ambitious Norway combated;
	So frown'd he once, when, in an angry parle,[5]
	He smote the sledded Polacks on the ice.
	'Tis strange.
MAR.	Thus twice before, and jump[6] at this dead hour,
	With martial stalk hath he gone by our watch.
HOR.	In what particular thought to work I know not;
	But, in the gross and scope[7] of my opinion,
	This bodes some strange eruption to our state.
MAR.	Good now, sit down, and tell me, he that knows,
	Why this same strict and most observant watch
	So nightly toils the subject of the land,[8]
	And why such daily cast[9] of brazen cannon,
	And foreign mart[10] for implements of war,
	Why such impress[11] of shipwrights, whose sore task
	Does not divide the Sunday from the week.
	What might be toward, that this sweaty haste
	Doth make the night joint-labourer with the day,
	Who is't that can inform me?
HOR.	That can I—
	At least the whisper goes so. Our last King,
	Whose image even but now appear'd to us,
	Was, as you know, by Fortinbras of Norway,
	Thereto prick'd on by a most emulate[12] pride,

---

[5] *parle*] parley, exchange.

[6] *jump*] exactly.

[7] *gross and scope*] general drift.

[8] *toils . . . land*] causes the people of this land to toil.

[9] *cast*] casting.

[10] *mart*] trading.

[11] *impress*] conscription.

[12] *emulate*] jealous, ambitious.

Dared to the combat; in which our valiant Hamlet—
For so this side of our known world esteem'd him—
Did slay this Fortinbras; who by a seal'd compact,
Well ratified by law and heraldry,
Did forfeit, with his life, all those his lands
Which he stood seized[13] of, to the conqueror;
Against the which, a moiety competent[14]
Was gaged by our King; which had return'd
To the inheritance of Fortinbras,
Had he been vanquisher; as, by the same covenant
And carriage of the article design'd,[15]
His fell to Hamlet. Now, sir, young Fortinbras,
Of unimproved[16] metal hot and full,
Hath in the skirts of Norway here and there
Shark'd up[17] a list of lawless resolutes,[18]
For food and diet to some enterprise
That hath a stomach in't; which is no other—
As it doth well appear unto our state—
But to recover of us, by strong hand
And terms compulsatory, those foresaid lands
So by his father lost. And this, I take it,
Is the main motive of our preparations,
The source of this our watch and the chief head
Of this post-haste and romage[19] in the land.

BER.   I think it be no other but e'en so.
Well may it sort[20] that this portentous figure
Comes armed through our watch, so like the King
That was and is the question of these wars.

HOR.   A mote it is to trouble the mind's eye.
In the most high and palmy[21] state of Rome,
A little ere the mightiest Julius fell,
The graves stood tenantless, and the sheeted dead
Did squeak and gibber in the Roman streets;
As stars with trains of fire and dews of blood,

---

[13] *seized*] possessed.
[14] *moiety competent*] sufficient portion.
[15] *carriage . . . design'd*] import of the aforementioned article.
[16] *unimproved*] unemployed, latent.
[17] *Shark'd up*] recruited haphazardly and illegally.
[18] *resolutes*] desperadoes.
[19] *romage*] bustle, activity.
[20] *sort*] be fitting.
[21] *palmy*] glorious.

Disasters[22] in the sun; and the moist star,[23]
Upon whose influence Neptune's empire stands,
Was sick almost to doomsday with eclipse.
And even the like precurse[24] of feared events,
As harbingers preceding still[25] the fates
And prologue to the omen coming on,
Have heaven and earth together demonstrated
Unto our climatures and countrymen.

Enter GHOST.

But soft, behold! Lo, where it comes again.
I'll cross[26] it, though it blast me. Stay, illusion.
If thou hast any sound or use of voice,
Speak to me;
If there be any good thing to be done,
That may to thee do ease and grace to me,
Speak to me;
If thou art privy to thy country's fate,
Which, happily,[27] foreknowing may avoid,
O, speak!
Or if thou hast uphoarded in thy life
Extorted treasure in the womb of earth,
For which, they say, you spirits oft walk in death,
Speak of it; stay and speak. [*The cock crows.*] Stop it, Marcellus.

MAR. Shall I strike at it with my partisan?[28]
HOR. Do, if it will not stand.
BER.   'Tis here.
HOR.   'Tis here.
MAR. 'Tis gone.   [*Exit* GHOST.
We do it wrong, being so majestical,
To offer it the show of violence;
For it is, as the air, invulnerable,
And our vain blows malicious mockery.[29]
BER. It was about to speak, when the cock crew.

---

[22] *Disasters*] ominous signs.
[23] *the moist star*] the moon.
[24] *precurse*] forerunning.
[25] *still*] always.
[26] *cross*] confront.
[27] *happily*] haply, by chance.
[28] *partisan*] long-handled spear.
[29] *malicious mockery*] a mere semblance of malice.

HOR.   And then it started like a guilty thing
Upon a fearful summons. I have heard,
The cock, that is the trumpet to the morn,
Doth with his lofty and shrill-sounding throat
Awake the god of day, and at his warning,
Whether in sea or fire, in earth or air,
The extravagant and erring[30] spirit hies
To his confine;[31] and of the truth herein
This present object made probation.[32]

MAR.   It faded on the crowing of the cock.
Some say that ever 'gainst[33] that season comes
Wherein our Saviour's birth is celebrated,
The bird of dawning singeth all night long;
And then, they say, no spirit dare stir abroad,
The nights are wholesome, then no planets strike,[34]
No fairy takes[35] nor witch hath power to charm,
So hallow'd and so gracious[36] is the time.

HOR.   So have I heard and do in part believe it.
But look, the morn, in russet mantle clad,
Walks o'er the dew of yon high eastward hill.
Break we our watch up; and by my advice,
Let us impart what we have seen tonight
Unto young Hamlet; for, upon my life,
This spirit, dumb to us, will speak to him.
Do you consent we shall acquaint him with it,
As needful in our loves, fitting our duty?

MAR.   Let's do't, I pray; and I this morning know
Where we shall find him most conveniently.   *[Exeunt.*

---

[30] *extravagant and erring*] wandering.
[31] *confine*] appointed territory.
[32] *probation*] proof.
[33] *'gainst*] just before.
[34] *strike*] blast, destroy.
[35] *takes*] charms.
[36] *gracious*] blessed.

SCENE II. *A room of state in the castle.*

Flourish. Enter the KING, QUEEN, HAMLET, POLONIUS, LAERTES,
VOLTIMAND, CORNELIUS, Lords, *and* Attendants.

KING.   Though yet of Hamlet our dear brother's death
        The memory be green, and that it us befitted
        To bear our hearts in grief and our whole kingdom
        To be contracted in one brow of woe,
        Yet so far hath discretion fought with nature
        That we with wisest sorrow think on him
        Together with remembrance of ourselves.
        Therefore our sometime sister, now our queen,
        The imperial jointress[1] to this warlike state,
        Have we, as 'twere with a defeated joy,
        With an auspicious and a dropping eye,
        With mirth in funeral and with dirge in marriage,
        In equal scale weighing delight and dole,
        Taken to wife. Nor have we herein barr'd
        Your better wisdoms, which have freely gone
        With this affair along. For all, our thanks.
        Now follows, that you know, young Fortinbras,
        Holding a weak supposal[2] of our worth,
        Or thinking by our late dear brother's death
        Our state to be disjoint and out of frame,
        Colleagued with this dream of his advantage,
        He hath not fail'd to pester us with message,
        Importing the surrender of those lands
        Lost by his father, with all bonds of law,
        To our most valiant brother. So much for him.
        Now for ourself, and for this time of meeting,
        Thus much the business is: we have here writ
        To Norway, uncle of young Fortinbras—
        Who, impotent and bed-rid, scarcely hears
        Of this his nephew's purpose—to suppress

---

[1] *jointress*] dowager.
[2] *weak supposal*] low opinion.

His further gait[3] herein, in that the levies,
The lists and full proportions, are all made
Out of his subject;[4] and we here dispatch
You, good Cornelius, and you, Voltimand,
For bearers of this greeting to old Norway,
Giving to you no further personal power
To business with the King more than the scope
Of these dilated[5] articles allow.
Farewell, and let your haste commend your duty.

COR. ⎫
VOL. ⎭   In that and all things will we show our duty.

KING.   We doubt it nothing. Heartily farewell.

                    [*Exeunt* VOLTIMAND *and* CORNELIUS.
And now, Laertes, what's the news with you?
You told us of some suit; what is't, Laertes?
You cannot speak of reason to the Dane,[6]
And lose your voice.[7] What wouldst thou beg, Laertes,
That shall not be my offer, not thy asking?
The head is not more native to the heart,
The hand more instrumental to the mouth,
Than is the throne of Denmark to thy father.
What wouldst thou have, Laertes?

LAER.   My dread lord,
Your leave and favour to return to France,
From whence though willingly I came to Denmark,
To show my duty in your coronation,
Yet now, I must confess, that duty done,
My thoughts and wishes bend again toward France
And bow them to your gracious leave and pardon.

KING.   Have you your father's leave? What says Polonius?

POL.   He hath, my lord, wrung from me my slow leave
By laboursome petition, and at last
Upon his will I seal'd my hard[8] consent.
I do beseech you, give him leave to go.

KING.   Take thy fair hour, Laertes; time be thine,
And thy best graces spend it at thy will.

---

[3] *gait*] proceeding.
[4] *Out of his subject*] at the expense of his people.
[5] *dilated*] detailed, copious.
[6] *the Dane*] the King of Denmark.
[7] *lose your voice*] speak in vain.
[8] *hard*] reluctant.

	But now, my cousin[9] Hamlet, and my son—
HAM.	[Aside] A little more than kin, and less than kind.
KING.	How is it that the clouds still hang on you?
HAM.	Not so, my lord; I am too much i' the sun.
QUEEN.	Good Hamlet, cast thy nighted colour off,
	And let thine eye look like a friend on Denmark.
	Do not for ever with thy vailed[10] lids
	Seek for thy noble father in the dust.
	Thou know'st 'tis common: all that lives must die,
	Passing through nature to eternity.
HAM.	Ay, madam, it is common.
QUEEN.	If it be,
	Why seems it so particular with thee?
HAM.	Seems, madam? Nay, it is. I know not 'seems.'
	'Tis not alone my inky cloak, good mother,
	Nor customary suits of solemn black,
	Nor windy suspiration of forced breath,
	No, nor the fruitful river in the eye,
	Nor the dejected haviour of the visage,
	Together with all forms, moods, shapes of grief,
	That can denote me truly. These indeed seem,
	For they are actions that a man might play;
	But I have that within which passeth show,
	These but the trappings and the suits of woe.
KING.	'Tis sweet and commendable in your nature, Hamlet,
	To give these mourning duties to your father;
	But, you must know, your father lost a father,
	That father lost, lost his, and the survivor bound
	In filial obligation for some term
	To do obsequious sorrow.[11] But to persever
	In obstinate condolement is a course
	Of impious stubbornness; 'tis unmanly grief;
	It shows a will most incorrect[12] to heaven,
	A heart unfortified, a mind impatient,
	An understanding simple and unschool'd;
	For what we know must be and is as common
	As any the most vulgar[13] thing to sense,

---

[9] *cousin*] close relation.
[10] *vailed*] lowered.
[11] *obsequious sorrow*] i.e., mourning appropriate for obsequies.
[12] *incorrect*] recalcitrant.
[13] *vulgar*] ordinary, commonplace.

Why should we in our peevish opposition
Take it to heart? Fie! 'tis a fault to heaven,
A fault against the dead, a fault to nature,
To reason most absurd, whose common theme
Is death of fathers, and who still[14] hath cried,
From the first corse till he that died today,
'This must be so.' We pray you, throw to earth
This unprevailing[15] woe, and think of us
As of a father; for let the world take note,
You are the most immediate[16] to our throne,
And with no less nobility of love
Than that which dearest father bears his son
Do I impart toward you. For your intent
In going back to school in Wittenberg,
It is most retrograde[17] to our desire,
And we beseech you, bend you to remain
Here in the cheer and comfort of our eye,
Our chiefest courtier, cousin and our son.

QUEEN. Let not thy mother lose her prayers, Hamlet.
      I pray thee, stay with us; go not to Wittenberg.
HAM.   I shall in all my best obey you, madam.
KING.   Why, 'tis a loving and a fair reply.
      Be as ourself in Denmark. Madam, come;
      This gentle and unforced accord of Hamlet
      Sits smiling to my heart; in grace whereof,
      No jocund health that Denmark drinks today,
      But the great cannon to the clouds shall tell,
      And the King's rouse[18] the heaven shall bruit[19] again,
      Re-speaking earthly thunder. Come away.

                  [*Flourish. Exeunt all but* HAMLET.

HAM.   O, that this too too sullied flesh would melt,
      Thaw and resolve itself into a dew,
      Or that the Everlasting had not fix'd
      His canon 'gainst self-slaughter! O God! God!
      How weary, stale, flat and unprofitable
      Seem to me all the uses of this world!

[14] *still*] always.
[15] *unprevailing*] unavailing, pointless.
[16] *most immediate*] next in succession.
[17] *retrograde*] contrary.
[18] *rouse*] drink, toast.
[19] *bruit*] announce.

Fie on't! ah fie! 'Tis an unweeded garden
That grows to seed; things rank and gross in nature
Possess it merely.[20] That it should come to this!
But two months dead—nay, not so much, not two—
So excellent a king, that was to this
Hyperion to a satyr, so loving to my mother
That he might not beteem[21] the winds of heaven
Visit her face too roughly. Heaven and earth,
Must I remember? Why, she would hang on him
As if increase of appetite had grown
By what it fed on; and yet, within a month—
Let me not think on't—Frailty, thy name is woman—
A little month, or ere those shoes were old
With which she follow'd my poor father's body,
Like Niobe, all tears—why she, even she—
O God! a beast that wants discourse of reason
Would have mourn'd longer—married with my uncle,
My father's brother, but no more like my father
Than I to Hercules. Within a month,
Ere yet the salt of most unrighteous tears
Had left the flushing in her galled eyes,
She married. O, most wicked speed, to post
With such dexterity to incestuous sheets!
It is not, nor it cannot come to good.
But break, my heart, for I must hold my tongue.

Enter HORATIO, MARCELLUS, *and* BERNARDO.

HOR.   Hail to your lordship.
HAM.   I am glad to see you well.
          Horatio—or I do forget myself.
HOR.   The same, my lord, and your poor servant ever.
HAM.   Sir, my good friend; I'll change that name[22] with you.
          And what make you from Wittenberg, Horatio?—
          Marcellus.
MAR.   My good lord.
HAM.   I am very glad to see you.—[*To* BER.] Good even, sir.—
          But what, in faith, make you from Wittenberg?
HOR.   A truant disposition, good my lord.
HAM.   I would not hear your enemy say so,

[20] *merely*] entirely.
[21] *beteem*] permit.
[22] *change that name*] exchange the name "servant."

              Nor shall you do my ear that violence,
              To make it truster of your own report
              Against yourself. I know you are no truant.
              But what is your affair in Elsinore?
              We'll teach you to drink deep ere you depart.

HOR.   My lord, I came to see your father's funeral.

HAM.   I pray thee, do not mock me, fellow-student;
              I think it was to see my mother's wedding.

HOR.   Indeed, my lord, it follow'd hard upon.

HAM.   Thrift, thrift, Horatio. The funeral baked meats
              Did coldly furnish forth the marriage tables.
              Would I had met my dearest[23] foe in heaven
              Or ever[24] I had seen that day, Horatio.
              My father—Methinks I see my father.

HOR.   O where, my lord?

HAM.   In my mind's eye, Horatio.

HOR.   I saw him once; he was a goodly king.

HAM.   He was a man, take him for all in all;
              I shall not look upon his like again.

HOR.   My lord, I think I saw him yesternight.

HAM.   Saw? Who?

HOR.   My lord, the King your father.

HAM.   The King my father?

HOR.   Season your admiration[25] for a while
              With an attent ear, till I may deliver,
              Upon the witness of these gentlemen,
              This marvel to you.

HAM.   For God's love, let me hear!

HOR.   Two nights together had these gentlemen,
              Marcellus and Bernardo, on their watch,
              In the dead vast and middle of the night,
              Been thus encounter'd. A figure like your father,
              Armed at point exactly,[26] cap-à-pie,[27]
              Appears before them, and with solemn march
              Goes slow and stately by them. Thrice he walk'd
              By their oppress'd and fear-surprised eyes
              Within his truncheon's length, whilst they, distill'd

---

[23] *dearest*] direst.
[24] *Or ever*] before.
[25] *Season your admiration*] temper your astonishment.
[26] *at point exactly*] correctly.
[27] *cap-à-pie*] head to foot.

> Almost to jelly with the act[28] of fear,
> Stand dumb, and speak not to him. This to me
> In dreadful secrecy impart they did;
> And I with them the third night kept the watch,
> Where, as they had deliver'd, both in time,
> Form of the thing, each word made true and good,
> The apparition comes. I knew your father;
> These hands are not more like.

HAM.   But where was this?
MAR.   My lord, upon the platform where we watch'd.
HAM.   Did you not speak to it?
HOR.   My lord, I did,
> But answer made it none. Yet once methought
> It lifted up it head and did address
> Itself to motion, like as it would speak.
> But even then the morning cock crew loud,
> And at the sound it shrunk in haste away
> And vanish'd from our sight.

HAM.   'Tis very strange.
HOR.   As I do live, my honour'd lord, 'tis true,
> And we did think it writ down in our duty
> To let you know of it.

HAM.   Indeed, indeed, sirs; but this troubles me.
> Hold you the watch tonight?

MAR. ⎱
BER. ⎰   We do, my lord.

HAM.   Arm'd, say you?

MAR. ⎱
BER. ⎰   Arm'd, my lord.

HAM.   From top to toe?

MAR. ⎱
BER. ⎰   My lord, from head to foot.

HAM.   Then saw you not his face?
HOR.   O, yes, my lord; he wore his beaver[29] up.
HAM.   What look'd he, frowningly?
HOR.   A countenance more in sorrow than in anger.
HAM.   Pale, or red?
HOR.   Nay, very pale.
HAM.   And fix'd his eyes upon you?

---

[28] *act*] effect.
[29] *beaver*] visor (covering lower part of the face).

HOR.	Most constantly.
HAM.	I would I had been there.
HOR.	It would have much amazed you.
HAM.	Very like, very like. Stay'd it long?
HOR.	While one with moderate haste might tell a hundred.
MAR. BER.	} Longer, longer.
HOR.	Not when I saw't.
HAM.	His beard was grizzled, no?
HOR.	It was as I have seen it in his life, A sable silver'd.
HAM.	I will watch tonight; Perchance 'twill walk again.
HOR.	I warrant it will.
HAM.	If it assume my noble father's person, I'll speak to it, though hell itself should gape And bid me hold my peace. I pray you all, If you have hitherto conceal'd this sight, Let it be tenable in your silence still, And whatsoever else shall hap tonight, Give it an understanding, but no tongue. I will requite your loves. So fare you well. Upon the platform, 'twixt eleven and twelve, I'll visit you.
ALL.	Our duty to your honour.
HAM.	Your loves, as mine to you. Farewell.

                        [*Exeunt all but* HAMLET.

My father's spirit in arms! All is not well.
I doubt[30] some foul play. Would the night were come.
Till then sit still, my soul. Foul deeds will rise,
Though all the earth o'erwhelm them, to men's eyes.   [*Exit.*

---

[30] *doubt*] suspect.

SCENE III. *A room in Polonius's house.*

Enter LAERTES *and* OPHELIA.

LAER.   My necessaries are embark'd. Farewell.
        And, sister, as the winds give benefit
        And convoy is assistant,[1] do not sleep,
        But let me hear from you.

OPH.   Do you doubt that?

LAER.   For Hamlet, and the trifling of his favour,
        Hold it a fashion, and a toy in blood,[2]
        A violet in the youth of primy[3] nature,
        Forward,[4] not permanent, sweet, not lasting,
        The perfume and suppliance[5] of a minute,
        No more.

OPH.   No more but so?

LAER.   Think it no more.
        For nature crescent[6] does not grow alone
        In thews[7] and bulk, but, as this temple[8] waxes,
        The inward service of the mind and soul
        Grows wide withal. Perhaps he loves you now,
        And now no soil nor cautel[9] doth besmirch
        The virtue of his will; but you must fear,
        His greatness weigh'd,[10] his will is not his own;
        For he himself is subject to his birth.
        He may not, as unvalued persons do,
        Carve for himself, for on his choice depends
        The safety and health of this whole state;
        And therefore must his choice be circumscribed

---

[1] *convoy is assistant*] means of conveyance are available.
[2] *toy in blood*] amorous whim.
[3] *primy*] flourishing.
[4] *Forward*] premature.
[5] *suppliance*] pastime, gratification.
[6] *crescent*] growing.
[7] *thews*] strength.
[8] *temple*] i.e., human body.
[9] *cautel*] deceit.
[10] *His greatness weigh'd*] his important position being considered.

Unto the voice and yielding[11] of that body
Whereof he is the head. Then if he says he loves you,
It fits your wisdom so far to believe it
As he in his particular act and place
May give his saying deed; which is no further
Than the main[12] voice of Denmark goes withal.
Then weigh what loss your honour may sustain
If with too credent ear you list[13] his songs,
Or lose your heart, or your chaste treasure open
To his unmaster'd importunity.
Fear it, Ophelia, fear it, my dear sister,
And keep you in the rear of your affection,
Out of the shot and danger of desire.
The chariest[14] maid is prodigal enough
If she unmask her beauty to the moon.
Virtue itself 'scapes not calumnious strokes.
The canker galls the infants of the spring
Too oft before their buttons[15] be disclosed,
And in the morn and liquid[16] dew of youth
Contagious blastments[17] are most imminent.
Be wary then; best safety lies in fear.
Youth to itself rebels, though none else near.

OPH. I shall the effect of this good lesson keep
As watchman to my heart. But, good my brother,
Do not, as some ungracious[18] pastors do,
Show me the steep and thorny way to heaven,
Whilst, like a puff'd and reckless libertine,
Himself the primrose path of dalliance treads
And recks not his own rede.[19]

LAER.   O, fear me not.
I stay too long. But here my father comes.

Enter POLONIUS.

A double blessing is a double grace;

---

[11] *yielding*] consent.
[12] *main*] general.
[13] *list*] listen to.
[14] *chariest*] most modest.
[15] *buttons*] buds.
[16] *liquid*] pure, limpid.
[17] *blastments*] blights.
[18] *ungracious*] impious.
[19] *recks not his own rede*] does not heed his own advice.

	Occasion smiles upon a second leave.
Pol.	Yet here, Laertes? Aboard, aboard, for shame!

POL.   Occasion smiles upon a second leave.
POL.   Yet here, Laertes? Aboard, aboard, for shame!
         The wind sits in the shoulder of your sail,
         And you are stay'd for. There, my blessing with thee.
         And these few precepts in thy memory
         Look thou character. [20] Give thy thoughts no tongue,
         Nor any unproportion'd thought his act.
         Be thou familiar, but by no means vulgar.
         Those friends thou hast, and their adoption tried, [21]
         Grapple them to thy soul with hoops of steel,
         But do not dull thy palm with entertainment
         Of each new-hatch'd unfledged comrade. Beware
         Of entrance to a quarrel; but being in,
         Bear't, that the opposed may beware of thee.
         Give every man thy ear, but few thy voice;
         Take each man's censure, [22] but reserve thy judgement.
         Costly thy habit [23] as thy purse can buy,
         But not express'd in fancy; rich, not gaudy;
         For the apparel oft proclaims the man;
         And they in France of the best rank and station
         Are of a most select and generous chief [24] in that.
         Neither a borrower nor a lender be;
         For loan oft loses both itself and friend,
         And borrowing dulls the edge of husbandry. [25]
         This above all: to thine own self be true,
         And it must follow, as the night the day,
         Thou canst not then be false to any man.
         Farewell. My blessing season this in thee.

LAER.   Most humbly do I take my leave, my lord.

POL.   The time invites you; go, your servants tend.

LAER.   Farewell, Ophelia, and remember well
         What I have said to you.

OPH.   'Tis in my memory lock'd,
         And you yourself shall keep the key of it.

LAER.   Farewell.   [*Exit.*

POL.   What is't, Ophelia, he hath said to you?

---

[20] *character*] inscribe.
[21] *tried*] justified.
[22] *censure*] opinion.
[23] *habit*] dress.
[24] *chief*] excellence.
[25] *husbandry*] economy, saving.

OPH.	So please you, something touching the Lord Hamlet.
POL.	Marry, well bethought.
	'Tis told me, he hath very oft of late
	Given private time to you, and you yourself
	Have of your audience been most free and bounteous.
	If it be so—as so 'tis put on[26] me,
	And that in way of caution—I must tell you,
	You do not understand yourself so clearly
	As it behoves my daughter and your honour.
	What is between you? Give me up the truth.
OPH.	He hath, my lord, of late made many tenders
	Of his affection to me.
POL.	Affection? Pooh! You speak like a green girl,
	Unsifted[27] in such perilous circumstance.
	Do you believe his tenders, as you call them?
OPH.	I do not know, my lord, what I should think.
POL.	Marry, I'll teach you. Think yourself a baby,
	That you have ta'en these tenders for true pay,
	Which are not sterling.[28] Tender yourself more dearly;[29]
	Or—not to crack the wind of the poor phrase,
	Running it thus—you'll tender me a fool.
OPH.	My lord, he hath importuned me with love
	In honourable fashion.
POL.	Ay, fashion you may call it. Go to, go to.
OPH.	And hath given countenance[30] to his speech, my lord,
	With almost all the holy vows of heaven.
POL.	Ay, springes[31] to catch woodcocks. I do know,
	When the blood burns, how prodigal the soul
	Lends the tongue vows. These blazes, daughter,
	Giving more light than heat, extinct in both,
	Even in their promise, as it is a-making,
	You must not take for fire. From this time
	Be something scanter of your maiden presence;
	Set your entreatments[32] at a higher rate

---

[26] *put on*] impressed upon.

[27] *unsifted*] inexperienced.

[28] *sterling*] of genuine value. Polonius is playing on two meanings of "tender": (1) to proffer affection; (2) to pay money.

[29] *Tender . . . dearly*] (1) Take care of yourself; (2) set a higher price on yourself.

[30] *countenance*] authority.

[31] *springes*] snares.

[32] *entreatments*] exchanges.

Than a command to parley.[33] For Lord Hamlet,
Believe so much in him, that he is young,
And with a larger tether may he walk
Than may be given you. In few,[34] Ophelia,
Do not believe his vows; for they are brokers,[35]
Not of that dye which their investments[36] show,
But mere implorators[37] of unholy suits,
Breathing[38] like sanctified and pious bawds,
The better to beguile. This is for all:
I would not, in plain terms, from this time forth,
Have you so slander any moment leisure,
As to give words or talk with the Lord Hamlet.
Look to't, I charge you. Come your ways.

OPH.   I shall obey, my lord.   [*Exeunt.*

SCENE IV. *The platform.*

Enter HAMLET, HORATIO, *and* MARCELLUS.

HAM.   The air bites shrewdly;[1] it is very cold.
HOR.   It is a nipping and an eager[2] air.
HAM.   What hour now?
HOR.   I think it lacks of twelve.
MAR.   No, it is struck.
HOR.   Indeed? I heard it not. It then draws near the season
        Wherein the spirit held his wont to walk.
               [*A flourish of trumpets, and ordnance shot off within.*
        What doth this mean, my lord?
HAM.   The King doth wake tonight and takes his rouse,[3]

---

[33] *command to parley*] invitation to talk.
[34] *In few*] in short.
[35] *brokers*] go-betweens, panders.
[36] *investments*] clothes.
[37] *implorators*] implorers.
[38] *Breathing*] speaking.

---

[1] *shrewdly*] keenly.
[2] *eager*] biting, bitter.
[3] *takes his rouse*] carouses.

Keeps wassail,[4] and the swaggering upspring[5] reels;
And as he drains his draughts of Rhenish down,
The kettle-drum and trumpet thus bray out
The triumph[6] of his pledge.

HOR.   Is it a custom?

HAM.   Ay, marry, is't;
But to my mind, though I am native here
And to the manner born, it is a custom
More honour'd in the breach than the observance.
This heavy-headed revel east and west
Makes us traduced and tax'd of[7] other nations.
They clepe[8] us drunkards, and with swinish phrase
Soil our addition;[9] and indeed it takes
From our achievements, though perform'd at height,
The pith and marrow of our attribute.[10]
So, oft it chances in particular men,[11]
That for some vicious mole of nature in them,
As in their birth—wherein they are not guilty,
Since nature cannot choose his origin—
By the o'ergrowth of some complexion,[12]
Oft breaking down the pales[13] and forts of reason,
Or by some habit that too much o'er-leavens[14]
The form of plausive[15] manners, that these men—
Carrying, I say, the stamp of one defect,
Being Nature's livery, or Fortune's star—
Their virtues else—be they as pure as grace,
As infinite as man may undergo—[16]
Shall in the general censure take corruption
From that particular fault. The dram of evil
Doth all the noble substance of a doubt[17]

---

[4] *keeps wassail*] carouses.
[5] *upspring*] wild German dance.
[6] *triumph*] celebration.
[7] *tax'd of*] censured by.
[8] *clepe*] call.
[9] *with swinish . . . addition*] by calling us swine sully our reputation.
[10] *attribute*] reputation.
[11] *particular men*] individuals.
[12] *complexion*] humor, trait.
[13] *pales*] palings.
[14] *o'er-leavens*] corrupts.
[15] *plausive*] pleasing.
[16] *undergo*] sustain.
[17] *of a doubt*] the text seems to be corrupt here.

To his own scandal.

Enter GHOST.

HOR.   Look, my lord, it comes.
HAM.   Angels and ministers of grace defend us!
            Be thou a spirit of health or goblin damn'd,
            Bring with thee airs from heaven or blasts from hell,
            Be thy intents wicked or charitable,
            Thou comest in such a questionable[18] shape
            That I will speak to thee. I'll call thee Hamlet,
            King, father, royal Dane. O, answer me!
            Let me not burst in ignorance, but tell
            Why thy canonized bones, hearsed[19] in death,
            Have burst their cerements, why the sepulchre,
            Wherein we saw thee quietly inurn'd,
            Hath oped his ponderous and marble jaws,
            To cast thee up again. What may this mean,
            That thou, dead corse, again, in complete steel,
            Revisits thus the glimpses of the moon,
            Making night hideous, and we fools of nature[20]
            So horridly to shake our disposition
            With thoughts beyond the reaches of our souls?
            Say, why is this? Wherefore? What should we do?
                                [GHOST *beckons* HAMLET.
HOR.   It beckons you to go away with it,
            As if it some impartment[21] did desire
            To you alone.
MAR.   Look, with what courteous action
            It waves you to a more removed ground.
            But do not go with it.
HOR.   No, by no means.
HAM.   It will not speak. Then I will follow it.
HOR.   Do not, my lord.
HAM.   Why, what should be the fear?
            I do not set my life at a pin's fee;
            And for my soul, what can it do to that,
            Being a thing immortal as itself?
            It waves me forth again. I'll follow it.

---

[18] *questionable*] inviting question.
[19] *hearsed*] coffined.
[20] *fools of nature*] beings limited to the understanding of things natural.
[21] *impartment*] communication.

HOR.   What if it tempt you toward the flood, my lord,
Or to the dreadful summit of the cliff
That beetles o'er[22] his base into the sea,
And there assume some other horrible form,
Which might deprive your sovereignty of reason
And draw you into madness? Think of it.
The very place puts toys of desperation,[23]
Without more motive, into every brain
That looks so many fathoms to the sea
And hears it roar beneath.

HAM.   It waves me still.
Go on; I'll follow thee.

MAR.   You shall not go, my lord.

HAM.   Hold off your hands.

HOR.   Be ruled; you shall not go.

HAM.   My fate cries out,
And makes each petty artery in this body
As hardy as the Nemean lion's[24] nerve.
Still am I call'd. Unhand me, gentlemen.
By heaven, I'll make a ghost of him that lets[25] me.
I say, away! Go on; I'll follow thee.

                                  [*Exeunt* GHOST *and* HAMLET.

HOR.   He waxes desperate with imagination.

MAR.   Let's follow. 'Tis not fit thus to obey him.

HOR.   Have after. To what issue will this come?

MAR.   Something is rotten in the state of Denmark.

HOR.   Heaven will direct it.

MAR.   Nay, let's follow him.   [*Exeunt.*

---

[22] *beetles o'er*] overhangs.
[23] *toys of desperation*] freakish thoughts of suicide.
[24] *Nemean lion's*] The Nemean lion was slain by Hercules as the first of his twelve labors.
[25] *lets*] hinders.

SCENE V. *Another part of the platform.*

Enter GHOST *and* HAMLET.

HAM.	Whither wilt thou lead me? Speak; I'll go no further.
GHOST.	Mark me.
HAM.	I will.
GHOST.	My hour is almost come,

When I to sulphurous and tormenting flames
Must render up myself.

HAM.	Alas, poor ghost!
GHOST.	Pity me not, but lend thy serious hearing

To what I shall unfold.

HAM.	Speak; I am bound to hear.
GHOST.	So art thou to revenge, when thou shalt hear.
HAM.	What?
GHOST.	I am thy father's spirit,

Doom'd for a certain term to walk the night,
And for the day confined to fast in fires,
Till the foul crimes done in my days of nature
Are burnt and purged away. But that I am forbid
To tell the secrets of my prison-house,
I could a tale unfold whose lightest word
Would harrow up thy soul, freeze thy young blood,
Make thy two eyes, like stars, start from their spheres,
Thy knotted and combined locks to part
And each particular hair to stand an end,
Like quills upon the fretful porpentine.
But this eternal blazon[1] must not be
To ears of flesh and blood. List, list, O, list!
If thou didst ever thy dear father love—

HAM.	O God!
GHOST.	Revenge his foul and most unnatural murder.
HAM.	Murder?
GHOST.	Murder most foul, as in the best it is,

But this most foul, strange, and unnatural.

HAM.	Haste me to know't, that I, with wings as swift

---

[1] *eternal blazon*] description of the afterlife.

As meditation or the thoughts of love,
May sweep to my revenge.

GHOST.   I find thee apt;
And duller shouldst thou be than the fat weed
That roots itself in ease on Lethe[2] wharf,
Wouldst thou not stir in this. Now, Hamlet, hear.
'Tis given out that, sleeping in my orchard,[3]
A serpent stung me; so the whole ear of Denmark
Is by a forged process[4] of my death
Rankly abused. But know, thou noble youth,
The serpent that did sting thy father's life
Now wears his crown.

HAM. O my prophetic soul! My uncle!

GHOST. Ay, that incestuous, that adulterate beast,
With witchcraft of his wit, with traitorous gifts—
O wicked wit and gifts that have the power
So to seduce!—won to his shameful lust
The will of my most seeming-virtuous queen.
O Hamlet, what a falling off was there!
From me, whose love was of that dignity
That it went hand in hand even with the vow
I made to her in marriage; and to decline
Upon a wretch, whose natural gifts were poor
To those of mine.
But virtue, as it never will be moved,
Though lewdness court it in a shape of heaven,
So lust, though to a radiant angel link'd,
Will sate itself in a celestial bed
And prey on garbage.
But, soft! methinks I scent the morning air;
Brief let me be. Sleeping within my orchard,
My custom always of the afternoon,
Upon my secure[5] hour thy uncle stole,
With juice of cursed hebenon in a vial,
And in the porches of my ears did pour
The leperous distilment, whose effect
Holds such an enmity with blood of man
That swift as quicksilver it courses through

---

[2] *Lethe*] the river of forgetfulness in the underworld.
[3] *orchard*] garden.
[4] *process*] account.
[5] *secure*] free from apprehension, unsuspecting.

The natural gates and alleys of the body,
And with a sudden vigour it doth posset[6]
And curd, like eager[7] droppings into milk,
The thin and wholesome blood. So did it mine;
And a most instant tetter[8] bark'd about,
Most lazar-like,[9] with vile and loathsome crust,
All my smooth body.
Thus was I, sleeping, by a brother's hand
Of life, of crown, of queen, at once dispatch'd,[10]
Cut off even in the blossoms of my sin,
Unhousel'd, disappointed, unaneled,[11]
No reckoning made, but sent to my account
With all my imperfections on my head.
O, horrible! O, horrible! most horrible!
If thou hast nature in thee, bear it not.
Let not the royal bed of Denmark be
A couch for luxury[12] and damned incest.
But, howsoever thou pursuest this act,
Taint not thy mind, nor let thy soul contrive
Against thy mother aught. Leave her to heaven,
And to those thorns that in her bosom lodge,
To prick and sting her. Fare thee well at once.
The glow-worm shows the matin[13] to be near,
And 'gins to pale his uneffectual fire.
Adieu, adieu, adieu. Remember me.   [*Exit.*

HAM.   O all you host of heaven! O earth! What else?
And shall I couple[14] hell? O, fie! Hold, hold, my heart;
And you, my sinews, grow not instant old,
But bear me stiffly up. Remember thee?
Ay, thou poor ghost, while memory holds a seat
In this distracted globe.[15] Remember thee?
Yea, from the table[16] of my memory

[6] *posset*] curdle, in the manner of a posset (a hot drink of spiced milk mixed with wine or ale).
[7] *eager*] sour.
[8] *tetter*] skin disease.
[9] *lazar-like*] like a leper.
[10] *dispatch'd*] deprived.
[11] *Unhousel'd, disappointed, unaneled*] not having received the sacrament, unprepared and not having received extreme unction.
[12] *luxury*] lechery.
[13] *matin*] morning.
[14] *couple*] include.
[15] *globe*] head.
[16] *table*] (writing) tablet.

I'll wipe away all trivial fond[17] records,
All saws[18] of books, all forms, all pressures[19] past,
That youth and observation copied there;
And thy commandment all alone shall live
Within the book and volume of my brain,
Unmix'd with baser matter. Yes, by heaven!
O most pernicious woman!
O villain, villain, smiling, damned villain!
My tables[20]—meet it is I set it down
That one may smile, and smile, and be a villain;
At least I'm sure it may be so in Denmark.   [*Writing.*
So, uncle, there you are. Now to my word.[21]
It is 'Adieu, adieu, remember me.'
I have sworn't.

HOR. ⎫
MAR. ⎭   [*Within*] My lord, my lord.

Enter HORATIO *and* MARCELLUS.

MAR.   Lord Hamlet.
HOR.   Heaven secure[22] him!
HAM.   So be it.
MAR.   Illo, ho, ho, my lord.
HAM.   Hillo, ho, ho, boy. Come, bird, come.
MAR.   How is't, my noble lord?
HOR.   What news, my lord?
HAM.   O, wonderful!
HOR.   Good my lord, tell it.
HAM.   No; you will reveal it.
HOR.   Not I, my lord, by heaven.
MAR.   Nor I, my lord.
HAM.   How say you, then; would heart of man once think it?
        But you'll be secret?

HOR. ⎫
MAR. ⎭   Ay, by heaven, my lord.

HAM.   There's ne'er a villain dwelling in all Denmark
        But he's an arrant knave.
HOR.   There needs no ghost, my lord, come from the grave

---

[17] *fond*] foolish.
[18] *saws*] maxims.
[19] *pressures*] impressions.
[20] *tables*] portable writing-tablets.
[21] *word*] watchword, motto.
[22] *secure*] protect.

	To tell us this.
HAM.	Why, right, you are i' the right;

And so, without more circumstance at all,
I hold it fit that we shake hands and part,
You, as your business and desire shall point you—
For every man hath business and desire,
Such as it is—and for my own poor part,
Look you, I'll go pray.

HOR.   These are but wild and whirling words, my lord.

HAM.   I'm sorry they offend you, heartily;
       Yes, faith, heartily.

HOR.   There's no offence, my lord.

HAM.   Yes, by Saint Patrick,[23] but there is, Horatio,
       And much offence too. Touching this vision here,
       It is an honest[24] ghost, that let me tell you.
       For your desire to know what is between us,
       O'ermaster't as you may. And now, good friends,
       As you are friends, scholars and soldiers,
       Give me one poor request.

HOR.   What is't, my lord? We will.

HAM.   Never make known what you have seen tonight.

HOR. ⎫
MAR. ⎭   My lord, we will not.

HAM.   Nay, but swear't.

HOR.   In faith,
       My lord, not I.

MAR.   Nor I, my lord, in faith.

HAM.   Upon my sword.[25]

MAR.   We have sworn, my lord, already.

HAM.   Indeed, upon my sword, indeed.

GHOST. [Beneath] Swear.

HAM.   Ah, ha, boy, say'st thou so? Art thou there, truepenny?[26]
       Come on. You hear this fellow in the cellarage.
       Consent to swear.

HOR.   Propose the oath, my lord.

HAM.   Never to speak of this that you have seen,
       Swear by my sword.

GHOST. [Beneath] Swear.

---

[23] *Saint Patrick*] The Irish saint was said to be the keeper of Purgatory.
[24] *honest*] real.
[25] *sword*] The sword's hilt forms a cross.
[26] *truepenny*] honest fellow.

HAM.   *Hic et ubique?*[27] Then we'll shift our ground.
      Come hither, gentlemen,
      And lay your hands again upon my sword.
      Never to speak of this that you have heard,
      Swear by my sword.

GHOST.   [*Beneath*] Swear.

HAM.   Well said, old mole. Canst work i' the earth so fast?
      A worthy pioner![28] Once more remove, good friends.

HOR.   O day and night, but this is wondrous strange.

HAM.   And therefore as a stranger give it welcome.
      There are more things in heaven and earth, Horatio,
      Than are dreamt of in your philosophy.
      But come;
      Here, as before, never, so help you mercy,
      How strange or odd soe'er I bear myself—
      As I perchance hereafter shall think meet
      To put an antic[29] disposition on—
      That you, at such times seeing me, never shall,
      With arms encumber'd[30] thus, or this head-shake,
      Or by pronouncing of some doubtful phrase,
      As 'Well, we know,' or 'We could, an if we would,'
      Or 'If we list to speak,' or 'There be, an if they might,'
      Or such ambiguous giving out,[31] to note[32]
      That you know aught of me; this not to do,
      So grace and mercy at your most need help you,
      Swear.

GHOST.   [*Beneath*] Swear.

HAM.   Rest, rest, perturbed spirit. [*They swear.*] So, gentlemen,
      With all my love I do commend me to you;
      And what so poor a man as Hamlet is
      May do to express his love and friending to you,
      God willing, shall not lack. Let us go in together;
      And still[33] your fingers on your lips, I pray.
      The time is out of joint. O cursed spite,
      That ever I was born to set it right!
      Nay, come, let's go together.   [*Exeunt.*

[27] *Hic et ubique*] here and everywhere.
[28] *pioner*] miner, digger.
[29] *antic*] odd, strange.
[30] *encumber'd*] folded.
[31] *giving out*] intimation.
[32] *note*] show.
[33] *still*] always.

ACT II.

SCENE I. *A room in Polonius's house.*

Enter POLONIUS *and* REYNALDO.

POL. Give him this money and these notes, Reynaldo.
REY. I will, my lord.
POL. You shall do marvellous wisely, good Reynaldo,
      Before you visit him, to make inquire
      Of his behaviour.
REY.   My lord, I did intend it.
POL. Marry, well said, very well said. Look you, sir,
      Inquire me first what Danskers[1] are in Paris,
      And how, and who, what means, and where they keep,[2]
      What company, at what expense, and finding
      By this encompassment[3] and drift of question
      That they do know my son, come you more nearer
      Than your particular demands will touch it.[4]
      Take[5] you, as 'twere, some distant knowledge of him,
      As thus, 'I know his father and his friends,
      And in part him.' Do you mark this, Reynaldo?
REY. Ay, very well, my lord.
POL. 'And in part him; but,' you may say, 'not well;
      But if't be he I mean, he's very wild,
      Addicted so and so;' and there put on him
      What forgeries you please—marry, none so rank
      As may dishonour him, take heed of that—
      But, sir, such wanton, wild and usual slips

---

[1] *Danskers*] Danes.
[2] *keep*] dwell.
[3] *encompassment*] roundabout way of talking.
[4] *come . . . it*] you will find out more than by asking direct questions.
[5] *Take*] assume.

	As are companions noted and most known
	To youth and liberty.
REY.	As gaming, my lord?
POL.	Ay, or drinking, fencing, swearing, quarrelling,
	Drabbing.[6] You may go so far.
REY.	My lord, that would dishonour him.
POL.	'Faith, no; as you may season it in the charge.

You must not put another scandal on him,
That he is open to incontinency.[7]
That's not my meaning; but breathe his faults so quaintly[8]
That they may seem the taints of liberty,
The flash and outbreak of a fiery mind,
A savageness in unreclaimed[9] blood,
Of general assault.[10]

REY.   But, my good lord—
POL.   Wherefore should you do this?
REY.   Ay, my lord,
    I would know that.
POL.   Marry, sir, here's my drift,
    And I believe it is a fetch of warrant:[11]
    You laying these slight sullies on my son,
    As 'twere a thing a little soil'd i' the working,
    Mark you,
    Your party in converse,[12] him you would sound,
    Having ever seen in the prenominate[13] crimes
    The youth you breathe of guilty, be assured
    He closes[14] with you in this consequence:
    'Good sir,' or so, or 'friend,' or 'gentleman,'
    According to the phrase or the addition[15]
    Of man and country.
REY.   Very good, my lord.
POL.   And then, sir, does he this—he does—what was I about to say?
                By the mass, I was about to say something. Where did I leave?

---

[6] *Drabbing*] whoring.
[7] *incontinency*] habitual licentiousness.
[8] *quaintly*] skillfully, delicately.
[9] *unreclaimed*] untamed.
[10] *Of general assault*] to which all young men are liable.
[11] *fetch of warrant*] justified stratagem.
[12] *converse*] conversation.
[13] *prenominate*] aforementioned.
[14] *closes*] agrees.
[15] *addition*] title.

REY.	At 'closes in the consequence,' at 'friend or so,' and 'gentle-man.'
POL.	At 'closes in the consequence,' ay, marry.
	He closes with you thus: 'I know the gentleman;
	I saw him yesterday,' or 't'other day,'
	Or then, or then, with such, or such, 'and, as you say,
	There was a[16] gaming,' 'there o'ertook in's rouse,'[17]
	'There falling out at tennis;' or perchance,
	'I saw him enter such a house of sale,'
	Videlicet,[18] a brothel, or so forth.
	See you now;
	Your bait of falsehood takes this carp of truth;
	And thus do we of wisdom and of reach,[19]
	With windlasses[20] and with assays of bias,[21]
	By indirections find directions out.
	So, by my former lecture and advice,
	Shall you my son. You have me, have you not?
REY.	My lord, I have.
POL.	God be wi' ye. Fare ye well.
REY.	Good my lord.
POL.	Observe his inclination in yourself.[22]
REY.	I shall, my lord.
POL.	And let him ply his music.
REY.	Well, my lord.
POL.	Farewell. [*Exit* REYNALDO.

Enter OPHELIA.

	How now, Ophelia, what's the matter?
OPH.	O, my lord, my lord, I have been so affrighted.
POL.	With what, i' the name of God?
OPH.	My lord, as I was sewing in my closet,
	Lord Hamlet, with his doublet all unbraced,[23]
	No hat upon his head, his stockings foul'd,
	Ungarter'd and down-gyved[24] to his ankle,

---

[16] *a*] he.

[17] *o'ertook in's rouse*] overcome by drinking.

[18] *Videlicet*] namely.

[19] *reach*] ability.

[20] *windlasses*] indirect advances.

[21] *assays of bias*] courses that resemble the curved path of a bowling ball.

[22] *Observe . . . yourself*](?) Behave as he does.

[23] *unbraced*] unbuttoned.

[24] *down-gyved*] fallen down and thereby resembling gyves (fetters).

	Pale as his shirt, his knees knocking each other,
	And with a look so piteous in purport
	As if he had been loosed out of hell
	To speak of horrors, he comes before me.
POL.	Mad for thy love?
OPH.	My lord, I do not know,
	But truly I do fear it.
POL.	What said he?
OPH.	He took me by the wrist and held me hard;

Then goes he to the length of all his arm,[25]
And with his other hand thus o'er his brow,
He falls to such perusal of my face
As he would draw it. Long stay'd he so.
At last, a little shaking of mine arm,
And thrice his head thus waving up and down,
He raised a sigh so piteous and profound
As it did seem to shatter all his bulk[26]
And end his being. That done, he lets me go,
And with his head over his shoulder turn'd,
He seem'd to find his way without his eyes;
For out o' doors he went without their helps,
And to the last bended their light on me.

POL. Come, go with me. I will go seek the King.
This is the very ecstasy[27] of love,
Whose violent property fordoes itself[28]
And leads the will to desperate undertakings
As oft as any passion under heaven
That does afflict our natures. I am sorry.
What, have you given him any hard words of late?

OPH. No, my good lord, but, as you did command,
I did repel his letters and denied
His access to me.

POL. That hath made him mad.
I am sorry that with better heed and judgement
I had not quoted[29] him. I fear'd he did but trifle
And meant to wrack thee. But beshrew my jealousy![30]

---

[25] *goes . . . arm*] withdraws to arm's length.
[26] *bulk*] body, in particular the trunk.
[27] *ecstasy*] madness.
[28] *Whose . . . itself*] the violent nature of which destroys itself.
[29] *quoted*] observed.
[30] *jealousy*] suspicion.

By heaven, it is as proper to our age
To cast beyond ourselves in our opinions
As it is common for the younger sort
To lack discretion. Come, go we to the King.
This must be known, which, being kept close, might move
More grief to hide than hate to utter love.[31]
Come.   [*Exeunt.*

SCENE II. *A room in the castle.*

Flourish. Enter KING, QUEEN, ROSENCRANTZ, GUILDENSTERN, *and* Attendants.

KING.   Welcome, dear Rosencrantz and Guildenstern.
          Moreover[1] that we much did long to see you,
          The need we have to use you did provoke
          Our hasty sending. Something have you heard
          Of Hamlet's transformation—so call it,
          Sith[2] nor the exterior nor the inward man
          Resembles that it was. What it should be,
          More than his father's death, that thus hath put him
          So much from the understanding of himself,
          I cannot dream of. I entreat you both
          That, being of so young days brought up with him
          And sith so neighbour'd to his youth and haviour,
          That you vouchsafe your rest[3] here in our court
          Some little time: so by your companies
          To draw him on to pleasures, and to gather
          So much as from occasion[4] you may glean,
          Whether aught to us unknown afflicts him thus
          That open'd lies within our remedy.
QUEEN.   Good gentlemen, he hath much talk'd of you,

---

[31] *might move . . . love*] might cause more grief by being concealed than hatred by being exposed as love.

---

[1] *Moreover*] besides the fact.
[2] *Sith*] since.
[3] *vouchsafe your rest*] agree to stay.
[4] *occasion*] opportunity.

                  And sure I am two men there are not living
                  To whom he more adheres. If it will please you
                  To show us so much gentry[5] and good will
                  As to expend your time with us awhile
                  For the supply and profit[6] of our hope,
                  Your visitation shall receive such thanks
                  As fits a king's remembrance.
ROS.   Both your Majesties
                  Might, by the sovereign power you have of us,
                  Put your dread pleasures more into command
                  Than to entreaty.
GUIL.   But we both obey,
                  And here give up ourselves, in the full bent[7]
                  To lay our service freely at your feet,
                  To be commanded.
KING.   Thanks, Rosencrantz and gentle Guildenstern.
QUEEN.   Thanks, Guildenstern and gentle Rosencrantz.
                  And I beseech you instantly to visit
                  My too much changed son. Go, some of you,
                  And bring these gentlemen where Hamlet is.
GUIL.   Heavens make our presence and our practices
                  Pleasant and helpful to him.
QUEEN.   Ay, amen.
       [*Exeunt* ROSENCRANTZ, GUILDENSTERN, *and some* Attendants.

Enter POLONIUS.

POL.   The ambassadors from Norway, my good lord,
                  Are joyfully return'd.
KING.   Thou still[8] hast been the father of good news.
POL.   Have I, my lord? I assure my good liege,
                  I hold my duty as I hold my soul,
                  Both to my God and to my gracious King.
                  And I do think, or else this brain of mine
                  Hunts not the trail of policy so sure
                  As it hath used to do, that I have found
                  The very cause of Hamlet's lunacy.
KING.   O, speak of that; that do I long to hear.
POL.   Give first admittance to the ambassadors.

---

[5] *gentry*] courtesy.
[6] *supply and profit*] support and fulfillment.
[7] *in the full bent*] to the utmost extent.
[8] *still*] always.

My news shall be the fruit to that great feast.

KING.   Thyself do grace to them, and bring them in.

                                         [Exit POLONIUS.

He tells me, my dear Gertrude, he hath found
The head and source of all your son's distemper.

QUEEN.   I doubt[9] it is no other but the main:
His father's death and our o'erhasty marriage.

KING.   Well, we shall sift him.[10]

Enter POLONIUS, *with* VOLTIMAND *and* CORNELIUS.

                        Welcome, my good friends.
Say, Voltimand, what from our brother Norway?

VOLT.   Most fair return of greetings and desires.
Upon our first,[11] he sent out to suppress
His nephew's levies, which to him appear'd
To be a preparation 'gainst the Polack,[12]
But better look'd into, he truly found
It was against your Highness; whereat grieved,
That so his sickness, age and impotence
Was falsely borne in hand,[13] sends out arrests
On Fortinbras; which he, in brief, obeys,
Receives rebuke from Norway, and in fine[14]
Makes vow before his uncle never more
To give the assay of arms[15] against your Majesty.
Whereon old Norway, overcome with joy,
Gives him three thousand crowns in annual fee
And his commission to employ those soldiers,
So levied as before, against the Polack,
With an entreaty, herein further shown,   *[Giving a paper.*
That it might please you to give quiet pass
Through your dominions for this enterprise,
On such regards of safety and allowance[16]

---

  [9] *doubt]* suspect.

[10] *sift him]* question him (Polonius).

[11] *our first]* i.e., our first mentioning the actions of Fortinbras.

[12] *the Polack]* the King of Poland.

[13] *borne in hand]* abused, deluded.

[14] *in fine]* in the end.

[15] *assay of arms]* attack.

[16] *safety and allowance]* safety of Denmark and permission for the Norwegian troops to pass
through.

     As therein are set down.

KING.   It likes us well,
And at our more consider'd time[17] we'll read,
Answer, and think upon this business.
Meantime we thank you for your well-took labour.
Go to your rest; at night we'll feast together.
Most welcome home.   [*Exeunt* VOLTIMAND *and* CORNELIUS.

POL.   This business is well ended.
My liege, and madam, to expostulate
What majesty should be, what duty is,
Why day is day, night night, and time is time,
Were nothing but to waste night, day and time.
Therefore, since brevity is the soul of wit
And tediousness the limbs and outward flourishes,
I will be brief. Your noble son is mad.
Mad call I it; for, to define true madness,
What is't but to be nothing else but mad?
But let that go.

QUEEN.   More matter, with less art.

POL.   Madam, I swear I use no art at all.
That he is mad, 'tis true; 'tis true 'tis pity;
And pity 'tis 'tis true—a foolish figure;
But farewell it, for I will use no art.
Mad let us grant him then. And now remains
That we find out the cause of this effect,
Or rather say, the cause of this defect,
For this effect defective comes by cause.
Thus it remains and the remainder thus:
Perpend;[18]
I have a daughter—have while she is mine—
Who in her duty and obedience, mark,
Hath given me this. Now gather and surmise.   [*Reads.*

To the celestial, and my soul's idol, the most beautified Ophelia—

That's an ill phrase, a vile phrase; 'beautified' is a vile phrase.
    But you shall hear: [*Reads.*

In her excellent white bosom, these, &c.

QUEEN.   Came this from Hamlet to her?
POL.   Good madam, stay awhile. I will be faithful.   [*Reads.*

---

[17] *more consider'd time*] convenience.
[18] *Perpend*] consider.

> Doubt thou the stars are fire,
>   Doubt that the sun doth move,
>   Doubt[19] truth to be a liar,
>   But never doubt I love.

O dear Ophelia, I am ill at these numbers.[20] I have not art to reckon[21] my groans. But that I love thee best, O most best, believe it. Adieu.

> Thine evermore, most dear lady, whilst this
>   machine[22] is to him, HAMLET.

This in obedience hath my daughter shown me;
And more above, hath his solicitings,
As they fell out by time, by means and place,
All given to mine ear.

KING.   But how hath she
Received his love?

POL.   What do you think of me?

KING. As of a man faithful and honourable.

POL. I would fain prove so. But what might you think,
When I had seen this hot love on the wing—
As I perceived it, I must tell you that,
Before my daughter told me—what might you,
Or my dear Majesty your queen here, think,
If I had play'd the desk or table-book,[23]
Or given my heart a winking,[24] mute and dumb,
Or look'd upon this love with idle sight;[25]
What might you think? No, I went round[26] to work,
And my young mistress thus I did bespeak:
'Lord Hamlet is a prince, out of thy star.
This must not be.' And then I prescripts gave her,
That she should lock herself from his resort,
Admit no messengers, receive no tokens.
Which done, she took the fruits of my advice;
And he, repulsed—a short tale to make—
Fell into a sadness, then into a fast,
Thence to a watch,[27] thence into a weakness,

[19] *Doubt*] suspect.
[20] *ill at these numbers*] not gifted in versifying.
[21] *reckon*] (1) count; (2) put into verse.
[22] *machine*] body.
[23] *play'd . . . table-book*] served as a go-between.
[24] *given . . . winking*] shut my eyes deliberately.
[25] *idle sight*] thoughtlessly.
[26] *round*] straight.

Thence to a lightness,[28] and by this declension[29]
Into the madness wherein now he raves
And all we mourn for.

KING.   Do you think 'tis this?

QUEEN. It may be; very like.

POL.   Hath there been such a time—I'ld fain know that—
That I have positively said ' 'Tis so,'
When it proved otherwise?

KING.   Not that I know.

POL.   [*Pointing to his head and shoulder*] Take this from this, if this
        be otherwise.
        If circumstances lead me, I will find
        Where truth is hid, though it were hid indeed
        Within the centre.[30]

KING.   How may we try it further?

POL.   You know, sometimes he walks four hours together
        Here in the lobby.

QUEEN.   So he does, indeed.

POL.   At such a time I'll loose my daughter to him.
        Be you and I behind an arras[31] then;
        Mark the encounter. If he love her not,
        And be not from his reason fall'n thereon,[32]
        Let me be no assistant for a state,
        But keep a farm and carters.

KING.   We will try it.

QUEEN. But look where sadly the poor wretch comes reading.

POL.   Away, I do beseech you both, away.
        I'll board[33] him presently.[34] O, give me leave.

                    [*Exeunt* KING, QUEEN, *and* Attendants.

Enter HAMLET, *reading*.

        How does my good Lord Hamlet?

HAM.   Well, God-a-mercy.

POL.   Do you know me, my lord?

HAM.   Excellent well. You are a fishmonger.

POL.   Not I, my lord.

---

[28] *lightness*] lightheadedness, mental derangement.
[29] *declension*] deterioration.
[30] *centre*] i.e., of the earth.
[31] *arras*] tapestry, named after the French town of Arras.
[32] *thereon*] on that account.
[33] *board*] accost, address.
[34] *presently*] immediately.

HAM.   Then I would you were so honest a man.

POL.   Honest, my lord?

HAM.   Ay, sir. To be honest, as this world goes, is to be one man picked out of ten thousand.

POL.   That's very true, my lord.

HAM.   For if the sun breed maggots in a dead dog, being a good kissing carrion[35]—Have you a daughter?

POL.   I have, my lord.

HAM.   Let her not walk i' the sun. Conception[36] is a blessing, but as your daughter may conceive—friend, look to't.

POL.   [Aside] How say you by that? Still[37] harping on my daughter. Yet he knew me not at first; he said I was a fishmonger. He is far gone. And truly in my youth I suffered much extremity for love, very near this. I'll speak to him again.—What do you read, my lord?

HAM.   Words, words, words.

POL.   What is the matter, my lord?

HAM.   Between who?

POL.   I mean, the matter that you read, my lord.

HAM.   Slanders, sir. For the satirical rogue says here that old men have grey beards, that their faces are wrinkled, their eyes purging[38] thick amber and plum-tree gum, and that they have a plentiful lack of wit, together with most weak hams—all which, sir, though I most powerfully and potently believe, yet I hold it not honesty[39] to have it thus set down; for yourself, sir, shall grow old as I am, if like a crab you could go backward.

POL.   [Aside] Though this be madness, yet there is method in't.— Will you walk out of the air, my lord?

HAM.   Into my grave?

POL.   Indeed, that's out of the air. [Aside] How pregnant sometimes his replies are!—a happiness that often madness hits on, which reason and sanity could not so prosperously be delivered of. I will leave him, and suddenly[40] contrive the means of meeting between him and my daughter.—My honourable lord, I will take my leave of you.

[35] *a good kissing carrion*] carrion good for kissing. "Carrion" can also have the meaning "live flesh."

[36] *Conception*] (1) forming concepts; (2) becoming pregnant.

[37] *Still*] always.

[38] *purging*] discharging.

[39] *honesty*] decency.

[40] *suddenly*] immediately.

HAM.	You cannot, sir, take from me anything that I will more willingly part withal—except my life, except my life, except my life.
POL.	Fare you well, my lord.
HAM.	These tedious old fools!

Enter ROSENCRANTZ *and* GUILDENSTERN.

POL.	You go to seek the Lord Hamlet. There he is.
ROS.	[*To Polonius*] God save you, sir. [*Exit* POLONIUS.
GUIL.	My honoured lord.
ROS.	My most dear lord.
HAM.	My excellent good friends. How dost thou, Guildenstern? Ah, Rosencrantz. Good lads, how do you both?
ROS.	As the indifferent[41] children of the earth.
GUIL.	Happy, in that we are not over-happy; on Fortune's cap we are not the very button.
HAM.	Nor the soles of her shoe?
ROS.	Neither, my lord.
HAM.	Then you live about her waist, or in the middle of her favours?
GUIL.	Faith, her privates[42] we.
HAM.	In the secret parts of Fortune? O, most true; she is a strumpet. What's the news?
ROS.	None, my lord, but that the world's grown honest.
HAM.	Then is doomsday near. But your news is not true. Let me question more in particular. What have you, my good friends, deserved at the hands of Fortune that she sends you to prison hither?
GUIL.	Prison, my lord?
HAM.	Denmark's a prison.
ROS.	Then is the world one.
HAM.	A goodly one, in which there are many confines, wards and dungeons, Denmark being one o' the worst.
ROS.	We think not so, my lord.
HAM.	Why, then 'tis none to you; for there is nothing either good or bad but thinking makes it so. To me it is a prison.
ROS.	Why, then your ambition makes it one: 'tis too narrow for your mind.
HAM.	O God, I could be bounded in a nutshell and count myself a king of infinite space were it not that I have bad dreams.

---

[41] *indifferent*] ordinary.
[42] *privates*] (1) persons not holding a public office; (2) genitalia.

GUIL.   Which dreams indeed are ambition; for the very substance of the ambitious is merely the shadow of a dream.

HAM.   A dream itself is but a shadow.

ROS.   Truly, and I hold ambition of so airy and light a quality that it is but a shadow's shadow.

HAM.   Then are our beggars bodies, and our monarchs and out-stretched heroes the beggars' shadows. Shall we to the court? For, by my fay, I cannot reason.

ROS. ⎫
GUIL. ⎭   We'll wait upon[43] you.

HAM.   No such matter. I will not sort[44] you with the rest of my servants; for, to speak to you like an honest man, I am most dreadfully attended. But, in the beaten way of friendship,[45] what make you at Elsinore?

ROS.   To visit you, my lord, no other occasion.

HAM.   Beggar that I am, I am even poor in thanks, but I thank you. And sure, dear friends, my thanks are too dear a halfpenny. Were you not sent for? Is it your own inclining? Is it a free visitation? Come, deal justly with me. Come, come. Nay, speak.

GUIL.   What should we say, my lord?

HAM.   Why, anything, but to the purpose. You were sent for; and there is a kind of confession in your looks which your modesties have not craft enough to colour. I know the good King and Queen have sent for you.

ROS.   To what end, my lord?

HAM.   That you must teach me. But let me conjure[46] you by the rights of our fellowship, by the consonancy of our youth, by the obligation of our ever-preserved love, and by what more dear a better proposer could charge you withal, be even[47] and direct with me whether you were sent for or no.

ROS.   [*Aside to* GUIL.] What say you?

HAM.   [*Aside*] Nay then, I have an eye of[48] you.—If you love me, hold not off.

GUIL.   My lord, we were sent for.

HAM.   I will tell you why. So shall my anticipation prevent your discovery,[49] and your secrecy to the King and Queen moult

---

[43] *wait upon*] escort.
[44] *sort*] class.
[45] *in the . . . friendship*] in the kind of plain language used among friends.
[46] *conjure*] entreat.
[47] *even*] honest.
[48] *of*] on.
[49] *prevent your discovery*] forestall your confession.

no feather. I have of late—but wherefore I know not—lost
all my mirth, forgone all custom of exercises, and indeed
it goes so heavily with my disposition that this goodly
frame,[50] the earth, seems to me a sterile promontory. This
most excellent canopy, the air, look you, this brave[51]
o'erhanging firmament, this majestical roof fretted[52] with
golden fire, why, it appears no other thing to me than a
foul and pestilent congregation of vapours. What a piece of
work is a man! How noble in reason, how infinite in
faculty, in form and moving how express and admirable, in
action how like an angel, in apprehension how like a
god—the beauty of the world, the paragon of animals! And
yet, to me, what is this quintessence of dust? Man delights
not me—no, nor woman neither, though by your smiling
you seem to say so.

ROS. My lord, there was no such stuff in my thoughts.

HAM. Why did you laugh then, when I said man delights not me?

ROS. To think, my lord, if you delight not in man, what lenten
entertainment[53] the players shall receive from you. We
coted[54] them on the way, and hither are they coming to offer
you service.

HAM. He that plays the king shall be welcome; his Majesty shall have
tribute of me. The adventurous knight shall use his foil and
target,[55] the lover shall not sigh gratis, the humorous man[56]
shall end his part in peace, the clown shall make those laugh
whose lungs are tickle o' the sere,[57] and the lady shall say her
mind freely, or the blank verse shall halt for't. What players
are they?

ROS. Even those you were wont to take such delight in, the tragedians of the city.

HAM. How chances it they travel? Their residence, both in reputation
and profit, was better both ways.

ROS. I think their inhibition[58] comes by the means of the late
innovation.

---

[50] *frame*] structure.
[51] *brave*] beautiful.
[52] *fretted*] adorned.
[53] *lenten entertainment*] poor reception.
[54] *coted*] passed by.
[55] *foil and target*] fencing sword and targe (light shield)
[56] *humorous man*] stage character representing the effect of one of the four "humours,"
particularly that of "choler."
[57] *are tickle o' the sere*] have a hair trigger; i.e., will laugh at anything.
[58] *inhibition*] prohibition (from acting in the town).

HAM.   Do they hold the same estimation they did when I was in the
        city? Are they so followed?

ROS.   No, indeed, are they not.

HAM.   How comes it? Do they grow rusty?

ROS.   Nay, their endeavour keeps in the wonted pace. But there is, sir,
        an eyrie of children, little eyases, [59] that cry out on the top of
        question and are most tyrannically[60] clapped for't. These
        are now the fashion, and so berattle the common stages[61]—
        so they call them—that many wearing rapiers are afraid of
        goose-quills, [62] and dare scarce come thither.

HAM.   What, are they children? Who maintains 'em? How are they
        escoted?[63] Will they pursue the quality[64] no longer than
        they can sing? Will they not say afterwards, if they should
        grow themselves to common players—as it is most like, if
        their means are no better—their writers do them wrong to
        make them exclaim against their own succession?[65]

ROS.   Faith, there has been much to do on both sides, and the nation
        holds it no sin to tarre[66] them to controversy. There was for a
        while no money bid for argument[67] unless the poet and the
        player went to cuffs[68] in the question. [69]

HAM.   Is't possible?

GUIL.   O, there has been much throwing about of brains.

HAM.   Do the boys carry it away?[70]

ROS.   Ay, that they do, my lord, Hercules and his load[71] too.

HAM.   It is not very strange; for my uncle is King of Denmark, and
        those that would make mows[72] at him while my father lived,
        give twenty, forty, fifty, a hundred ducats apiece for his
        picture in little. 'Sblood, there is something in this more
        than natural, if philosophy could find it out.

                                            [*Flourish of trumpets within.*

---

[59] *eyases*] young hawks.

[60] *tyrannically*] violently.

[61] *berattle the common stages*] berate the public playhouses.

[62] *many . . . goose-quills*] gallants are afraid of being satirized.

[63] *escoted*] supported.

[64] *quality*] (acting) profession.

[65] *succession*] i.e., future profession.

[66] *tarre*] incite.

[67] *argument*] plots for plays.

[68] *went to cuffs*] attacked one another.

[69] *in the question*] concerning the controversy.

[70] *carry it away*] win.

[71] *Hercules and his load*] perhaps a reference to the Globe theatre, the sign of which portrayed
     Hercules supporting the earth.

[72] *mows*] faces.

GUIL.   There are the players.

HAM.   Gentlemen, you are welcome to Elsinore. Your hands, come then. The appurtenance of welcome is fashion and ceremony. Let me comply with you in this garb,[73] lest my extent[74] to the players—which, I tell you, must show fairly outwards—should more appear like entertainment than yours. You are welcome. But my uncle-father and aunt-mother are deceived.

GUIL.   In what, my dear lord?

HAM.   I am but mad north-north-west. When the wind is southerly I know a hawk from a handsaw.

Enter POLONIUS.

POL.   Well be with you, gentlemen.

HAM.   Hark you, Guildenstern, and you too—at each ear a hearer. That great baby you see there is not yet out of his swaddling clouts.

ROS.   Happily[75] he's the second time come to them; for they say an old man is twice a child.

HAM.   I will prophesy he comes to tell me of the players. Mark it. You say right, sir; o' Monday morning; 'twas so, indeed.

POL.   My lord, I have news to tell you.

HAM.   My lord, I have news to tell you. When Roscius[76] was an actor in Rome—

POL.   The actors are come hither, my lord.

HAM.   Buzz, buzz.

POL.   Upon my honour—

HAM.   Then came each actor on his ass—

POL.   The best actors in the world, either for tragedy, comedy, history, pastoral, pastoral-comical, historical-pastoral, tragical-historical, tragical-comical-historical-pastoral, scene individable,[77] or poem unlimited.[78] Seneca cannot be too heavy, nor Plautus too light. For the law of writ and the liberty, these are the only men.

HAM.   O Jephthah, judge of Israel,[79] what a treasure hadst thou!

POL.   What a treasure had he, my lord?

[73] *garb*] manner.

[74] *extent*] welcome.

[75] *Happily*] haply, perhaps.

[76] *Roscius*] the most celebrated actor of ancient Rome.

[77] *individable*] unclassifiable.

[78] *unlimited*] undefined.

[79] *Jephthah, judge of Israel*] a Biblical figure who sacrificed his own daughter.

HAM.   Why,

> One fair daughter, and no more,
> The which he loved passing[80] well.

POL.   [*Aside*] Still on my daughter.
HAM.   Am I not i' the right, old Jephthah?
POL.   If you call me Jephthah, my lord, I have a daughter that I love
   passing well.
HAM.   Nay, that follows not.
POL.   What follows, then, my lord?
HAM.   Why,

> As by lot God wot,

and then, you know,

> It came to pass, as most like it was—

The first row[81] of the pious chanson will show you more; for
look where my abridgement[82] comes.

Enter the Players.

You are welcome, masters. Welcome, all. I am glad to see
thee well. Welcome, good friends. O, my old friend! Why,
thy face is valanced[83] since I saw thee last. Comest thou to
beard[84] me in Denmark? What, my young lady[85] and mistress! By'r lady, your ladyship is nearer to heaven than when
I saw you last, by the altitude of a chopine.[86] Pray God, your
voice, like a piece of uncurrent gold, be not cracked within
the ring.[87] Masters, you are all welcome. We'll e'en to't like
French falconers, fly at any thing we see.[88] We'll have a
speech straight. Come, give us a taste of your quality.
Come, a passionate speech.
FIRST PLAY.   What speech, my good lord?

---

[80] *passing*] exceedingly.
[81] *row*] stanza.
[82] *abridgement*] (1) entertainment; (2) reason for cutting short the conversation with Polonius.
[83] *valanced*] fringed (bearded).
[84] *beard*] face, defy (with the obvious pun on the actor's new facial hair).
[85] *my young lady*] a boy who would play a woman's role.
[86] *chopine*] a woman's thick-soled shoe.
[87] *cracked within the ring*] A coin that had been clipped within the ring surrounding the
sovereign's head was not legal tender.
[88] *French . . . see*] Falcons were trained to attack only one kind of quarry. Hamlet is thus
expressing his overenthusiasm.

HAM.   I heard thee speak me a speech once, but it was never acted, or,
if it was, not above once; for the play, I remember, pleased
not the million, 'twas caviare to the general.[89] But it was—
as I received it, and others, whose judgements in such
matters cried in the top of[90] mine—an excellent play, well
digested[91] in the scenes, set down with as much modesty[92]
as cunning.[93] I remember, one said there were no sallets[94]
in the lines to make the matter savoury, nor no matter in
the phrase that might indict the author of affection,[95] but
called it an honest method, as wholesome as sweet, and by
very much more handsome than fine. One speech in it I
chiefly loved: 'twas Æneas' tale to Dido, and thereabout
of it especially where he speaks of Priam's slaughter.[96] If it
live in your memory, begin at this line—let me see, let
me see—
The rugged Pyrrhus, like th' Hyrcanian beast—[97]
It is not so. It begins with Pyrrhus—
The rugged Pyrrhus, he whose sable arms,[98]
Black as his purpose, did the night resemble
When he lay couched in the ominous horse,[99]
Hath now this dread and black complexion smear'd
With heraldry more dismal. Head to foot
Now is he total gules,[100] horridly trick'd[101]
With blood of fathers, mothers, daughters, sons,
Baked and impasted with the parching streets,
That lend a tyrannous and a damned light
To their lord's murder. Roasted in wrath and fire,
And thus o'er-sized[102] with coagulate gore,
With eyes like carbuncles, the hellish Pyrrhus
Old grandsire Priam seeks.
So, proceed you.

[89] *caviare to the general*] i.e., too rich for common taste.

[90] *in the top of*] with more authority than.

[91] *digested*] arranged.

[92] *modesty*] restraint.

[93] *cunning*] skill.

[94] *sallets*] salad, relish; here, offensive language.

[95] *affection*] affectation.

[96] *Priam's slaughter*] for the account of the sacking of Troy, see Virgil's *Aeneid*, II.

[97] *Hyrcanian beast*] tiger (from Hyrcania, a region on the southeast coast of the Caspian sea).

[98] *sable arms*] black armor.

[99] *the ominous horse*] the Trojan horse.

[100] *gules*] a heraldic term for red.

[101] *trick'd*] a heraldic term; here, adorned.

[102] *o'ersized*] smeared.

POL.   'Fore God, my lord, well spoken, with good accent and good
            discretion.
FIRST PLAY.   Anon he finds him
            Striking too short at Greeks. His antique sword,
            Rebellious to his arm, lies where it falls,
            Repugnant[103] to command. Unequal match'd,
            Pyrrhus at Priam drives, in rage strikes wide,
            But with the whiff and wind of his fell[104] sword
            The unnerved father falls. Then senseless[105] Ilium,
            Seeming to feel this blow, with flaming top
            Stoops to his base, and with a hideous crash
            Takes prisoner Pyrrhus' ear. For, lo! his sword,
            Which was declining on the milky head
            Of reverend Priam, seem'd i' the air to stick.
            So, as a painted tyrant, Pyrrhus stood,
            And like a neutral to his will and matter,[106]
            Did nothing.
            But as we often see, against[107] some storm,
            A silence in the heavens, the rack[108] stand still,
            The bold winds speechless and the orb below
            As hush as death, anon the dreadful thunder
            Doth rend the region,[109] so after Pyrrhus' pause
            Aroused vengeance[110] sets him new a-work,
            And never did the Cyclops' hammers fall
            On Mars's armour, forged for proof[111] eterne,
            With less remorse[112] than Pyrrhus' bleeding sword
            Now falls on Priam.
            Out, out, thou strumpet, Fortune! All you gods,
            In general synod take away her power,
            Break all the spokes and fellies[113] from her wheel,
            And bowl the round nave[114] down the hill of heaven
            As low as to the fiends.
POL.   This is too long.

[103] *Repugnant*] refractory.
[104] *fell*] fierce.
[105] *senseless*] insensate.
[106] *matter*] purpose, aim.
[107] *against*] before.
[108] *rack*] clouds.
[109] *region*] sky, air.
[110] *vengeance*] Achilles, Pyrrhus' father, had been killed by Paris, Priam's son.
[111] *proof*] tested and found impenetrable.
[112] *remorse*] compassion.
[113] *fellies*] rim.
[114] *nave*] hub.

HAM.   It shall to the barber's, with your beard. Prithee, say on. He's for
              a jig[115] or a tale of bawdry, or he sleeps. Say on; come to
              Hecuba.
FIRST PLAY.   But who, O, who had seen the mobled[116] queen—
HAM.   'The mobled queen?'
POL.   That's good; 'mobled queen' is good.
FIRST PLAY.   Run barefoot up and down, threatening the flames
              With bisson rheum,[117] a clout upon that head
              Where late the diadem stood, and for a robe,
              About her lank and all o'er-teemed[118] loins,
              A blanket, in the alarm of fear caught up;
              Who this had seen, with tongue in venom steep'd
              'Gainst Fortune's state would treason have pronounced.
              But if the gods themselves did see her then,
              When she saw Pyrrhus make malicious sport
              In mincing with his sword her husband's limbs,
              The instant burst of clamour that she made,
              Unless things mortal move them not at all,
              Would have made milch[119] the burning eyes of heaven
              And passion in the gods.
POL.   Look whether he has not turned his colour and has tears in's
              eyes. Prithee, no more.
HAM.   'Tis well. I'll have thee speak out the rest of this soon. Good my
              lord, will you see the players well bestowed?[120] Do you hear,
              let them be well used, for they are the abstract[121] and brief
              chronicles of the time. After your death you were better have
              a bad epitaph than their ill report while you live.
POL.   My lord, I will use them according to their desert.
HAM.   God's bodykins, man, much better. Use every man after his
              desert, and who shall 'scape whipping? Use them after your
              own honour and dignity: the less they deserve, the more
              merit is in your bounty. Take them in.
POL.   Come, sirs.
HAM.   Follow him, friends. We'll hear a play tomorrow.
                   [*Exit* POLONIUS *with all the* Players *but the* First.]
              Dost thou hear me, old friend? Can you play *The Murder of
              Gonzago?*

---

[115] *jig*] a farcical metrical composition with singing and dancing.
[116] *mobled*] with head muffled.
[117] *bisson rheum*] blinding tears.
[118] *o'er-teemed*] worn out by childbearing.
[119] *milch*] shed milky tears.
[120] *bestowed*] lodged.
[121] *abstract*] summary.

FIRST PLAY.   Ay, my lord.
HAM.   We'll ha't tomorrow night. You could, for a need,[122] study a
             speech of some dozen or sixteen lines, which I would set
             down and insert in't, could you not?
FIRST PLAY.   Ay, my lord.
HAM.   Very well. Follow that lord, and look you mock him not. [*Exit*
             FIRST PLAYER.] My good friends, I'll leave you till night.
             You are welcome to Elsinore.
ROS.   Good my lord.
HAM.   Ay, so. God be wi' ye.
                         [*Exeunt* ROSENCRANTZ *and* GUILDENSTERN.
                              Now I am alone.
             O, what a rogue and peasant slave am I!
             Is it not monstrous that this player here,
             But in a fiction, in a dream of passion,
             Could force his soul so to his own conceit
             That from her working all his visage wann'd,
             Tears in his eyes, distraction in's aspect,
             A broken voice, and his whole function suiting
             With forms to his conceit?[123] And all for nothing!
             For Hecuba!
             What's Hecuba to him, or he to Hecuba,
             That he should weep for her? What would he do,
             Had he the motive and the cue for passion
             That I have? He would drown the stage with tears
             And cleave the general ear with horrid speech,
             Make mad the guilty and appal the free,[124]
             Confound the ignorant, and amaze[125] indeed
             The very faculties of eyes and ears.
             Yet I,
             A dull and muddy-mettled[126] rascal, peak,[127]
             Like John-a-dreams, unpregnant of[128] my cause,
             And can say nothing; no, not for a king,
             Upon whose property and most dear life
             A damn'd defeat was made. Am I a coward?
             Who calls me villain, breaks my pate across,
             Plucks off my beard and blows it in my face,

[122] *for a need*] if necessary.
[123] *his whole . . . conceit*] his entire being producing gestures to match his conception.
[124] *free*] innocent.
[125] *amaze*] confuse.
[126] *muddy-mettled*] dull-spirited.
[127] *peak*] mope.
[128] *unpregnant of*] indifferent to.

Tweaks me by the nose, gives me the lie i' the throat,
As deep as to the lungs? Who does me this?
Ha!
'Swounds, I should take it: for it cannot be
But I am pigeon-liver'd and lack gall
To make oppression bitter,[129] or ere this
I should have fatted all the region kites[130]
With this slave's offal. Bloody, bawdy villain!
Remorseless, treacherous, lecherous, kindless[131] villain!
Why, what an ass am I! This is most brave,
That I, the son of a dear father murder'd,
Prompted to my revenge by heaven and hell,
Must, like a whore, unpack my heart with words,
And fall a-cursing, like a very drab,[132]
A scullion![133] Fie upon't! Foh!
About,[134] my brain! Hum, I have heard
That guilty creatures, sitting at a play,
Have by the very cunning of the scene
Been struck so to the soul that presently[135]
They have proclaim'd their malefactions.
For murder, though it have no tongue, will speak
With most miraculous organ. I'll have these players
Play something like the murder of my father
Before mine uncle. I'll observe his looks,
I'll tent[136] him to the quick. If he but blench,[137]
I know my course. The spirit that I have seen
May be the devil, and the devil hath power
To assume a pleasing shape, yea, and perhaps
Out of my weakness and my melancholy,
As he is very potent with such spirits,[138]
Abuses me to damn me. I'll have grounds
More relative[139] than this. The play's the thing
Wherein I'll catch the conscience of the King.   [*Exit.*

---

[129] *pigeon-liver'd . . . bitter*] Pigeons were thought not to produce gall, and therefore to be without malice.
[130] *region kites*] kites of the air.
[131] *kindless*] unnatural.
[132] *drab*] prostitute.
[133] *scullion*] kitchen servant.
[134] *About*] get active.
[135] *presently*] immediately.
[136] *tent*] probe, search.
[137] *blench*] start, flinch.
[138] *spirits*] humors.
[139] *relative*] to the purpose, conclusive.

ACT III.

Scene I. *A room in the castle.*

Enter King, Queen, Polonius, Ophelia, Rosencrantz, *and* Guildenstern.

KING.	And can you by no drift of conference[1]
	Get from him why he puts on this confusion,
	Grating so harshly all his days of quiet
	With turbulent and dangerous lunacy?
Ros.	He does confess he feels himself distracted,
	But from what cause he will by no means speak.
Guil.	Nor do we find him forward to be sounded;
	But, with a crafty madness, keeps aloof,
	When we would bring him on to some confession
	Of his true state.
Queen.	Did he receive you well?
Ros.	Most like a gentleman.
Guil.	But with much forcing of his disposition.
Ros.	Niggard of question,[2] but of our demands
	Most free in his reply.
Queen.	Did you assay him
	To any pastime?[3]
Ros.	Madam, it so fell out that certain players
	We o'er-raught[4] on the way. Of these we told him,
	And there did seem in him a kind of joy
	To hear of it. They are about the court,
	And, as I think, they have already order

---

[1] *drift of conference*] turn of conversation.
[2] N*iggard of question*] sparing in conversation.
[3] *assay . . . pastime*] tempt him with any form of entertainment.
[4] *o'er-raught*] overtook.

This night to play before him.

POL.   'Tis most true;
And he beseech'd me to entreat your Majesties
To hear and see the matter.

KING.   With all my heart; and it doth much content me
To hear him so inclined.
Good gentlemen, give him a further edge,[5]
And drive his purpose on to these delights.

ROS.   We shall, my lord.
                    [*Exeunt* ROSENCRANTZ *and* GUILDENSTERN.

KING.   Sweet Gertrude, leave us too;
For we have closely[6] sent for Hamlet hither,
That he, as 'twere by accident, may here
Affront[7] Ophelia.
Her father and myself, lawful espials,[8]
Will so bestow ourselves that, seeing unseen,
We may of their encounter frankly judge,
And gather by him, as he is behaved,
If't be the affliction of his love or no
That thus he suffers for.

QUEEN.   I shall obey you.
And for your part, Ophelia, I do wish
That your good beauties be the happy cause
Of Hamlet's wildness; so shall I hope your virtues
Will bring him to his wonted way again,
To both your honours.

OPH.   Madam, I wish it may. [*Exit* QUEEN.

POL.   Ophelia, walk you here. Gracious,[9] so please you,
We will bestow ourselves. [*To* OPHELIA.] Read on this book,
That show of such an exercise[10] may colour
Your loneliness.[11] We are oft to blame in this—
'Tis too much proved—that with devotion's visage
And pious action we do sugar o'er
The devil himself.

KING.   [*Aside*] O, 'tis too true.

---

[5] *edge*] incitement.
[6] *closely*] secretly.
[7] *Affront*] encounter.
[8] *espials*] spies.
[9] *Gracious*] Your Grace.
[10] *exercise*] act of religious devotion.
[11] *colour Your loneliness*] make your being alone seem plausible.

> How smart a lash that speech doth give my conscience.
> The harlot's cheek, beautied with plastering art,
> Is not more ugly to the thing that helps it
> Than is my deed to my most painted word.
> O heavy burden!

POL.   I hear him coming. Let's withdraw, my lord.

                        [*Exeunt* KING *and* POLONIUS.

Enter HAMLET.

HAM.   To be, or not to be, that is the question:
> Whether 'tis nobler in the mind to suffer
> The slings and arrows of outrageous fortune,
> Or to take arms against a sea of troubles,
> And by opposing end them. To die: to sleep;
> No more; and by a sleep to say we end
> The heart-ache and the thousand natural shocks
> That flesh is heir to; 'tis a consummation
> Devoutly to be wish'd. To die, to sleep;
> To sleep; perchance to dream. Ay, there's the rub;[12]
> For in that sleep of death what dreams may come,
> When we have shuffled off[13] this mortal coil,[14]
> Must give us pause—there's the respect
> That makes calamity of so long life.[15]
> For who would bear the whips and scorns of time,
> The oppressor's wrong, the proud man's contumely,
> The pangs of disprized[16] love, the law's delay,
> The insolence of office, and the spurns
> That patient merit of the unworthy takes,
> When he himself might his quietus[17] make
> With a bare bodkin?[18] Who would fardels[19] bear,
> To grunt and sweat under a weary life,
> But that the dread of something after death,
> The undiscover'd country from whose bourn[20]
> No traveller returns, puzzles the will,

[12] *rub*] obstacle (a bowling term for anything blocking or deflecting the course of the bowl).
[13] *shuffled off*] cast off.
[14] *coil*] (1) turmoil; (2) (?) rope.
[15] *of so long life*] so long-lived.
[16] *disprized*] undervalued.
[17] *quietus*] final settlement of an account.
[18] *bare bodkin*] mere dagger.
[19] *fardels*] burdens, packs.
[20] *bourn*] boundary.

And makes us rather bear those ills we have
Than fly to others that we know not of?
Thus conscience[21] does make cowards of us all,
And thus the native hue of resolution
Is sicklied o'er with the pale cast of thought,
And enterprises of great pitch[22] and moment
With this regard their currents turn awry
And lose the name of action. Soft you now,
The fair Ophelia! Nymph, in thy orisons[23]
Be all my sins remember'd.

OPH.   Good my lord,
How does your honour for this many a day?

HAM. I humbly thank you: well.

OPH. My lord, I have remembrances of yours
That I have longed long to redeliver.
I pray you, now receive them.

HAM.   No, not I.
I never gave you aught.

OPH. My honour'd lord, you know right well you did;
And with them words of so sweet breath composed
As made the things more rich. Their perfume lost,
Take these again; for to the noble mind
Rich gifts wax poor when givers prove unkind.
There, my lord.

HAM. Ha, ha! Are you honest?[24]

OPH. My lord?

HAM. Are you fair?

OPH. What means your lordship?

HAM. That if you be honest and fair, your honesty should admit no
discourse to your beauty.

OPH. Could beauty, my lord, have better commerce than with honesty?

HAM. Ay, truly; for the power of beauty will sooner transform honesty from what it is to a bawd than the force of honesty can translate beauty into his likeness. This was sometime a paradox, but now the time gives it proof. I did love you once.

OPH. Indeed, my lord, you made me believe so.

---

[21] *conscience*] (1) consciousness; (2) conscience.
[22] *pitch*] height.
[23] *orisons*] prayers.
[24] *honest*] (1) truthful; (2) chaste.

HAM.   You should not have believed me; for virtue cannot so inocu-
        late[25] our old stock but we shall relish of it.[26] I loved you not.

OPH.   I was the more deceived.

HAM.   Get thee to a nunnery. Why, wouldst thou be a breeder of
        sinners? I am myself indifferent[27] honest, but yet I could
        accuse me of such things that it were better my mother had
        not borne me. I am very proud, revengeful, ambitious, with
        more offences at my beck[28] than I have thoughts to put them
        in, imagination to give them shape, or time to act them in.
        What should such fellows as I do crawling between heaven
        and earth? We are arrant knaves all. Believe none of us. Go
        thy ways to a nunnery. Where's your father?

OPH.   At home, my lord.

HAM.   Let the doors be shut upon him, that he may play the fool
        nowhere but in's own house. Farewell.

OPH.   O, help him, you sweet heavens!

HAM.   If thou dost marry, I'll give thee this plague for thy dowry: be
        thou as chaste as ice, as pure as snow, thou shalt not escape
        calumny. Get thee to a nunnery, farewell. Or, if thou wilt
        needs marry, marry a fool; for wise men know well enough
        what monsters[29] you make of them. To a nunnery, go; and
        quickly too. Farewell.

OPH.   O heavenly powers, restore him!

HAM.   I have heard of your paintings too, well enough. God hath given
        you one face, and you make yourselves another. You jig, you
        amble, and you lisp, and nickname God's creatures, and
        make your wantonness your ignorance. Go to, I'll no more
        on't; it hath made me mad. I say, we will have no more mar-
        riages. Those that are married already—all but one—shall
        live; the rest shall keep as they are. To a nunnery, go. [*Exit.*

OPH.   O, what a noble mind is here o'erthrown!
        The courtier's, soldier's, scholar's, eye, tongue, sword,
        The expectancy and rose of the fair state,
        The glass of fashion and the mould of form,
        The observed[30] of all observers, quite, quite down!
        And I, of ladies most deject and wretched,

---

[25] *inoculate*] graft.
[26] *of it*] i.e., of the old, sinful nature.
[27] *indifferent*] moderately.
[28] *at my beck*] ready to be committed.
[29] *monsters*] i.e., cuckolds (having grown horns).
[30] *observed*] revered, respected.

That suck'd the honey of his music vows,
Now see that noble and most sovereign reason
Like sweet bells jangled out of tune and harsh,
That unmatch'd form and feature of blown[31] youth
Blasted with ecstasy.[32] O, woe is me,
To have seen what I have seen, see what I see!

Enter KING *and* POLONIUS.

KING.   Love? His affections do not that way tend;
          Nor what he spake, though it lack'd form a little,
          Was not like madness. There's something in his soul
          O'er which his melancholy sits on brood,
          And I do doubt[33] the hatch and the disclose
          Will be some danger; which for to prevent,
          I have in quick determination
          Thus set it down: he shall with speed to England,
          For the demand of our neglected tribute.
          Haply the seas and countries different
          With variable objects shall expel
          This something-settled matter in his heart,
          Whereon his brains still[34] beating puts him thus
          From fashion of himself.[35] What think you on't?
POL.   It shall do well. But yet do I believe
          The origin and commencement of his grief
          Sprung from neglected love. How now, Ophelia?
          You need not tell us what Lord Hamlet said;
          We heard it all. My lord, do as you please;
          But, if you hold it fit, after the play,
          Let his queen mother all alone entreat him
          To show his grief. Let her be round[36] with him;
          And I'll be placed, so please you, in the ear
          Of all their conference. If she find him not,
          To England send him, or confine him where
          Your wisdom best shall think.
KING.   It shall be so.
          Madness in great ones must not unwatch'd go.   [*Exeunt.*

---

[31] *blown*] in full blossom.
[32] *ecstasy*] madness.
[33] *doubt*] fear.
[34] *still*] constantly.
[35] *From fashion of himself*] out of his normal manner.
[36] *be round*] speak plainly.

SCENE II. *A hall in the castle.*

Enter HAMLET *and* Players.

HAM.   Speak the speech, I pray you, as I pronounced it to you,
        trippingly on the tongue. But if you mouth it, as many of
        your players do, I had as lief the town-crier spoke my lines.
        Nor do not saw the air too much with your hand, thus; but
        use all gently: for in the very torrent, tempest, and, as I may
        say, whirlwind of your passion, you must acquire and beget a
        temperance that may give it smoothness. O, it offends me to
        the soul to hear a robustious periwig-pated fellow tear a
        passion to tatters, to very rags, to split the ears of the ground-
        lings,[1] who, for the most part, are capable of[2] nothing but
        inexplicable dumb-shows and noise. I would have such a
        fellow whipped for o'erdoing Termagant.[3] It out-Herods
        Herod.[4] Pray you, avoid it.

FIRST PLAY.   I warrant your honour.

HAM.   Be not too tame neither, but let your own discretion be your
        tutor. Suit the action to the word, the word to the action,
        with this special observance, that you o'erstep not the mod-
        esty of nature. For anything so overdone is from the purpose
        of playing, whose end, both at the first and now, was and is,
        to hold, as 'twere, the mirror up to nature, to show virtue
        her own feature, scorn her own image, and the very age
        and body of the time his form and pressure.[5] Now this
        overdone or come tardy off,[6] though it make the unskilful
        laugh, cannot but make the judicious grieve, the censure[7]
        of the which one must in your allowance o'erweigh a whole
        theatre of others. O, there be players that I have seen play,
        and heard others praise, and that highly, not to speak it pro-
        fanely, that neither having the accent of Christians nor the

---

[1] *groundlings*] those spectators who stood in the pit of the theater.

[2] *capable of*] responsive to.

[3] *Termagant*] a legendary Muslim deity, presented as a violently noisy character in medieval
    dramas.

[4] *Herod*] Herod was presented as a ranting tyrant in medieval dramas.

[5] *pressure*] stamped impression.

[6] *come tardy off*] performed inadequately.

[7] *censure*] critical judgement.

          gait of Christian, pagan, nor man, have so strutted and
          bellowed, that I have thought some of Nature's journeymen[8]
          had made men, and not made them well, they imitated
          humanity so abominably.

FIRST PLAY.   I hope we have reformed that indifferently[9] with us, sir.

HAM.   O, reform it altogether. And let those that play your clowns
          speak no more than is set down for them; for there be of
          them that will themselves laugh, to set on some quantity of
          barren spectators to laugh too, though in the meantime
          some necessary question of the play be then to be consid-
          ered. That's villanous, and shows a most pitiful ambition in
          the fool that uses it. Go, make you ready. [*Exeunt* Players.

Enter POLONIUS, ROSENCRANTZ, *and* GUILDENSTERN.

          How now, my lord! Will the King hear this piece of work?

POL.   And the Queen too, and that presently.[10]

HAM.   Bid the players make haste.   [*Exit* POLONIUS.
          Will you two help to hasten them?

ROS. ⎫
GUIL. ⎭   We will, my lord.

               [*Exeunt* ROSENCRANTZ *and* GUILDENSTERN.

HAM.   What ho, Horatio!

Enter HORATIO.

HOR.   Here, sweet lord, at your service.

HAM.   Horatio, thou art e'en as just a man
          As e'er my conversation coped[11] withal.

HOR.   O, my dear lord—

HAM.   Nay, do not think I flatter;
          For what advancement may I hope from thee,
          That no revenue hast but thy good spirits,
          To feed and clothe thee? Why should the poor be flatter'd?
          No, let the candied tongue lick absurd[12] pomp,
          And crook the pregnant[13] hinges of the knee
          Where thrift[14] may follow fawning. Dost thou hear?

     [8] *journeymen*] hired workmen.
     [9] *indifferently*] tolerably well.
   [10] *presently*] immediately.
   [11] *coped*] encountered.
   [12] *absurd*] insipid.
   [13] *pregnant*] ready.
   [14] *thrift*] profit.

Since my dear soul was mistress of her choice,
And could of men distinguish her election,
Sh'hath seal'd thee for herself; for thou hast been
As one, in suffering all, that suffers nothing,
A man that Fortune's buffets and rewards
Hast ta'en with equal thanks; and blest are those
Whose blood[15] and judgement are so well commeddled[16]
That they are not a pipe for Fortune's finger
To sound what stop she please. Give me that man
That is not passion's slave, and I will wear him
In my heart's core, ay, in my heart of heart,
As I do thee. Something too much of this.
There is a play tonight before the King.
One scene of it comes near the circumstance
Which I have told thee of my father's death.
I prithee, when thou seest that act afoot,
Even with the very comment[17] of thy soul
Observe my uncle. If his occulted guilt
Do not itself unkennel in one speech,
It is a damned ghost that we have seen,
And my imaginations are as foul
As Vulcan's stithy.[18] Give him heedful note;
For I mine eyes will rivet to his face,
And after we will both our judgements join
In censure of his seeming.[19]

HOR.   Well, my lord.
If he steal aught the whilst this play is playing,
And 'scape detecting, I will pay the theft.

HAM.   They are coming to the play. I must be idle.[20]
Get you a place.

Danish march. A flourish. Enter KING, QUEEN, POLONIUS, OPHELIA,
ROSENCRANTZ, GUILDENSTERN, *and other Lords attendant, with the
Guard carrying torches.*

KING.   How fares our cousin Hamlet?

---

[15] *blood*] passion.
[16] *commeddled*] commingled.
[17] *the very comment*] the most searching judgment.
[18] *Vulcan's stithy*] the smithy of Vulcan, god of fire and metalworking.
[19] *In censure of his seeming*] in judgment of his behavior.
[20] *idle*] unoccupied, distracted.

HAM.   Excellent, i' faith; of the chameleon's dish.[21] I eat the air, promise-crammed. You cannot feed capons so.

KING.   I have nothing with this answer, Hamlet. These words are not mine.[22]

HAM.   No, nor mine now. [*To* POLONIUS] My lord, you played once i' the university, you say?

POL.   That did I, my lord, and was accounted a good actor.

HAM.   What did you enact?

POL.   I did enact Julius Cæsar. I was killed i' the Capitol. Brutus killed me.

HAM.   It was a brute part of him to kill so capital a calf there. Be the players ready?

ROS.   Ay, my lord; they stay upon your patience.

QUEEN.   Come hither, my dear Hamlet, sit by me.

HAM.   No, good mother, here's metal more attractive.

POL.   [*To the* KING] O, ho! do you mark that?

HAM.   Lady, shall I lie in your lap? [*Lying down at* OPHELIA's *feet*.

OPH.   No, my lord.

HAM.   I mean, my head upon your lap?

OPH.   Ay, my lord.

HAM.   Do you think I meant country matters?

OPH.   I think nothing, my lord.

HAM.   That's a fair thought to lie between maids' legs.

OPH.   What is, my lord?

HAM.   Nothing.

OPH.   You are merry, my lord.

HAM.   Who, I?

OPH.   Ay, my lord.

HAM.   O God, your only jig-maker. What should a man do but be merry? For, look you, how cheerfully my mother looks, and my father died within's two hours.

OPH.   Nay, 'tis twice two months, my lord.

HAM.   So long? Nay then, let the devil wear black, for I'll have a suit of sables. O heavens, die two months ago, and not forgotten yet! Then there's hope a great man's memory may outlive his life half a year. But, by'r lady, he must build churches then, or else shall he suffer not thinking on, with the hobby-horse,[23] whose epitaph is, 'For, O, for, O, the hobby-horse is forgot.'

---

[21] *the chameleon's dish*] Chameleons were said to feed on air. Hamlet deliberately misinterprets "fare" to mean "feed."

[22] *are not mine*] do not correspond to my question.

[23] *hobby-horse*] a character in the morris dance.

Hautboys play. The dumb-show enters.

Enter a King *and a* Queen *very lovingly, the* Queen *embracing him, and he her. She kneels and makes show of protestation unto him. He takes her up and declines his head upon her neck; lays him down upon a bank of flowers. She, seeing him asleep, leaves him. Anon comes in a fellow, takes off his crown, kisses it, and pours poison in the* King's *ears, and exit. The* Queen *returns, finds the* King *dead, and makes passionate action. The* Poisoner, *with some two or three* Mutes, *comes in again, seeming to lament with her. The dead body is carried away. The* Poisoner *wooes the* Queen *with gifts. She seems loath and unwilling awhile, but in the end accepts his love.*   [*Exeunt.*

OPH. What means this, my lord?
HAM. Marry, this is miching mallecho.[24] It means mischief.
OPH. Belike this show imports the argument[25] of the play.

Enter PROLOGUE.

HAM. We shall know by this fellow. The players cannot keep counsel;
   they'll tell all.
OPH. Will he tell us what this show meant?
HAM. Ay, or any show that you'll show him. Be not you ashamed to
   show, he'll not shame to tell you what it means.
OPH. You are naught,[26] you are naught. I'll mark the play.
PRO.   For us, and for our tragedy,
       Here stooping to your clemency,
       We beg your hearing patiently.
HAM. Is this a prologue, or the posy[27] of a ring?
OPH. 'Tis brief, my lord.
HAM. As woman's love.

Enter two Players, KING *and* QUEEN.

P. KING. Full thirty times hath Phœbus' cart[28] gone round
    Neptune's salt wash and Tellus' orbed ground,[29]
    And thirty dozen moons with borrowed sheen
    About the world have times twelve thirties been,
    Since love our hearts and Hymen[30] did our hands
    Unite commutual in most sacred bands.

---

[24] *miching mallecho*] insidious mischief.
[25] *argument*] plot.
[26] *naught*] worthless, indecent.
[27] *posy*] a motto inscribed on a ring.
[28] *Phœbus' cart*] the chariot of the sun-god.
[29] *Tellus' orbed ground*] the earth.
[30] *Hymen*] the god of marriage.

P. QUEEN.   So many journeys may the sun and moon
           Make us again count o'er ere love be done.
           But, woe is me, you are so sick of late,
           So far from cheer and from your former state,
           That I distrust[31] you. Yet, though I distrust,
           Discomfort you, my lord, it nothing must.
           For women's fear and love hold quantity,[32]
           In neither aught, or in extremity.
           Now, what my love is, proof hath made you know,
           And as my love is sized, my fear is so.
           Where love is great, the littlest doubts are fear,
           Where little fears grow great, great love grows there.
P. KING.   Faith, I must leave thee, love, and shortly too.
           My operant[33] powers their functions leave to do,[34]
           And thou shalt live in this fair world behind,
           Honour'd, beloved; and haply one as kind
           For husband shalt thou—
P. QUEEN.   O, confound the rest!
           Such love must needs be treason in my breast.
           In second husband let me be accurst,
           None wed the second but who kill'd the first.
HAM.   [*Aside*] Wormwood, wormwood.
P. QUEEN.   The instances[35] that second marriage move
           Are base respects of thrift,[36] but none of love.
           A second time I kill my husband dead
           When second husband kisses me in bed.
P. KING.   I do believe you think what now you speak,
           But what we do determine oft we break.
           Purpose is but the slave to memory,
           Of violent birth but poor validity,
           Which now, like fruit unripe, sticks on the tree,
           But fall unshaken when they mellow be.
           Most necessary 'tis that we forget
           To pay ourselves what to ourselves is debt.
           What to ourselves in passion we propose,
           The passion ending, doth the purpose lose.

---

[31] *distrust*] feel concern for.
[32] *hold quantity*] are in proportion to one another.
[33] *operant*] active.
[34] *leave to do*] cease to carry out.
[35] *instances*] motives.
[36] *thrift*] profit, gain.

The violence of either grief or joy
Their own enactures[37] with themselves destroy.
Where joy most revels, grief doth most lament;
Grief joys, joy grieves, on slender accident.
This world is not for aye, nor 'tis not strange
That even our loves should with our fortunes change,
For 'tis a question left us yet to prove,
Whether love lead fortune or else fortune love.
The great man down, you mark his favourite flies,
The poor advanced makes friends of enemies.
And hitherto doth love on fortune tend;
For who not needs shall never lack a friend,
And who in want a hollow friend doth try
Directly seasons him[38] his enemy.
But, orderly to end where I begun,
Our wills and fates do so contrary run,
That our devices still[39] are overthrown;
Our thoughts are ours, their ends none of our own.
So think thou wilt no second husband wed,
But die thy thoughts when thy first lord is dead.

P. QUEEN.   Nor earth to me give food nor heaven light,
Sport and repose lock from me day and night,
To desperation turn my trust and hope,
An anchor's cheer[40] in prison be my scope,
Each opposite, that blanks[41] the face of joy,
Meet what I would have well and it destroy,
Both here and hence pursue me lasting strife,
If, once a widow, ever I be wife.

HAM.   If she should break it now.

P. KING.   'Tis deeply sworn. Sweet, leave me here awhile.
My spirits grow dull, and fain I would beguile
The tedious day with sleep.   [*Sleeps.*

P. QUEEN.   Sleep rock thy brain,
And never come mischance between us twain.   [*Exit.*

HAM.   Madam, how like you this play?

QUEEN.   The lady doth protest too much, methinks.

HAM.   O, but she'll keep her word.

---

[37] *enactures*] fulfillments.
[38] *seasons him*] ripens him into.
[39] *still*] always.
[40] *anchor's cheer*] anchorite's fare.
[41] *blanks*] blanches, makes pale.

KING.   Have you heard the argument? Is there no offence in't?

HAM.   No, no, they do but jest, poison in jest. No offence i' the world.

KING.   What do you call the play?

HAM.   *The Mousetrap.* Marry, how? Tropically.[42] This play is the image of a murder done in Vienna. Gonzago is the Duke's name; his wife, Baptista. You shall see anon. 'Tis a knavish piece of work, but what o' that? Your Majesty, and we that have free[43] souls, it touches us not. Let the galled jade[44] wince, our withers are unwrung.[45]

Enter LUCIANUS.

This is one Lucianus, nephew to the King.

OPH.   You are as good as a chorus, my lord.

HAM.   I could interpret between you and your love, if I could see the puppets dallying.

OPH.   You are keen,[46] my lord, you are keen.

HAM.   It would cost you a groaning[47] to take off my edge.[48]

OPH.   Still better, and worse.

HAM.   So you mistake[49] your husbands. Begin, murderer. Pox, leave thy damnable faces and begin. Come, the croaking raven doth bellow for revenge.

LUC.   Thoughts black, hands apt, drugs fit, and time agreeing, Confederate season, else no creature seeing; Thou mixture rank, of midnight weeds collected, With Hecate's ban[50] thrice blasted, thrice infected, Thy natural magic and dire property, On wholesome life usurp[51] immediately.

[*Pours the poison into the sleeper's ear.*

HAM.   He poisons him i' the garden for his estate. His name's Gonzago. The story is extant, and written in very choice Italian. You shall see anon how the murderer gets the love of Gonzago's wife.

OPH.   The King rises.

---

[42] *Tropically*] metaphorically.
[43] *free*] innocent.
[44] *galled jade*] horse rubbed sore (by a saddle or harness).
[45] *unwrung*] not pinched.
[46] *keen*] bitter.
[47] *groaning*] i.e., sexual intercourse.
[48] *edge*] i.e., sexual appetite.
[49] *mistake*] take in error.
[50] *Hecate's ban*] the curse of Hecate, goddess of magic and the underworld.
[51] *usurp*] encroach.

HAM.   What, frighted with false fire?[52]
QUEEN.   How fares my lord?
POL.   Give o'er the play.
KING.   Give me some light. Away!
POL.   Lights, lights, lights! [*Exeunt all but* HAMLET *and* HORATIO.
HAM.   Why, let the stricken deer go weep,
                          The hart ungalled play;
                For some must watch, while some must sleep,
                          Thus runs the world away.

        Would not this, sir, and a forest of feathers—if the rest of my
           fortunes turn Turk with me—with two Provincial roses[53] on
           my razed[54] shoes, get me a fellowship in a cry[55] of players,
           sir?
HOR.   Half a share.
HAM.   A whole one, I.

                     For thou dost know, O Damon dear,
                          This realm dismantled was
                     Of Jove himself; and now reigns here
                          A very, very—pajock.[56]

HOR.   You might have rhymed.
HAM.   O good Horatio, I'll take the ghost's word for a thousand pound.
           Didst perceive?
HOR.   Very well, my lord.
HAM.   Upon the talk of the poisoning?
HOR.   I did very well note him.
HAM.   Ah, ha! Come, some music; come, the recorders.

                     For if the King like not the comedy,
                     Why then, belike, he likes it not, perdy.[57]

        Come, some music.

Enter ROSENCRANTZ *and* GUILDENSTERN.

GUIL.   Good my lord, vouchsafe me a word with you.
HAM.   Sir, a whole history.

---

[52] *false fire*] discharge of blank shots.
[53] *Provincial roses*] roses from Provins or from Provence.
[54] *razed*] slashed (in patterns). The feathers and decorated shoes were regularly part of an
     actor's costume.
[55] *cry*] pack.
[56] *pajock*] (?) peacock.
[57] *perdy*] a colloquial form of *pardieu*.

GUIL. The King, sir—

HAM. Ay, sir, what of him?

GUIL. Is in his retirement marvellous distempered.

HAM. With drink, sir?

GUIL. No, my lord, rather with choler.

HAM. Your wisdom should show itself more richer to signify this to the doctor; for, for me to put him to his purgation would perhaps plunge him into far more choler.

GUIL. Good my lord, put your discourse into some frame, and start not so wildly from my affair.

HAM. I am tame, sir. Pronounce.

GUIL. The Queen, your mother, in most great affliction of spirit, hath sent me to you.

HAM. You are welcome.

GUIL. Nay, good my lord, this courtesy is not of the right breed. If it shall please you to make me a wholesome answer, I will do your mother's commandment; if not, your pardon and my return shall be the end of my business.

HAM. Sir, I cannot.

GUIL. What, my lord?

HAM. Make you a wholesome answer. My wit's diseased. But, sir, such answer as I can make, you shall command, or rather, as you say, my mother. Therefore no more, but to the matter. My mother, you say—

ROS. Then thus she says: your behaviour hath struck her into amazement and admiration. [58]

HAM. O wonderful son, that can so astonish a mother! But is there no sequel at the heels of this mother's admiration? Impart.

ROS. She desires to speak with you in her closet, ere you go to bed.

HAM. We shall obey, were she ten times our mother. Have you any further trade with us?

ROS. My lord, you once did love me.

HAM. So I do still, by these pickers and stealers. [59]

ROS. Good my lord, what is your cause of distemper? You do surely bar the door upon your own liberty if you deny your griefs to your friend.

HAM. Sir, I lack advancement.

ROS. How can that be, when you have the voice of the King himself for your succession in Denmark?

---

[58] *admiration*] astonishment.

[59] *pickers and stealers*] i.e., hands.

HAM.   Ay, sir, but 'while the grass grows'—the proverb is something musty.

Enter Players *with recorders.*

    O, the recorders! Let me see one. To withdraw[60] with you:— why do you go about to recover the wind of[61] me, as if you would drive me into a toil?[62]

GUIL.   O, my lord, if my duty be too bold, my love is too unmannerly.

HAM.   I do not well understand that. Will you play upon this pipe?

GUIL.   My lord, I cannot.

HAM.   I pray you.

GUIL.   Believe me, I cannot.

HAM.   I do beseech you.

GUIL.   I know no touch of it, my lord.

HAM.   It is as easy as lying. Govern these ventages with your fingers and thumb, give it breath with your mouth, and it will discourse most eloquent music. Look you, these are the stops.

GUIL.   But these cannot I command to any utterance of harmony. I have not the skill.

HAM.   Why, look you now, how unworthy a thing you make of me. You would play upon me, you would seem to know my stops, you would pluck out the heart of my mystery, you would sound me from my lowest note to the top of my compass; and there is much music, excellent voice, in this little organ; yet cannot you make it speak. 'Sblood, do you think I am easier to be played on than a pipe? Call me what instrument you will, though you can fret me, yet you cannot play upon me.

Enter POLONIUS.

    God bless you, sir.

POL.   My lord, the Queen would speak with you, and presently.[63]

HAM.   Do you see yonder cloud that's almost in shape of a camel?

POL.   By the mass, and 'tis like a camel, indeed.

HAM.   Methinks it is like a weasel.

POL.   It is backed like a weasel.

HAM.   Or like a whale?

---

[60] *withdraw*] i.e., to speak a word in private.
[61] *recover the wind of*] a hunting metaphor meaning "to get upwind of."
[62] *toil*] net.
[63] *presently*] immediately.

POL.   Very like a whale.

HAM.   Then I will come to my mother by and by. [*Aside*] They fool
        me to the top of my bent. [64]—I will come by and by.

POL.   I will say so.   [*Exit* POLONIUS.

HAM.   'By and by' is easily said. Leave me, friends.

                           [*Exeunt all but* HAMLET.

        'Tis now the very witching time of night,
        When churchyards yawn, and hell itself breathes out
        Contagion to this world. Now could I drink hot blood,
        And do such bitter business as the day
        Would quake to look on. Soft, now to my mother.
        O heart, lose not thy nature. Let not ever
        The soul of Nero [65] enter this firm bosom.
        Let me be cruel, not unnatural.
        I will speak daggers to her, but use none.
        My tongue and soul in this be hypocrites;
        How in my words soever she be shent, [66]
        To give them seals never my soul consent.   [*Exit.*

SCENE III. *A room in the castle.*

Enter KING, ROSENCRANTZ, *and* GUILDENSTERN.

KING.   I like him not, nor stands it safe with us
        To let his madness range. Therefore prepare you.
        I your commission will forthwith dispatch,
        And he to England shall along with you.
        The terms of our estate may not endure
        Hazard so near us as doth hourly grow
        Out of his brows.

GUIL.   We will ourselves provide. [1]
        Most holy and religious fear it is
        To keep those many many bodies safe

---

[64] *the top of my bent*] to the utmost limit.
[65] *Nero*] the Roman emperor who put his mother, Agrippina, to death.
[66] *shent*] reproached.

---

[1] *provide*] equip.

That live and feed upon your Majesty.

ROS.   The single and peculiar[2] life is bound
With all the strength and armour of the mind
To keep itself from noyance,[3] but much more
That spirit upon whose weal depends and rests
The lives of many. The cess[4] of majesty
Dies not alone, but like a gulf[5] doth draw
What's near it with it. It is a massy wheel,
Fix'd on the summit of the highest mount,
To whose huge spokes ten thousand lesser things
Are mortised and adjoin'd; which, when it falls,
Each small annexment, petty consequence,
Attends the boisterous ruin. Never alone
Did the King sigh, but with a general groan.

KING.   Arm you,[6] I pray you, to this speedy voyage,
For we will fetters put about this fear,
Which now goes too free-footed.

ROS. ⎫
GUIL. ⎭   We will haste us.

                [Exeunt ROSENCRANTZ *and* GUILDENSTERN.

Enter POLONIUS.

POL.   My lord, he's going to his mother's closet.
Behind the arras I'll convey myself,
To hear the process.[7] I'll warrant she'll tax him home.
And, as you said, and wisely was it said,
'Tis meet that some more audience than a mother,
Since nature makes them partial, should o'erhear
The speech, of vantage.[8] Fare you well, my liege.
I'll call upon you ere you go to bed,
And tell you what I know.

KING.   Thanks, dear my lord.

                      [Exit POLONIUS.

O, my offence is rank, it smells to heaven.
It hath the primal eldest curse upon't,
A brother's murder. Pray can I not,

---

2 *peculiar*] particular, individual.
3 *noyance*] harm.
4 *cess*] decease.
5 *gulf*] whirlpool.
6 *Arm you*] prepare, equip yourselves.
7 *process*] proceedings.
8 *of vantage*] besides.

Though inclination be as sharp as will;
My stronger guilt defeats my strong intent,
And, like a man to double business bound,
I stand in pause where I shall first begin,
And both neglect. What if this cursed hand
Were thicker than itself with brother's blood,
Is there not rain enough in the sweet heavens
To wash it white as snow? Whereto serves mercy
But to confront the visage of offence?
And what's in prayer but this twofold force,
To be forestalled ere we come to fall,
Or pardon'd being down? Then I'll look up.
My fault is past. But O, what form of prayer
Can serve my turn? 'Forgive me my foul murder?'
That cannot be, since I am still possess'd
Of those effects for which I did the murder—
My crown, mine own ambition and my queen.
May one be pardon'd and retain the offence?[9]
In the corrupted currents of this world
Offence's gilded hand may shove by justice,
And oft 'tis seen the wicked prize itself
Buys out the law. But 'tis not so above:
There is no shuffling,[10] there the action lies
In his true nature, and we ourselves compell'd
Even to the teeth and forehead of[11] our faults
To give in evidence. What then? What rests?
Try what repentance can. What can it not?
Yet what can it when one can not repent?
O wretched state, O bosom black as death,
O limed soul, that struggling to be free
Art more engaged! Help, angels! Make assay.
Bow, stubborn knees, and, heart with strings of steel,
Be soft as sinews of the new-born babe.
All may be well.   [*Retires and kneels.*

Enter HAMLET.

HAM.   Now might I do it pat, now he is praying.
          And now I'll do't. And so he goes to heaven;

---

[9] *offence*] the fruits of the crime.
[10] *shuffling*] trickery.
[11] *to the teeth and forehead of*] face to face with.

And so am I revenged. That would be scann'd:[12]
A villain kills my father, and for that,
I, his sole son, do this same villain send
To heaven.
O, this is hire and salary, not revenge.
He took my father grossly, full of bread,
With all his crimes broad blown,[13] as flush[14] as May;
And how his audit stands who knows save heaven?
But in our circumstance[15] and course of thought,
'Tis heavy with him. And am I then revenged,
To take him in the purging of his soul,
When he is fit and season'd for his passage?
No.
Up, sword, and know thou a more horrid hent.[16]
When he is drunk asleep, or in his rage,
Or in the incestuous pleasure of his bed,
At game, a-swearing, or about some act
That has no relish of salvation in't,
Then trip him, that his heels may kick at heaven
And that his soul may be as damn'd and black
As hell, whereto it goes. My mother stays.
This physic[17] but prolongs thy sickly days.   [*Exit.*

KING.   [*Rising*] My words fly up, my thoughts remain below.
Words without thoughts never to heaven go.   [*Exit.*

---

[12] *would be scann'd*] needs to be examined.
[13] *broad blown*] in full bloom.
[14] *flush*] lusty, in its prime.
[15] *in our circumstance*] viewed from our earthly perspective.
[16] *hent*] seizing, opportunity for seizing.
[17] *physic*] i.e., praying.

SCENE IV. *The Queen's closet.*

Enter QUEEN *and* POLONIUS.

POL.   He will come straight. Look you lay home to him. [1]
        Tell him his pranks have been too broad[2] to bear with,
        And that your grace hath screen'd and stood between
        Much heat and him. I'll silence me even here.
        Pray you, be round[3] with him.
QUEEN.   I'll warrant you,
        Fear me not. Withdraw, I hear him coming.
                        [POLONIUS *hides behind the arras.*

Enter HAMLET.

HAM.   Now, mother, what's the matter?
QUEEN. Hamlet, thou hast thy father much offended.
HAM.   Mother, you have my father much offended.
QUEEN. Come, come, you answer with an idle tongue.
HAM.   Go, go, you question with a wicked tongue.
QUEEN. Why, how now, Hamlet?
HAM.   What's the matter now?
QUEEN. Have you forgot me?
HAM.   No, by the rood, not so.
        You are the Queen, your husband's brother's wife,
        And—would it were not so—you are my mother.
QUEEN. Nay, then, I'll set those to you that can speak.
HAM.   Come, come, and sit you down; you shall not budge.
        You go not till I set you up a glass
        Where you may see the inmost part of you.
QUEEN. What wilt thou do? Thou wilt not murder me?
        Help, help, ho!
POL.   [*Behind*] What, ho! Help, help, help!
HAM.   [*Drawing*] How now, a rat? Dead for a ducat, dead.
                        [*Makes a pass through the arras.*
POL.   [*Behind*] O, I am slain!   [*Falls and dies.*
QUEEN.   O me, what hast thou done?

---

[1] *lay home to him*] speak bluntly with him.
[2] *broad*] unrestrained.
[3] *round*] plain-spoken.

HAM.   Nay, I know not. Is it the King?
QUEEN.   O, what a rash and bloody deed is this!
HAM.   A bloody deed. Almost as bad, good mother,
            As kill a king and marry with his brother.
QUEEN.   As kill a king?
HAM.   Ay, lady, 'twas my word.
                            [*Lifts up the arras and discovers* POLONIUS.
            Thou wretched, rash, intruding fool, farewell.
            I took thee for thy better. Take thy fortune.
            Thou find'st to be too busy is some danger.—
            Leave wringing of your hands. Peace, sit you down,
            And let me wring your heart; for so I shall,
            If it be made of penetrable stuff,
            If damned custom have not braz'd[4] it so,
            That it be proof[5] and bulwark against sense.[6]
QUEEN.   What have I done, that thou darest wag thy tongue
            In noise so rude against me?
HAM.   Such an act
            That blurs the grace and blush of modesty,
            Calls virtue hypocrite, takes off the rose
            From the fair forehead of an innocent love,
            And sets a blister[7] there, makes marriage vows
            As false as dicers' oaths—O, such a deed
            As from the body of contraction[8] plucks
            The very soul, and sweet religion makes
            A rhapsody[9] of words. Heaven's face doth glow,
            Yea, this solidity and compound mass
            With tristful visage, as against the doom,[10]
            Is thought-sick at the act.
QUEEN.   Ay me, what act,
            That roars so loud and thunders in the index?[11]
HAM.   Look here upon this picture, and on this,
            The counterfeit presentment[12] of two brothers.
            See what a grace was seated on this brow:

    [4] *braz'd*] coated with brass, hardened.
    [5] *proof*] impenetrable.
    [6] *sense*] reason.
    [7] *blister*] prostitutes were branded on the forehead.
    [8] *contraction*] the marriage contract.
    [9] *rhapsody*] cento, amalgam of empty words.
    [10] *against the doom*] in expectation of the Judgment Day.
    [11] *index*] preface, prologue.
    [12] *counterfeit presentment*] representation, portrait.

Hyperion's curls, the front[13] of Jove himself,
An eye like Mars, to threaten and command,
A station[14] like the herald Mercury
New-lighted on a heaven-kissing hill,
A combination and a form indeed
Where every god did seem to set his seal
To give the world assurance of a man.
This was your husband. Look you now, what follows.
Here is your husband: like a mildew'd ear,
Blasting[15] his wholesome brother. Have you eyes?
Could you on this fair mountain leave[16] to feed,
And batten on this moor? Ha, have you eyes?
You cannot call it love, for at your age
The heyday in the blood is tame, it's humble,
And waits upon the judgement; and what judgement
Would step from this to this? Sense[17] sure you have,
Else could you not have motion, but sure that sense
Is apoplex'd, for madness would not err,
Nor sense to ecstasy[18] was ne'er so thrall'd
But it reserved some quantity of choice,
To serve in such a difference. What devil was't
That thus hath cozen'd you at hoodman-blind?[19]
Eyes without feeling, feeling without sight,
Ears without hands or eyes, smelling sans all,
Or but a sickly part of one true sense
Could not so mope.[20]
O shame, where is thy blush? Rebellious hell,
If thou canst mutine in a matron's bones,
To flaming youth let virtue be as wax
And melt in her own fire. Proclaim no shame
When the compulsive ardour gives the charge,[21]
Since frost itself as actively doth burn,
And reason panders will.

QUEEN.   O Hamlet, speak no more.

---

[13] *front*] forehead.
[14] *station*] stance.
[15] *Blasting*] blighting, causing to wither.
[16] *leave*] cease.
[17] *Sense*] the faculties and act of perception.
[18] *ecstasy*] delusion, madness.
[19] *hoodman-blind*] blindman's buff.
[20] *mope*] act without thought.
[21] *gives the charge*] attacks.

Thou turn'st mine eyes into my very soul,
And there I see such black and grained[22] spots
As will not leave their tinct.

HAM.   Nay, but to live
In the rank sweat of an enseamed[23] bed,
Stew'd in corruption, honeying and making love
Over the nasty sty—

QUEEN.   O, speak to me no more.
These words like daggers enter in my ears.
No more, sweet Hamlet.

HAM.   A murderer and a villain,
A slave that is not twentieth part the tithe
Of your precedent lord, a vice[24] of kings,
A cutpurse of the empire and the rule,
That from a shelf the precious diadem stole
And put it in his pocket—

QUEEN.   No more.
HAM.   A king of shreds and patches—

Enter GHOST.

Save me, and hover o'er me with your wings,
You heavenly guards! What would your gracious figure?

QUEEN.   Alas, he's mad.
HAM.   Do you not come your tardy son to chide,
That, lapsed in time and passion, lets go by
The important[25] acting of your dread command?
O, say!

GHOST.   Do not forget. This visitation
Is but to whet thy almost blunted purpose.
But look, amazement on thy mother sits.
O, step between her and her fighting soul.
Conceit[26] in weakest bodies strongest works.
Speak to her, Hamlet.

HAM.   How is it with you, lady?
QUEEN.   Alas, how is't with you,
That you do bend your eye on vacancy
And with the incorporal air do hold discourse?

---

[22] *grained*] dyed in grain, which was a red dye made from the dried bodies of insects.
[23] *enseamed*] filthy.
[24] *vice*] the buffoon-like character of Morality plays.
[25] *important*] urgent.
[26] *Conceit*] imagination.

	Forth at your eyes your spirits wildly peep,
	And, as the sleeping soldiers in the alarm,[27]
	Your bedded hair, like life in excrements,[28]
	Start up and stand an end. O gentle son,
	Upon the heat and flame of thy distemper
	Sprinkle cool patience. Whereon do you look?
HAM.	On him, on him. Look you how pale he glares.
	His form and cause conjoin'd, preaching to stones,
	Would make them capable.[29]—Do not look upon me,
	Lest with this piteous action you convert
	My stern effects.[30] Then what I have to do
	Will want true colour—tears perchance for blood.
QUEEN.	To whom do you speak this?
HAM.	Do you see nothing there?
QUEEN.	Nothing at all; yet all that is I see.
HAM.	Nor did you nothing hear?
QUEEN.	No, nothing but ourselves.
HAM.	Why, look you there. Look how it steals away.
	My father, in his habit[31] as he lived.
	Look where he goes, even now, out at the portal. [*Exit* GHOST.
QUEEN.	This is the very coinage of your brain.
	This bodily creation ecstasy[32]
	Is very cunning in.
HAM.	Ecstasy?
	My pulse, as yours, doth temperately keep time,
	And makes as healthful music. It is not madness
	That I have utter'd. Bring me to the test,
	And I the matter will re-word, which madness
	Would gambol[33] from. Mother, for love of grace,
	Lay not that flattering unction[34] to your soul,
	That not your trespass but my madness speaks.
	It will but skin[35] and film the ulcerous place,
	Whiles rank corruption, mining all within,
	Infects unseen. Confess yourself to heaven,
	Repent what's past, avoid what is to come,

[27] *in the alarm*] at the call to arms.
[28] *excrements*] growths out from the body.
[29] *capable*] responsive.
[30] *effects*] intended actions.
[31] *his habit*] appearance.
[32] *ecstasy*] madness.
[33] *gambol*] skip, shy away.
[34] *unction*] salve, ointment.
[35] *skin*] cover with skin.

And do not spread the compost on the weeds,
To make them ranker. Forgive me this my virtue,
For in the fatness of these pursy[36] times
Virtue itself of vice must pardon beg,
Yea, curb[37] and woo for leave to do him good.

QUEEN. O Hamlet, thou hast cleft my heart in twain.

HAM.   O, throw away the worser part of it
And live the purer with the other half.
Good night. But go not to my uncle's bed.
Assume[38] a virtue, if you have it not.
That monster, custom, who all sense doth eat,
Of habits evil, is angel yet in this,
That to the use of actions fair and good
He likewise gives a frock or livery,
That aptly is put on. Refrain tonight
And that shall lend a kind of easiness
To the next abstinence, the next more easy;
For use almost can change the stamp of nature
And either master the devil, or throw him out
With wondrous potency. Once more, good night;
And when you are desirous to be blest,
I'll blessing beg of you. For this same lord, [*Pointing to* POLONIUS.
I do repent. But heaven hath pleased it so,
To punish me with this, and this with me,
That I must be their scourge and minister.
I will bestow[39] him, and will answer well
The death I gave him. So, again, good night.
I must be cruel, only to be kind.
This bad begins, and worse remains behind.[40]
One word more, good lady.

QUEEN.   What shall I do?

HAM.   Not this, by no means, that I bid you do:
Let the bloat King tempt you again to bed,
Pinch wanton on your cheek, call you his mouse,
And let him, for a pair of reechy[41] kisses,
Or paddling[42] in your neck with his damn'd fingers,
Make you to ravel all this matter out,

[36] *pursy*] flabby.
[37] *curb*] bow.
[38] *Assume*] take on, adopt.
[39] *bestow*] dispose of.
[40] *behind*] i.e., to come.
[41] *reechy*] filthy, stinking.
[42] *paddling*] playing amorously.

That I essentially am not in madness,
But mad in craft. 'Twere good you let him know;
For who, that's but a queen, fair, sober, wise,
Would from a paddock,[43] from a bat, a gib,[44]
Such dear concernings hide? Who would do so?
No, in despite of sense and secrecy,
Unpeg the basket on the house's top,
Let the birds fly, and like the famous ape,[45]
To try conclusions, in the basket creep
And break your own neck down.

QUEEN.   Be thou assured, if words be made of breath
And breath of life, I have no life to breathe
What thou hast said to me.

HAM.   I must to England; you know that?

QUEEN.   Alack,
I had forgot. 'Tis so concluded on.

HAM.   There's letters seal'd, and my two schoolfellows,
Whom I will trust as I will adders fang'd,
They bear the mandate. They must sweep my way,
And marshal me to knavery.[46] Let it work;
For 'tis the sport to have the enginer[47]
Hoist[48] with his own petard;[49] and't shall go hard
But I will delve one yard below their mines,
And blow them at the moon. O, 'tis most sweet
When in one line[50] two crafts[51] directly meet.
This man shall set me packing.[52]
I'll lug the guts into the neighbour room.
Mother, good night indeed. This counsellor
Is now most still, most secret and most grave,
Who was in life a foolish prating knave.
Come, sir, to draw toward an end with you.
Good night, mother.

                    [*Exeunt severally*; HAMLET *dragging in* POLONIUS.

---

[43] *paddock*] toad.
[44] *gib*] tomcat.
[45] *famous ape*] the ape, seeing the birds flying, imitates them and ends badly.
[46] *marshal me to knavery*] lead me to suffer knavery.
[47] *enginer*] creator of military hardware.
[48] *Hoist*] blown up.
[49] *petard*] explosive device.
[50] *in one line*] head on.
[51] *crafts*] plots.
[52] *packing*] (1) off in a hurry; (2) plotting.

ACT IV.

SCENE I. *A room in the castle.*

Enter KING, QUEEN, ROSENCRANTZ, *and* GUILDENSTERN.

KING.   There's matter in these sighs, these profound heaves;
        You must translate. 'Tis fit we understand them.
        Where is your son?

QUEEN. Bestow this place on us a little while.
                    [*Exeunt* ROSENCRANTZ *and* GUILDENSTERN.
        Ah, mine own lord, what have I seen tonight!

KING.   What, Gertrude? How does Hamlet?

QUEEN. Mad as the sea and wind, when both contend
        Which is the mightier. In his lawless fit,
        Behind the arras hearing something stir,
        Whips out his rapier, cries 'A rat, a rat!'
        And in this brainish[1] apprehension kills
        The unseen good old man.

KING.   O heavy deed!
        It had been so with us, had we been there.
        His liberty is full of threats to all,
        To you yourself, to us, to everyone.
        Alas, how shall this bloody deed be answer'd?
        It will be laid to us, whose providence
        Should have kept short,[2] restrain'd and out of haunt,[3]
        This mad young man. But so much was our love,
        We would not understand what was most fit,
        But, like the owner of a foul disease,
        To keep it from divulging,[4] let it feed

---

[1] *brainish*] brainsick.
[2] *short*] i.e., on a short leash.
[3] *out of haunt*] away from any public place.
[4] *divulging*] becoming known.

          Even on the pith of life. Where is he gone?

QUEEN. To draw apart the body he hath kill'd,

          O'er whom—his very madness, like some ore[5]

          Among a mineral[6] of metals base,

          Shows itself pure—he weeps for what is done.

KING.   O Gertrude, come away.

          The sun no sooner shall the mountains touch,

          But we will ship him hence; and this vile deed

          We must, with all our majesty and skill,

          Both countenance and excuse. Ho, Guildenstern!

Enter ROSENCRANTZ *and* GUILDENSTERN.

          Friends both, go join you with some further aid.

          Hamlet in madness hath Polonius slain,

          And from his mother's closet hath he dragg'd him.

          Go seek him out, speak fair, and bring the body

          Into the chapel. I pray you, haste in this.

                    [*Exeunt* ROSENCRANTZ *and* GUILDENSTERN.

          Come, Gertrude, we'll call up our wisest friends,

          And let them know, both what we mean to do,

          And what's untimely done. So . . . slander,[7]

          Whose whisper o'er the world's diameter

          As level[8] as the cannon to his blank[9]

          Transports his poison'd shot, may miss our name

          And hit the woundless[10] air. O, come away.

          My soul is full of discord and dismay.   [*Exeunt.*

---

[5] *ore*] precious metal, perhaps gold.

[6] *mineral*] mine.

[7] *So . . . slander*] a defective line.

[8] *level*] straight.

[9] *blank*] target.

[10] *woundless*] invulnerable.

SCENE II. *Another room in the castle.*

Enter HAMLET.

HAM. Safely stowed.

ROS. ⎫
GUIL. ⎭ [*Within*] Hamlet! Lord Hamlet!

HAM. But soft, what noise? Who calls on Hamlet? O, here they come.

Enter ROSENCRANTZ *and* GUILDENSTERN.

ROS. What have you done, my lord, with the dead body?

HAM. Compounded it with dust, whereto 'tis kin.

ROS. Tell us where 'tis, that we may take it thence and bear it to the chapel.

HAM. Do not believe it.

ROS. Believe what?

HAM. That I can keep your counsel and not mine own. Besides, to be demanded of a sponge—what replication[1] should be made by the son of a king?

ROS. Take you me for a sponge, my lord?

HAM. Ay, sir, that soaks up the King's countenance,[2] his rewards, his authorities. But such officers do the King best service in the end. He keeps them, like an ape, in the corner of his jaw— first mouthed, to be last swallowed. When he needs what you have gleaned, it is but squeezing you, and, sponge, you shall be dry again.

ROS. I understand you not, my lord.

HAM. I am glad of it. A knavish speech sleeps in a foolish ear.

ROS. My lord, you must tell us where the body is, and go with us to the King.

HAM. The body is with the King, but the King is not with the body. The King is a thing—

GUIL. A thing, my lord?

HAM. Of nothing. Bring me to him.   [*Exeunt.*

---

[1] *replication*] reply.
[2] *countenance*] patronage, favor.

SCENE III. *Another room in the castle.*

Enter KING, *attended.*

KING.   I have sent to seek him, and to find the body.
        How dangerous is it that this man goes loose!
        Yet must not we put the strong law on him.
        He's loved of the distracted[1] multitude,
        Who like not in their judgement, but their eyes;
        And where 'tis so, the offender's scourge[2] is weigh'd,
        But never the offence. To bear all smooth and even,
        This sudden sending him away must seem
        Deliberate pause.[3] Diseases desperate grown
        By desperate appliance[4] are relieved,
        Or not at all.

Enter ROSENCRANTZ.

        How now, what hath befall'n?
ROS.   Where the dead body is bestow'd, my lord,
        We cannot get from him.
KING.   But where is he?
ROS.   Without, my lord; guarded, to know your pleasure.
KING.   Bring him before us.
ROS.   Ho, Guildenstern! Bring in my lord.

Enter HAMLET *and* GUILDENSTERN.

KING.   Now, Hamlet, where's Polonius?
HAM.   At supper.
KING.   At supper? Where?
HAM.   Not where he eats, but where he is eaten. A certain convoca-
        tion of politic worms are e'en at him. Your worm is your
        only emperor for diet. We fat all creatures else to fat us, and
        we fat ourselves for maggots. Your fat king and your lean
        beggar is but variable service,[5] two dishes, but to one table.
        That's the end.

---

[1] *distracted*] irrational, unthinking.
[2] *scourge*] punishment.
[3] *Deliberate pause*] the result of careful consideration.
[4] *appliance*] cure, treatment.
[5] *service*] course (of food).

KING.   Alas, alas!
HAM.   A man may fish with the worm that hath eat of a king, and eat
         of the fish that hath fed of that worm.
KING.   What dost thou mean by this?
HAM.   Nothing but to show you how a king may go a progress[6]
         through the guts of a beggar.
KING.   Where is Polonius?
HAM.   In heaven. Send thither to see. If your messenger find him not
         there, seek him i' the other place yourself. But indeed, if you
         find him not within this month, you shall nose him as you
         go up the stairs into the lobby.
KING.   [To some Attendants] Go seek him there.
HAM.   He will stay till you come.   [Exeunt Attendants.
KING.   Hamlet, this deed, for thine especial safety—
         Which we do tender,[7] as we dearly grieve
         For that which thou hast done—must send thee hence
         With fiery quickness. Therefore prepare thyself.
         The bark is ready and the wind at help,[8]
         The associates tend,[9] and everything is bent
         For England.
HAM.   For England?
KING.   Ay, Hamlet.
HAM.   Good.
KING.   So is it, if thou knew'st our purposes.
HAM.   I see a cherub that sees them. But, come; for England. Fare-
         well, dear mother.
KING.   Thy loving father, Hamlet.
HAM.   My mother. Father and mother is man and wife, man and wife
         is one flesh, and so, my mother. Come, for England. [Exit.
KING.   Follow him at foot.[10] Tempt him with speed aboard.
         Delay it not. I'll have him hence tonight.
         Away, for every thing is seal'd and done
         That else leans on the affair. Pray you, make haste.
                        [Exeunt ROSENCRANTZ and GUILDENSTERN.
         And, England,[11] if my love thou hold'st at aught—
         As my great power thereof may give thee sense,
         Since yet thy cicatrice looks raw and red

---

[6] progress] journey made by a sovereign.
[7] tender] hold dear.
[8] at help] favorable.
[9] tend] attend, are in waiting.
[10] at foot] closely.
[11] England] the King of England.

After the Danish sword, and thy free awe
Pays homage to us—thou mayst not coldly set[12]
Our sovereign process;[13] which imports at full, ·
By letters congruing to[14] that effect,
The present[15] death of Hamlet. Do it, England;
For like the hectic[16] in my blood he rages,
And thou must cure me. Till I know 'tis done,
Howe'er my haps, my joys were ne'er begun.   [*Exit.*

SCENE IV. *A plain in Denmark.*

Enter FORTINBRAS, *a* Captain *and* Soldiers, *marching.*

FOR.   Go, captain, from me greet the Danish king.
         Tell him that by his license Fortinbras
         Craves the conveyance of a promised march
         Over his kingdom. You know the rendezvous.
         If that his Majesty would aught with us,
         We shall express our duty in his eye;[1]
         And let him know so.
CAP.   I will do't, my lord.
FOR.   Go softly on.   [*Exeunt* FORTINBRAS *and* Soldiers.

Enter HAMLET, ROSENCRANTZ, GUILDENSTERN, *and others.*

HAM.   Good sir, whose powers are these?
CAP.   They are of Norway, sir.
HAM.   How purposed, sir, I pray you?
CAP.   Against some part of Poland.
HAM.   Who commands them, sir?
CAP.   The nephew to old Norway, Fortinbras.
HAM.   Goes it against the main of Poland, sir,
         Or for some frontier?

---

[12] *coldly set*] regard with indifference.
[13] *process*] mandate.
[14] *congruing to*] in accordance with.
[15] *present*] immediate.
[16] *hectic*] fever.

---

[1] *express . . . eye*] pay our respects to him in person.

CAP.   Truly to speak, and with no addition,
        We go to gain a little patch of ground
        That hath in it no profit but the name.
        To pay five ducats, five, I would not farm[2] it,
        Nor will it yield to Norway or the Pole
        A ranker[3] rate, should it be sold in fee.[4]
HAM.   Why, then the Polack never will defend it.
CAP.   Yes, it is already garrison'd.
HAM.   Two thousand souls and twenty thousand ducats
        Will not debate the question of this straw!
        This is the imposthume[5] of much wealth and peace,
        That inward breaks, and shows no cause without
        Why the man dies. I humbly thank you, sir.
CAP.   God be wi' you, sir.   [Exit.
ROS.   Will't please you go, my lord?
HAM.   I'll be with you straight. Go a little before.
                                    [Exeunt all but HAMLET.
        How all occasions do inform against me,
        And spur my dull revenge. What is a man,
        If his chief good and market of his time
        Be but to sleep and feed? A beast, no more.
        Sure, he that made us with such large discourse,[6]
        Looking before and after, gave us not
        That capability and godlike reason
        To fust[7] in us unused. Now, whether it be
        Bestial oblivion, or some craven scruple
        Of thinking too precisely on the event—
        A thought which, quarter'd, hath but one part wisdom
        And ever three parts coward—I do not know
        Why yet I live to say this thing's to do,
        Sith I have cause, and will, and strength, and means,
        To do't. Examples gross as earth exhort me:
        Witness this army, of such mass and charge,[8]
        Led by a delicate and tender prince,
        Whose spirit with divine ambition puff'd
        Makes mouths at the invisible event,

[2] *farm*] take the lease of.
[3] *ranker*] greater.
[4] *in fee*] outright, freehold.
[5] *imposthume*] abscess.
[6] *discourse*] faculty of reason.
[7] *fust*] grow moldy.
[8] *charge*] expense, cost.

Exposing what is mortal and unsure
To all that fortune, death and danger dare,
Even for an eggshell. Rightly to be great
Is not to stir without great argument,
But greatly to find quarrel in a straw
When honour's at the stake. How stand I then,
That have a father kill'd, a mother stain'd,
Excitements of my reason and my blood,
And let all sleep, while to my shame I see
The imminent death of twenty thousand men,
That for a fantasy and trick[9] of fame
Go to their graves like beds, fight for a plot
Whereon the numbers cannot try the cause,[10]
Which is not tomb enough and continent
To hide the slain? O, from this time forth,
My thoughts be bloody, or be nothing worth.   [*Exit.*

SCENE V. *Elsinore. A room in the castle.*

Enter QUEEN, HORATIO, *and a* Gentleman.

QUEEN. I will not speak with her.
GENT.   She is importunate,
      Indeed distract.[1] Her mood will needs be pitied.
QUEEN. What would she have?
GENT. She speaks much of her father, says she hears
      There's tricks i' the world, and hems and beats her heart,
      Spurns enviously[2] at straws, speaks things in doubt,[3]
      That carry but half sense. Her speech is nothing,
      Yet the unshaped use of it doth move
      The hearers to collection.[4] They aim at it,
      And botch the words up fit to their own thoughts,
      Which, as her winks and nods and gestures yield them,

---

[9] *trick*] trifle.
[10] *Whereon . . . cause*] i.e., the disputed territory is not large enough to be the battlefield.

---

[1] *distract*] mad.
[2] *enviously*] spitefully.
[3] *in doubt*] ambiguously.
[4] *collection*] make inferences.

Indeed would make one think there might be thought,
Though nothing sure, yet much unhappily.[5]

HOR.   'Twere good she were spoken with, for she may strew
Dangerous conjectures in ill-breeding minds.

QUEEN.   Let her come in.   [*Exit* Gentleman.
[*Aside*] To my sick soul, as sin's true nature is,
Each toy[6] seems prologue to some great amiss.[7]
So full of artless jealousy[8] is guilt,
It spills[9] itself in fearing to be spilt.

Enter Gentleman, *with* OPHELIA.

OPH.   Where is the beauteous Majesty of Denmark?

QUEEN.   How now, Ophelia?

OPH.   [*Sings*] How should I your true love know
                        From another one?
                      By his cockle hat and staff
                      And his sandal shoon.[10]

QUEEN.   Alas, sweet lady, what imports this song?

OPH.   Say you? Nay, pray you, mark.

            [*Sings*] He is dead and gone, lady,
                        He is dead and gone;
                      At his head a grass-green turf,
                        At his heels a stone.

         Oh, oh!

QUEEN.   Nay, but, Ophelia—

OPH.   Pray you, mark.

            [*Sings*] White his shroud as the mountain snow—

Enter KING.

QUEEN.   Alas, look here, my lord.

OPH.   [*Sings*]   Larded[11] with sweet flowers,
                      Which bewept to the grave did go
                      With true-love showers.

---

[5] *unhappily*] mischievously.

[6] *toy*] trifle.

[7] *great amiss*] calamity.

[8] *jealousy*] apprehension.

[9] *spills*] destroys.

[10] *cockle hat . . . shoon*] The lover is dressed as a pilgrim. *Shoon* is the archaic plural of "shoe."

[11] *Larded*] garnished, adorned.

KING.   How do you, pretty lady?

OPH.   Well, God 'ild you.[12] They say the owl was a baker's daughter. Lord, we know what we are, but know not what we may be. God be at your table.

KING.   Conceit upon her father.

OPH.   Pray you, let's have no words of this; but when they ask you what it means, say you this:

> [*Sings*] Tomorrow is Saint Valentine's day,
>   All in the morning betime,
> And I a maid at your window,
>   To be your Valentine.
>
> Then up he rose, and donn'd his clothes,
>   And dupp'd[13] the chamber door,
> Let in the maid, that out a maid
>   Never departed more.

KING.   Pretty Ophelia—

OPH.   Indeed, without an oath, I'll make an end on't.

> [*Sings*] By Gis[14] and by Saint Charity,
>   Alack, and fie for shame!
> Young men will do't, if they come to't,
>   By Cock,[15] they are to blame.
>
> Quoth she, 'Before you tumbled me,
>   You promised me to wed.'

He answers:

> 'So would I ha' done, by yonder sun,
>   An thou hadst not come to my bed.'

KING.   How long hath she been thus?

OPH.   I hope all will be well. We must be patient. But I cannot choose but weep, to think they should lay him i' the cold ground. My brother shall know of it. And so I thank you for your good counsel. Come, my coach. Good night, ladies; good night, sweet ladies; good night, good night.   [*Exit.*

KING.   Follow her close. Give her good watch, I pray you.

                                       [*Exit* HORATIO.

     O, this is the poison of deep grief; it springs

[12] *God 'ild you*] God yield (reward) you.
[13] *dupp'd*] opened.
[14] *Gis*] a corruption of "Jesus."
[15] *Cock*] a corruption of "God."

All from her father's death. O Gertrude, Gertrude,
When sorrows come, they come not single spies,[16]
But in battalions. First, her father slain;
Next, your son gone, and he most violent author
Of his own just remove; the people muddied,
Thick and unwholesome in their thoughts and whispers,
For good Polonius' death; and we have done but greenly,[17]
In hugger-mugger[18] to inter him; poor Ophelia
Divided from herself and her fair judgement,
Without the which we are pictures, or mere beasts;
Last, and as much containing as all these,
Her brother is in secret come from France,
Feeds on his wonder,[19] keeps himself in clouds,
And wants not buzzers[20] to infect his ear
With pestilent speeches of his father's death;
Wherein necessity, of matter beggar'd,
Will nothing stick[21] our person to arraign[22]
In ear and ear. O my dear Gertrude, this,
Like to a murdering-piece,[23] in many places
Gives me superfluous death.   [A *noise within.*

QUEEN.   Alack, what noise is this?
KING.   Where are my Switzers?[24] Let them guard the door.

Enter another Gentleman.

            What is the matter?
GENT.   Save yourself, my lord.
        The ocean, overpeering of his list,[25]
        Eats not the flats with more impetuous haste
        Than young Laertes, in a riotous head,[26]
        O'erbears your officers. The rabble call him lord;
        And, as the world were now but to begin,
        Antiquity forgot, custom not known—

---

[16] *spies*] advance guards.
[17] *greenly*] foolishly.
[18] *In hugger-mugger*] clandestinely.
[19] *wonder*] bewilderment.
[20] *wants not buzzers*] does not lack rumor-mongers.
[21] *nothing stick*] not hesitate.
[22] *arraign*] accuse.
[23] *murdering-piece*] a type of cannon firing grapeshot.
[24] *Switzers*] Swiss mercenaries, used as a personal bodyguard.
[25] *overpeering of his list*] rising above its boundary.
[26] *head*] armed force.

The ratifiers and props of every word—
They cry 'Choose we! Laertes shall be king.'
Caps, hands and tongues applaud it to the clouds,
'Laertes shall be king, Laertes king.'
QUEEN.　　How cheerfully on the false trail they cry.[27]
　　　　　　O, this is counter, you false Danish dogs!　　　[*Noise within.*
KING.　　The doors are broke.

Enter LAERTES, *armed*; Danes *following.*

LAER.　　Where is this King? Sirs, stand you all without.
DANES.　　No, let's come in.
LAER.　　　　　　　　　I pray you, give me leave.
DANES.　　We will, we will.
LAER.　　I thank you. Keep the door.　　　[*They retire without the door.*
　　　　　　　　　　　　　　O thou vile king,
　　　　　　Give me my father.
QUEEN.　　　　　　　　　Calmly, good Laertes.
LAER.　　That drop of blood that's calm proclaims me bastard,
　　　　　　Cries cuckold to my father, brands the harlot
　　　　　　Even here, between the chaste unsmirched brows
　　　　　　Of my true mother.
KING.　　　　　　　　　What is the cause, Laertes,
　　　　　　That thy rebellion looks so giant-like?
　　　　　　Let him go, Gertrude. Do not fear[28] our person.
　　　　　　There's such divinity doth hedge a king
　　　　　　That treason can but peep to what it would,
　　　　　　Acts little of his will. Tell me, Laertes,
　　　　　　Why thou art thus incensed. Let him go, Gertrude.
　　　　　　Speak, man.
LAER.　　Where is my father?
KING.　　　　　　　　Dead.
QUEEN.　　　　　　　　　But not by him.
KING.　　Let him demand his fill.
LAER.　　How came he dead? I'll not be juggled with.
　　　　　　To hell, allegiance! Vows, to the blackest devil!
　　　　　　Conscience and grace, to the profoundest pit!
　　　　　　I dare damnation. To this point I stand,
　　　　　　That both the worlds I give to negligence,

---

[27] *cry*] make the sound of hounds.
[28] *fear*] fear for.

             Let come what comes; only I'll be revenged
             Most throughly[29] for my father.
KING.   Who shall stay you?
LAER.   My will, not all the world.
             And for my means, I'll husband them so well,
             They shall go far with little.
KING.   Good Laertes,
             If you desire to know the certainty
             Of your dear father's death, is't writ in your revenge
             That, swoopstake,[30] you will draw both friend and foe,
             Winner and loser?
LAER.   None but his enemies.
KING.   Will you know them then?
LAER.   To his good friends thus wide I'll ope my arms,
             And, like the kind[31] life-rendering pelican,
             Repast them with my blood.
KING.   Why, now you speak
             Like a good child and a true gentleman.
             That I am guiltless of your father's death,
             And am most sensibly[32] in grief for it,
             It shall as level to your judgement pierce
             As day does to your eye.
DANES. [*Within*]   Let her come in.
LAER.   How now, what noise is that?

Enter OPHELIA.

             O heat, dry up my brains! Tears seven times salt,
             Burn out the sense and virtue[33] of mine eye!
             By heaven, thy madness shall be paid with weight,
             Till our scale turn the beam. O rose of May!
             Dear maid, kind sister, sweet Ophelia!
             O heavens, is't possible a young maid's wits
             Should be as mortal as an old man's life?
             Nature is fine in love, and where 'tis fine
             It sends some precious instance[34] of itself
             After the thing it loves.

---

[29] *throughly*] thoroughly.
[30] *swoopstake*] sweepstake; i.e., indiscriminately.
[31] *kind*] behaving in accordance with its nature.
[32] *sensibly*] feelingly.
[33] *virtue*] power.
[34] *instance*] specimen, sample.

OPH.   [*Sings*] They bore him barefaced on the bier;
                          And in his grave rain'd many a tear—

            Fare you well, my dove.
LAER.   Hadst thou thy wits, and didst persuade revenge,
            It could not move thus.
OPH.   You must sing 'down a-down,' and you 'Call him a-down-a.'
            O, how the wheel[35] becomes it! It is the false steward that
            stole his master's daughter.
LAER.   This nothing's more than matter.
OPH.   There's rosemary, that's for remembrance. Pray you, love, re-
            member. And there is pansies, that's for thoughts.
LAER.   A document in madness: thoughts and remembrance fitted.
OPH.   There's fennel for you, and columbines.[36] There's rue for you,
            and here's some for me. We may call it herb of grace[37] o'
            Sundays. O, you must wear your rue with a difference.[38]
            There's a daisy.[39] I would give you some violets,[40] but they
            withered all when my father died. They say a made a good
            end—

            [*Sings*] For bonny sweet Robin is all my joy.

LAER.   Thought[41] and affliction, passion,[42] hell itself,
            She turns to favour and to prettiness.
OPH.   [*Sings*] And will a not come again?
                              And will a not come again?
                                No, no, he is dead,
                                Go to thy death-bed,
                              He never will come again.

                              His beard was as white as snow,
                              All flaxen was his poll.
                                He is gone, he is gone,
                                And we cast away moan.
                              God ha' mercy on his soul.

            And of[43] all Christian souls, I pray God. God be wi' you.
                                                              [*Exit*

---

[35] *wheel*] poetic refrain, burden.
[36] *fennel . . . columbines*] plants signifying infidelity.
[37] *rue . . . herb of grace*] plant signifying repentance.
[38] *a difference*] a mark of distinction, in heraldry.
[39] *daisy*] signifying unhappy love.
[40] *violets*] signifying faithfulness.
[41] *Thought*] sorrow, melancholy thought.
[42] *passion*] grief.
[43] *of*] on.

LAER.   Do you see this, O God?
KING.   Laertes, I must commune with your grief,
         Or you deny me right. Go but apart,
         Make choice of whom your wisest friends you will,
         And they shall hear and judge 'twixt you and me.
         If by direct or by collateral[44] hand
         They find us touch'd,[45] we will our kingdom give,
         Our crown, our life, and all that we call ours,
         To you in satisfaction. But if not,
         Be you content to lend your patience to us,
         And we shall jointly labour with your soul
         To give it due content.
LAER.   Let this be so.
         His means of death, his obscure funeral—
         No trophy,[46] sword, nor hatchment[47] o'er his bones,
         No noble rite nor formal ostentation—[48]
         Cry to be heard, as 'twere from heaven to earth,
         That I must call't in question.
KING.   So you shall.
         And where the offence is, let the great axe fall.
         I pray you, go with me.   [*Exeunt.*

SCENE VI. *Another room in the castle.*

Enter HORATIO *and a* Servant.

HOR.   What are they that would speak with me?
SERV.   Seafaring men, sir. They say they have letters for you.
HOR.   Let them come in.   [*Exit* Servant.
         I do not know from what part of the world
         I should be greeted, if not from Lord Hamlet.

Enter Sailors.

FIRST SAIL.   God bless you, sir.

---

44 *collateral*] indirect.
45 *touch'd*] implicated.
46 *trophy*] memorial.
47 *hatchment*] armorial escutcheon.
48 *ostentation*] ceremony.

HOR. Let him bless thee too.

FIRST SAIL. He shall, sir, an't please him. There's a letter for you, sir. It comes from the ambassador that was bound for England—if your name be Horatio, as I am let to know it is.

HOR. [*Reads*] Horatio, when thou shalt have overlooked[1] this, give these fellows some means to the King. They have letters for him. Ere we were two days old at sea, a pirate of very warlike appointment gave us chase. Finding ourselves too slow of sail, we put on a compelled valour, and in the grapple I boarded them. On the instant they got clear of our ship; so I alone became their prisoner. They have dealt with me like thieves of mercy; but they knew what they did: I am to do a turn for them. Let the King have the letters I have sent, and repair thou to me with as much speed as thou wouldest fly death. I have words to speak in thine ear will make thee dumb, yet are they much too light for the bore[2] of the matter. These good fellows will bring thee where I am. Rosencrantz and Guildenstern hold their course for England. Of them I have much to tell thee. Farewell.

        He that thou knowest thine, HAMLET.

Come, I will make you way for these your letters,
And do't the speedier, that you may direct me
To him from whom you brought them.   [*Exeunt.*

SCENE VII. *Another room in the castle.*

Enter KING *and* LAERTES.

KING. Now must your conscience my acquittance seal,
And you must put me in your heart for friend,
Sith you have heard, and with a knowing ear,
That he which hath your noble father slain
Pursued my life.

LAER.   It well appears. But tell me
Why you proceeded not against these feats,[1]
So crimeful and so capital[2] in nature,

---

[1] *overlooked*] looked over, read.
[2] *too light for the bore*] i.e., Hamlet's words are like shot too light for the bore of the gun.

---

[1] *feats*] wicked deeds.
[2] *capital*] punishable by death.

As by your safety, wisdom, all things else,
You mainly[3] were stirr'd up.

KING.   O, for two special reasons,
Which may to you perhaps seem much unsinew'd,
But yet to me they're strong. The Queen his mother
Lives almost by his looks; and for myself—
My virtue or my plague, be it either which—
She's so conjunctive[4] to my life and soul
That, as the star moves not but in his sphere,
I could not but by her. The other motive,
Why to a public count[5] I might not go,
Is the great love the general gender[6] bear him,
Who, dipping all his faults in their affection,
Would, like the spring that turneth wood to stone,
Convert his gyves[7] to graces; so that my arrows,
Too slightly timber'd for so loud a wind,
Would have reverted to my bow again
And not where I had aim'd them.

LAER.   And so have I a noble father lost,
A sister driven into desperate terms,[8]
Whose worth, if praises may go back again,[9]
Stood challenger on mount of all the age
For her perfections. But my revenge will come.

KING.   Break not your sleeps for that. You must not think
That we are made of stuff so flat and dull
That we can let our beard be shook with danger
And think it pastime. You shortly shall hear more.
I loved your father, and we love ourself.
And that, I hope, will teach you to imagine—

Enter a Messenger, *with letters.*

How now? What news?

MESS.   Letters, my lord, from Hamlet.
This to your Majesty; this to the Queen.

KING.   From Hamlet? Who brought them?

MESS.   Sailors, my lord, they say. I saw them not.

---

[3] *mainly*] mightily.
[4] *conjunctive*] closely joined.
[5] *count*] reckoning, account.
[6] *general gender*] common people.
[7] *gyves*] chains, fetters; here, deficiencies.
[8] *terms*] circumstances.
[9] *go back again*] i.e., to what she was before she lapsed into madness.

	They were given me by Claudio. He received them
	Of him that brought them.
KING.	Laertes, you shall hear them.—
	Leave us. [*Exit* Messenger.

[*Reads*] High and mighty, you shall know I am set naked[10] on your kingdom. Tomorrow shall I beg leave to see your kingly eyes, when I shall, first asking your pardon, thereunto recount the occasion of my sudden and more strange return.

HAMLET.

	What should this mean? Are all the rest come back?
	Or is it some abuse,[11] and no such thing?
LAER.	Know you the hand?
KING.	'Tis Hamlet's character.[12] 'Naked'—
	And in a postscript here, he says 'Alone.'
	Can you advise me?
LAER.	I'm lost in it, my lord. But let him come.
	It warms the very sickness in my heart
	That I shall live and tell him to his teeth,
	'Thus diest thou.'
KING.	If it be so, Laertes—
	As how should it be so, how otherwise?—
	Will you be ruled by me?
LAER.	Ay, my lord,
	So you will not o'errule me to a peace.
KING.	To thine own peace. If he be now return'd,
	As checking at[13] his voyage, and that he means
	No more to undertake it, I will work him
	To an exploit now ripe in my device,
	Under the which he shall not choose but fall;
	And for his death no wind of blame shall breathe,
	But even his mother shall uncharge[14] the practice,[15]
	And call it accident.
LAER.	My lord, I will be ruled;
	The rather, if you could devise it so
	That I might be the organ.
KING.	It falls right.

[10] *naked*] destitute.
[11] *abuse*] deception.
[12] *character*] handwriting.
[13] *checking at*] turning from.
[14] *uncharge*] acquit of blame.
[15] *practice*] devious stratagem.

You have been talk'd of since your travel much,
And that in Hamlet's hearing, for a quality
Wherein, they say, you shine. Your sum of parts
Did not together pluck such envy from him,
As did that one, and that in my regard
Of the unworthiest siege.[16]

LAER.   What part is that, my lord?
KING.   A very ribbon in the cap of youth,
Yet needful too; for youth no less becomes
The light and careless livery that it wears
Than settled age his sables and his weeds,
Importing health and graveness. Two months since,
Here was a gentleman of Normandy—
I've seen myself, and served against, the French,
And they can well[17] on horseback; but this gallant
Had witchcraft in't. He grew unto his seat,
And to such wondrous doing brought his horse
As had he been incorpsed and demi-natured
With the brave beast. So far he topp'd my thought
That I, in forgery[18] of shapes and tricks,
Come short of what he did.

LAER.   A Norman was't?
KING.   A Norman.
LAER.   Upon my life, Lamord.
KING.   The very same.
LAER.   I know him well. He is the brooch indeed
And gem of all the nation.
KING.   He made confession of[19] you,
And gave you such a masterly report,
For art and exercise in your defence,[20]
And for your rapier most especial,
That he cried out, 'twould be a sight indeed
If one could match[21] you. The scrimers[22] of their nation,
He swore, had neither motion, guard, nor eye,
If you opposed them. Sir, this report of his

[16] *siege*] rank.
[17] *can well*] are skillful.
[18] *forgery*] invention.
[19] *made confession of*] spoke of.
[20] *defence*] swordmanship.
[21] *match*] engage in a match with.
[22] *scrimers*] fencers.

            Did Hamlet so envenom with his envy
            That he could nothing do but wish and beg
            Your sudden coming o'er, to play with him.
            Now, out of this—

LAER.   What out of this, my lord?
KING.   Laertes, was your father dear to you?
            Or are you like the painting of a sorrow,
            A face without a heart?

LAER.   Why ask you this?
KING.   Not that I think you did not love your father,
            But that I know love is begun by time,
            And that I see, in passages of proof,[23]
            Time qualifies[24] the spark and fire of it.
            There lives within the very flame of love
            A kind of wick or snuff that will abate it;
            And nothing is at a like goodness still,[25]
            For goodness, growing to a pleurisy,
            Dies in his own too much. That we would do,
            We should do when we would; for this 'would' changes
            And hath abatements and delays as many
            As there are tongues, are hands, are accidents,
            And then this 'should' is like a spendthrift sigh
            That hurts by easing. But, to the quick o' the ulcer:
            Hamlet comes back; what would you undertake
            To show yourself your father's son in deed
            More than in words?

LAER.   To cut his throat i' the church.
KING.   No place indeed should murder sanctuarize.[26]
            Revenge should have no bounds. But, good Laertes,
            Will you do this, keep close within your chamber.
            Hamlet return'd shall know you are come home.
            We'll put on[27] those shall praise your excellence
            And set a double varnish on the fame
            The Frenchman gave you, bring you in fine[28] together
            And wager on your heads. He, being remiss,[29]
            Most generous and free from all contriving,

---

[23] *passages of proof*] reliable instances.
[24] *qualifies*] diminishes.
[25] *still*] always.
[26] *sanctuarize*] give sanctuary to.
[27] *put on*] set to work.
[28] *in fine*] in the end.
[29] *remiss*] unsuspecting.

Will not peruse the foils, so that with ease,
Or with a little shuffling, you may choose
A sword unbated,[30] and in a pass[31] of practice
Requite him for your father.

LAER.   I will do't.
And for that purpose I'll anoint my sword.
I bought an unction[32] of a mountebank,
So mortal that but dip a knife in it,
Where it draws blood no cataplasm[33] so rare,
Collected from all simples[34] that have virtue
Under the moon, can save the thing from death
That is but scratch'd withal. I'll touch my point
With this contagion that, if I gall[35] him slightly,
It may be death.

KING.   Let's further think of this,
Weigh what convenience both of time and means
May fit us to our shape.[36] If this should fail,
And that our drift[37] look through our bad performance,
'Twere better not assay'd. Therefore this project
Should have a back or second that might hold
If this did blast in proof.[38] Soft, let me see.
We'll make a solemn wager on your cunnings—[39]
I ha't!
When in your motion you are hot and dry—
As make your bouts more violent to that end—
And that he calls for drink, I'll have prepared him
A chalice for the nonce; whereon but sipping,
If he by chance escape your venom'd stuck,[40]
Our purpose may hold there. But stay, what noise?

Enter QUEEN.

                    How now, sweet Queen?
QUEEN.   One woe doth tread upon another's heel,

---

[30] *unbated*] unblunted (without a button on the point).
[31] *pass*] a single thrust or a bout.
[32] *unction*] ointment.
[33] *cataplasm*] plaster, poultice.
[34] *simples*] medicinal herbs.
[35] *gall*] wound.
[36] *shape*] form of proceeding.
[37] *drift*] scheme.
[38] *blast in proof*] fail when put to the test.
[39] *your cunnings*] your respective skill.
[40] *stuck*] thrust.

| | So fast they follow. Your sister's drown'd, Laertes. |

LAER.   Drown'd? O, where?

QUEEN.   There is a willow grows aslant a brook,
That shows his hoary leaves in the glassy stream.
Therewith fantastic garlands did she make
Of crow-flowers, [41] nettles, daisies, and long purples, [42]
That liberal [43] shepherds give a grosser name,
But our cold [44] maids do dead men's fingers call them.
There, on the pendent boughs her crownet weeds
Clambering to hang, an envious [45] sliver broke;
When down her weedy trophies and herself
Fell in the weeping brook. Her clothes spread wide,
And mermaid-like awhile they bore her up;
Which time she chanted snatches of old lauds, [46]
As one incapable [47] of her own distress,
Or like a creature native and indued
Unto [48] that element. But long it could not be
Till that her garments, heavy with their drink,
Pull'd the poor wretch from her melodious lay
To muddy death.

LAER.   Alas, then she is drown'd.

QUEEN.   Drown'd, drown'd.

LAER.   Too much of water hast thou, poor Ophelia,
And therefore I forbid my tears. But yet
It is our trick; [49] nature her custom holds,
Let shame say what it will. When these are gone,
The woman will be out. [50] Adieu, my lord.
I have a speech of fire that fain would blaze,
But that this folly douts it. [51]   [*Exit.*

KING.   Let's follow, Gertrude.
How much I had to do to calm his rage.
Now fear I this will give it start again;
Therefore let's follow.   [*Exeunt.*

[41] *crow-flowers*] ragged robins.
[42] *long purples*] *Orchis mascula.*
[43] *liberal*] licentious.
[44] *cold*] chaste.
[45] *envious*] spiteful.
[46] *lauds*] hymns.
[47] *incapable*] unaware.
[48] *indued Unto*] suited to live in.
[49] *our trick*] in our nature.
[50] *When . . . out*] i.e., when I have shed these tears the woman in me will have been cast off, too.
[51] *this folly douts it*] this weeping extinguishes it.

ACT V.

SCENE I. *A churchyard.*

Enter two Clowns, *with spades, &c.*

FIRST CLO. Is she to be buried in Christian burial that wilfully seeks her own salvation?[1]

SEC. CLO. I tell thee she is; and therefore make her grave straight.[2] The crowner[3] hath sat on her, and finds it Christian burial.

FIRST CLO. How can that be, unless she drowned herself in her own defence?

SEC. CLO. Why, 'tis found so.

FIRST CLO. It must be *se offendendo*;[4] it cannot be else. For here lies the point: if I drown myself wittingly, it argues an act, and an act hath three branches: it is to act, to do, and to perform; argal,[5] she drowned herself wittingly.

SEC. CLO. Nay, but hear you, Goodman Delver—

FIRST CLO. Give me leave. Here lies the water—good. Here stands the man—good. If the man go to this water and drown himself, it is, will he, nill he, he goes. Mark you that. But if the water come to him and drown him, he drowns not himself; argal, he that is not guilty of his own death shortens not his own life.

SEC. CLO. But is this law?

FIRST CLO. Ay, marry, is't; crowner's quest[6] law.

---

[1] *Christian burial . . . salvation*] The Clowns assume that Ophelia has committed suicide and that therefore she cannot be buried in consecrated ground. *Salvation* is a blunder for "damnation."

[2] *straight*] straightaway.

[3] *crowner*] coroner.

[4] *se offendendo*] a blunder for *se defendendo* (in self-defense).

[5] *argal*] an uneducated pronunciation of "ergo."

[6] *quest*] inquest.

SEC. CLO.   Will you ha' the truth on't? If this had not been a gentle-woman, she should have been buried out o' Christian burial.

FIRST CLO.   Why, there thou say'st. And the more pity that great folk should have countenance in this world to drown or hang themselves, more than their even[7] Christian. Come, my spade. There is no ancient gentlemen but gardeners, ditchers and grave-makers: they hold up[8] Adam's profession.

SEC. CLO.   Was he a gentleman?

FIRST CLO.   A was the first that ever bore arms.

SEC. CLO.   Why, he had none.

FIRST CLO.   What, art a heathen? How dost thou understand the Scripture? The Scripture says Adam digged. Could he dig without arms? I'll put another question to thee. If thou answerest me not to the purpose, confess thyself—

SEC. CLO.   Go to.

FIRST CLO.   What is he that builds stronger than either the mason, the shipwright, or the carpenter?

SEC. CLO.   The gallows-maker; for that frame outlives a thousand tenants.

FIRST CLO.   I like thy wit well, in good faith. The gallows does well. But how does it well? It does well to those that do ill. Now, thou dost ill to say the gallows is built stronger than the church; argal, the gallows may do well to thee. To't again, come.

SEC. CLO.   'Who builds stronger than a mason, a shipwright, or a carpenter?'

FIRST CLO.   Ay, tell me that, and unyoke.[9]

SEC. CLO.   Marry, now I can tell.

FIRST CLO.   To't.

SEC. CLO.   Mass, I cannot tell.

Enter HAMLET *and* HORATIO, *afar off.*

FIRST CLO.   Cudgel thy brains no more about it, for your dull ass will not mend his pace with beating, and when you are asked this question next, say 'A grave-maker.' The houses that he makes last till doomsday. Go, get thee to Yaughan. Fetch me a stoup of liquor.

                [*Exit* Sec. Clown; First Clown *digs, and sings.*

[7] *even*] fellow.
[8] *hold up*] continue.
[9] *unyoke*] i.e., then your work is done.

> In youth, when I did love, did love,
> > Methought it was very sweet,
> To contract,[10] O, the time, for-a my behove,[11]
> > O, methought, there-a was nothing-a meet.

HAM.   Has this fellow no feeling of his business, that he sings at grave-making?

HOR.   Custom hath made it in him a property of easiness.[12]

HAM.   'Tis e'en so. The hand of little employment hath the daintier sense.

FIRST CLO.   [Sings] But age, with his stealing steps,
> > Hath claw'd me in his clutch,
> > And hath shipped me intil[13] the land,
> > > As if I had never been such. [Throws up a skull.]

HAM.   That skull had a tongue in it, and could sing once. How the knave jowls[14] it to the ground, as if it were Cain's jawbone, that did the first murder. It might be the pate of a politician, which this ass now o'er-offices,[15] one that would circumvent God, might it not?

HOR.   It might, my lord.

HAM.   Or of a courtier, which could say 'Good morrow, sweet lord. How dost thou, sweet lord?' This might be my Lord Such-a-one, that praised my Lord Such-a-one's horse, when he meant to beg it, might it not?

HOR.   Ay, my lord.

HAM.   Why, e'en so; and now my Lady Worm's, chapless,[16] and knocked about the mazard[17] with a sexton's spade. Here's fine revolution, an we had the trick[18] to see't. Did these bones cost no more the breeding, but to play at loggats[19] with 'em? Mine ache to think on't.

FIRST CLO.   [Sings] A pickaxe, and a spade, a spade,
> > For and[20] a shrouding-sheet;
> > O, a pit of clay for to be made
> > > For such a guest is meet. [Throws up another skull.]

---

[10] *contract*] shorten (probably a blunder by the Clown).

[11] *behove*] behoof, advantage.

[12] *property of easiness*] activity that does not trouble the mind.

[13] *intil*] to.

[14] *jowls*] throws, dashes.

[15] *o'er-offices*] lords over (by virtue of his office as grave digger).

[16] *chapless*] without a jaw.

[17] *mazard*] head.

[18] *trick*] knack, art.

[19] *loggats*] a game in which small logs are thrown at a stake.

[20] *For and*] and moreover.

HAM.   There's another. Why may not that be the skull of a lawyer? Where be his quiddities now, his quillets,[21] his cases, his tenures, and his tricks? Why does he suffer this rude knave now to knock him about the sconce with a dirty shovel, and will not tell him of his action of battery? Hum! This fellow might be in's time a great buyer of land, with his statutes, his recognizances, his fines, his double vouchers, his recoveries.[22] Is this the fine[23] of his fines and the recovery of his recoveries, to have his fine pate full of fine dirt? Will his vouchers vouch[24] him no more of his purchases, and double ones too, than the length and breadth of a pair of indentures?[25] The very conveyances of his lands will hardly lie in this box;[26] and must the inheritor[27] himself have no more, ha?

HOR.   Not a jot more, my lord.

HAM.   Is not parchment made of sheepskins?

HOR.   Ay, my lord, and of calfskins too.

HAM.   They are sheep and calves which seek out assurance in that. I will speak to this fellow. Whose grave's this, sirrah?

FIRST CLO.   Mine, sir.

[*Sings*]   O, a pit of clay for to be made
            For such a guest is meet.

HAM.   I think it be thine indeed, for thou liest in't.

FIRST CLO.   You lie out on't, sir, and therefore 'tis not yours. For my part, I do not lie in't, and yet it is mine.

HAM.   Thou dost lie in't, to be in't and say 'tis thine. 'Tis for the dead, not for the quick; therefore thou liest.

FIRST CLO.   'Tis a quick lie, sir; 'twill away again from me to you.

HAM.   What man dost thou dig it for?

FIRST CLO.   For no man, sir.

HAM.   What woman then?

FIRST CLO.   For none, neither.

HAM.   Who is to be buried in't?

FIRST CLO.   One that was a woman, sir, but, rest her soul, she's dead.

---

[21] *quiddities . . . quillets*] subtle arguments.
[22] *statutes . . . recoveries*] legal terms relating to the transfer and mortgaging of land.
[23] *fine*] end.
[24] *vouch*] guarantee.
[25] *indentures*] contracts.
[26] *box*] coffin.
[27] *inheritor*] possessor, owner.

HAM.   How absolute[28] the knave is! We must speak by the card,[29] or
            equivocation will undo us. By the Lord, Horatio, this three
            years I have taken note of it: the age is grown so picked[30] that
            the toe of the peasant comes so near the heel of the courtier,
            he galls his kibe.[31] How long hast thou been a grave-maker?

FIRST CLO. Of all the days i' the year, I came to't that day that our last
            King Hamlet o'ercame Fortinbras.

HAM.   How long is that since?

FIRST CLO. Cannot you tell that? Every fool can tell that. It was that
            very day that young Hamlet was born—he that is mad and
            sent into England.

HAM.   Ay, marry, why was he sent into England?

FIRST CLO. Why, because a was mad. A shall recover his wits there; or,
            if a do not, 'tis no great matter there.

HAM.   Why?

FIRST CLO. 'Twill not be seen in him there. There the men are as mad
            as he.

HAM.   How came he mad?

FIRST CLO. Very strangely, they say.

HAM.   How 'strangely'?

FIRST CLO. Faith, e'en with losing his wits.

HAM.   Upon what ground?

FIRST CLO. Why, here in Denmark. I have been sexton here, man and
            boy, thirty years.

HAM.   How long will a man lie i' the earth ere he rot?

FIRST CLO. I'faith, if a be not rotten before a die—as we have many
            pocky corses nowadays that will scarce hold the laying
            in[32]—a will last you some eight year or nine year. A tanner
            will last you nine year.

HAM.   Why he more than another?

FIRST CLO. Why, sir, his hide is so tanned with his trade that a will
            keep out water a great while; and your water is a sore decayer
            of your whoreson dead body. Here's a skull, now. This skull
            has lain in the earth three and twenty years.

HAM.   Whose was it?

FIRST CLO. A whoreson mad fellow's it was. Whose do you think it
            was?

---

[28] *absolute*] strict.
[29] *by the card*] with the utmost precision.
[30] *picked*] refined.
[31] *galls his kibe*] chafes the sore on his heel.
[32] *hold the laying in*] remain in one piece until after the burial.

HAM.   Nay, I know not.

FIRST CLO.   A pestilence on him for a mad rogue! A poured a flagon of Rhenish on my head once. This same skull, sir, was Yorick's skull, the King's jester.

HAM.   [*Takes the skull*] This?

FIRST CLO.   E'en that.

HAM.   Alas, poor Yorick. I knew him, Horatio: a fellow of infinite jest, of most excellent fancy. He hath borne me on his back a thousand times; and now, how abhorred in my imagination it is! My gorge rises at it. Here hung those lips that I have kissed I know not how oft. Where be your gibes now, your gambols, your songs, your flashes of merriment, that were wont to set the table on a roar? Not one now to mock your own grinning? Quite chop-fallen? Now get you to my lady's chamber, and tell her, let her paint an inch thick, to this favour[33] she must come. Make her laugh at that. Prithee, Horatio, tell me one thing.

HOR.   What's that, my lord?

HAM.   Dost thou think Alexander looked o' this fashion i' the earth?

HOR.   E'en so.

HAM.   And smelt so? Pah!   [*Puts down the skull.*

HOR.   E'en so, my lord.

HAM.   To what base uses we may return, Horatio! Why, may not imagination trace the noble dust of Alexander till he find it stopping a bung-hole?

HOR.   'Twere to consider too curiously[34] to consider so.

HAM.   No, faith, not a jot; but to follow him thither with modesty[35] enough and likelihood to lead it, as thus: Alexander died, Alexander was buried, Alexander returneth into dust, the dust is earth, of earth we make loam, and why of that loam, whereto he was converted, might they not stop a beer-barrel?
Imperious[36] Cæsar, dead and turn'd to clay,
Might stop a hole to keep the wind away.
O, that that earth, which kept the world in awe,
Should patch a wall to expel the winter's flaw![37]
But soft, but soft awhile! Here comes the King,
The Queen, the courtiers.

---

[33] *favour*] appearance.
[34] *curiously*] minutely.
[35] *modestly*] moderation.
[36] *Imperious*] imperial.
[37] *flaw*] gust of wind.

Enter Priests, *&c. in procession; the Corpse of Ophelia,* LAERTES, *and* Mourners *following;* KING, QUEEN, *their trains, &c.*

                              Who is this they follow?
          And with such maimed rites? This doth betoken
          The corse they follow did with desperate hand
          Fordo[38] its own life. 'Twas of some estate.[39]
          Couch we[40] awhile and mark.   [*Retiring with* HORATIO.

LAER.   What ceremony else?
HAM.   That is Laertes, a very noble youth. Mark.
LAER.   What ceremony else?
PRIEST.   Her obsequies have been as far enlarged
          As we have warranty. Her death was doubtful;
          And, but that great command o'ersways the order,
          She should in ground unsanctified have lodged
          Till the last trumpet; for charitable prayers,
          Shards,[41] flints and pebbles should be thrown on her.
          Yet here she is allow'd her virgin crants,[42]
          Her maiden strewments[43] and the bringing home
          Of bell and burial.[44]

LAER.   Must there no more be done?
PRIEST.   No more be done.
          We should profane the service of the dead
          To sing a requiem and such rest to her
          As to peace-parted souls.

LAER.   Lay her i' the earth,
          And from her fair and unpolluted flesh
          May violets spring. I tell thee, churlish priest,
          A ministering angel shall my sister be
          When thou liest howling.

HAM.   What, the fair Ophelia!
QUEEN.   [*Scattering flowers*] Sweets to the sweet. Farewell.
          I hoped thou shouldst have been my Hamlet's wife;
          I thought thy bride-bed to have deck'd, sweet maid,
          And not have strew'd thy grave.

LAER.   O, treble woe

---

[38] *Fordo*] destroy.
[39] *estate*] rank.
[40] *Couch we*] let us remain hidden.
[41] *Shards*] fragments of pottery.
[42] *crants*] garlands.
[43] *strewments*] strewing of flowers.
[44] *bringing home . . . burial*] laying to rest to the sound of the knell.

Fall ten times treble on that cursed head
Whose wicked deed thy most ingenious sense
Deprived thee of! Hold off the earth awhile,
Till I have caught her once more in mine arms.

> *[Leaps into the grave.*

Now pile your dust upon the quick and dead,
Till of this flat a mountain you have made
To o'ertop old Pelion or the skyish head
Of blue Olympus.

HAM.   *[Advancing]* What is he whose grief
Bears such an emphasis, whose phrase of sorrow
Conjures the wandering stars[45] and makes them stand
Like wonder-wounded hearers? This is I,
Hamlet the Dane.

LAER.   The devil take thy soul!   *[Grappling with him.*

HAM.   Thou pray'st not well.
I prithee, take thy fingers from my throat;
For, though I am not splenative[46] and rash,
Yet have I in me something dangerous,
Which let thy wisdom fear. Hold off thy hand.

KING.   Pluck them asunder.

QUEEN.   Hamlet, Hamlet!

ALL.   Gentlemen!

HOR.   Good my lord, be quiet.

HAM.   Why, I will fight with him upon this theme
Until my eyelids will no longer wag.

QUEEN.   O my son, what theme?

HAM.   I loved Ophelia. Forty thousand brothers
Could not, with all their quantity of love,
Make up my sum. What wilt thou do for her?

KING.   O, he is mad, Laertes.

QUEEN.   For love of God, forbear[47] him.

HAM.   'Swounds, show me what thou'lt do.
Woo't[48] weep, woo't fight, woo't fast, woo't tear thyself,
Woo't drink up eisel,[49] eat a crocodile?
I'll do't. Dost thou come here to whine,
To outface me with leaping in her grave?

---

[45] *wandering stars]* planets.
[46] *splenative]* hot-tempered, impetuous.
[47] *forbear]* leave alone.
[48] *Woo't]* will you.
[49] *eisel]* vinegar.

Be buried quick[50] with her, and so will I.
And, if thou prate of mountains, let them throw
Millions of acres on us, till our ground,
Singeing his pate against the burning zone,[51]
Make Ossa like a wart. Nay, an thou'lt mouth,
I'll rant as well as thou.

QUEEN.   This is mere madness;
And thus awhile the fit will work on him.
Anon, as patient as the female dove
When that her golden couplets are disclosed,[52]
His silence will sit drooping.

HAM.   Hear you, sir;
What is the reason that you use me thus?
I loved you ever. But it is no matter.
Let Hercules himself do what he may,
The cat will mew, and dog will have his day.   [Exit.

KING.   I pray thee, good Horatio, wait upon him. [Exit HORATIO.
[To LAERTES] Strengthen your patience in our last night's
  speech;
We'll put the matter to the present push. —[53]
Good Gertrude, set some watch over your son.
This grave shall have a living monument.
An hour of quiet shortly shall we see;
Till then, in patience our proceeding be.   [Exeunt.

SCENE II. *A hall in the castle.*

Enter HAMLET *and* HORATIO.

HAM.   So much for this, sir. Now shall you see the other.
        You do remember all the circumstance?
HOR.   Remember it, my lord!
HAM.   Sir, in my heart there was a kind of fighting
        That would not let me sleep. Methought I lay

---

[50] *quick*] alive.
[51] *burning zone*] sun's sphere or orbit.
[52] *disclosed*] hatched.
[53] *to the present push*] into immediate action.

Worse than the mutines in the bilboes.[1] Rashly—
And praised be rashness for it: let us know
Our indiscretion sometime serves us well
When our deep plots do pall; and that should learn us
There's a divinity that shapes our ends,
Rough-hew them how we will—

HOR.   That is most certain.

HAM.   Up from my cabin,
My sea-gown scarf'd about me, in the dark
Groped I to find out them,[2] had my desire,
Finger'd[3] their packet, and in fine[4] withdrew
To mine own room again, making so bold,
My fears forgetting manners, to unseal
Their grand commission, where I found, Horatio—
O royal knavery!—an exact command,
Larded[5] with many several sorts of reasons
Importing Denmark's health and England's too,
With, ho! such bugs and goblins in my life,[6]
That on the supervise,[7] no leisure bated,[8]
No, not to stay the grinding of the axe,
My head should be struck off.

HOR.   Is't possible?

HAM.   Here's the commission. Read it at more leisure.
But wilt thou hear now how I did proceed?

HOR.   I beseech you.

HAM.   Being thus benetted round with villanies—
Or[9] I could make a prologue to my brains,
They had begun the play—I sat me down,
Devised a new commission, wrote it fair.[10]
I once did hold it, as our statists[11] do,
A baseness to write fair, and labour'd much
How to forget that learning; but, sir, now
It did me yeoman's service. Wilt thou know

---

[1] *mutines in the bilboes*] mutineers in shackles.
[2] *them*] Rosencrantz and Guildenstern.
[3] *Finger'd*] pilfered.
[4] *in fine*] finally.
[5] *Larded*] garnished.
[6] *such bugs . . . life*] such imaginary dangers, should I be allowed to live.
[7] *supervise*] perusal (of Claudius' missive).
[8] *no leisure bated*] with no delay.
[9] *Or*] before.
[10] *fair*] in a legible hand.
[11] *statists*] statesmen.

	The effect of what I wrote?
Hor.	Ay, good my lord.
Ham.	An earnest conjuration from the King,

HAM. An earnest conjuration from the King,
As England was his faithful tributary,
As love between them like the palm might flourish,
As peace should still[12] her wheaten garland wear
And stand a comma 'tween their amities,
And many such-like 'As'es of great charge,[13]
That on the view and knowing of these contents,
Without debatement further, more or less,
He should the bearers put to sudden death,
Not shriving-time[14] allow'd.

HOR.   How was this seal'd?

HAM. Why, even in that was heaven ordinant.[15]
I had my father's signet in my purse,
Which was the model of that Danish seal;
Folded the writ up in the form of the other,
Subscribed it, gave't the impression, placed it safely,
The changeling never known. Now, the next day
Was our sea-fight; and what to this was sequent
Thou know'st already.

HOR. So Guildenstern and Rosencrantz go to't.

HAM. Why, man, they did make love to this employment.
They are not near my conscience. Their defeat
Does by their own insinuation grow.
'Tis dangerous when the baser nature comes
Between the pass[16] and fell incensed points
Of mighty opposites.

HOR.   Why, what a king is this!

HAM. Does it not, think thee, stand me now upon—[17]
He that hath kill'd my king and whored my mother,
Popp'd in between the election and my hopes,
Thrown out his angle[18] for my proper[19] life,
And with such cozenage[20]—is't not perfect conscience
To quit him with this arm? And is't not to be damn'd

---

[12] *still*] always.
[13] *charge*] importance. There is a pun on "asses," and the load they carry.
[14] *shriving-time*] time for absolution.
[15] *ordinant*] ordaining, directing.
[16] *pass*] sword thrust.
[17] *stand me now upon*] put me under obligation.
[18] *angle*] fishhook.
[19] *proper*] own.
[20] *cozenage*] deceit.

To let this canker of our nature come
In further evil?

HOR. It must be shortly known to him from England
What is the issue of the business there.

HAM. It will be short. The interim is mine;
And a man's life's no more than to say 'One.'
But I am very sorry, good Horatio,
That to Laertes I forgot myself;
For by the image of my cause I see
The portraiture of his. I'll court his favours.
But, sure, the bravery[21] of his grief did put me
Into a towering passion.

HOR. Peace, who comes here?

Enter OSRIC.

OSR. Your lordship is right welcome back to Denmark.

HAM. I humbly thank you, sir. Dost know this water-fly?

HOR. No, my good lord.

HAM. Thy state is the more gracious,[22] for 'tis a vice to know him. He
hath much land, and fertile. Let a beast be lord of beasts,
and his crib[23] shall stand at the king's mess. 'Tis a chuff,[24]
but, as I say, spacious in the possession of dirt.

OSR. Sweet lord, if your lordship were at leisure, I should impart a
thing to you from his Majesty.

HAM. I will receive it, sir, with all diligence of spirit. Put your bonnet
to his right use: 'tis for the head.

OSR. I thank your lordship, it is very hot.

HAM. No, believe me, 'tis very cold; the wind is northerly.

OSR. It is indifferent[25] cold, my lord, indeed.

HAM. But yet methinks it is very sultry and hot for my complexion.[26]

OSR. Exceedingly, my lord. It is very sultry, as 'twere—I cannot tell
how. But, my lord, his Majesty bade me signify to you that
he has laid a great wager on your head. Sir, this is the
matter—

HAM. I beseech you, remember—

[HAMLET *moves him to put on his hat.*

---

[21] *bravery*] bravado, ostentation.
[22] *gracious*] virtuous.
[23] *crib*] manger, trough.
[24] *chuff*] a wealthy, but dull, person.
[25] *indifferent*] moderately.
[26] *complexion*] temperament, constitution.

OSR.   Nay, good my lord; for mine ease, in good faith. Sir, here is
         newly come to court Laertes—believe me, an absolute gen-
         tleman, full of most excellent differences, [27] of very soft
         society and great showing. [28] Indeed, to speak feelingly[29] of
         him, he is the card or calendar of gentry, [30] for you shall find
         in him the continent[31] of what part a gentleman would see.

HAM.   Sir, his definement suffers no perdition[32] in you, though, I
         know, to divide him inventorially would dizzy the arithme-
         tic of memory, and yet but yaw neither, [33] in respect of his
         quick sail. But, in the verity of extolment, I take him to be a
         soul of great article, [34] and his infusion[35] of such dearth[36]
         and rareness as, to make true diction of him, his semblable
         is his mirror, [37] and who else would trace[38] him, his um-
         brage, [39] nothing more.

OSR.   Your lordship speaks most infallibly of him.

HAM.   The concernancy, [40] sir? Why do we wrap the gentleman in our
         more rawer breath?[41]

OSR.   Sir?

HOR.   Is't not possible to understand in another tongue?[42] You will
         do't, sir, really.

HAM.   What imports the nomination[43] of this gentleman?

OSR.   Of Laertes?

HOR.   His purse is empty already; all's golden words are spent.

HAM.   Of him, sir.

OSR.   I know you are not ignorant—

HAM.   I would you did, sir. Yet, in faith, if you did, it would not much
         approve[44] me. Well, sir?

---

[27] *differences*] extraordinary qualities.
[28] *soft society . . . showing*] distinguished appearance.
[29] *feelingly*] perceptively.
[30] *card or calendar of gentry*] epitome of courtesy.
[31] *continent*] container.
[32] *perdition*] loss.
[33] *but yaw neither*] steer out of course nevertheless.
[34] *article*] i.e., matter to be listed on an inventory.
[35] *infusion*] quality.
[36] *dearth*] rarity.
[37] *his semblable is his mirror*] the only person like him is his own reflection.
[38] *trace*] follow.
[39] *umbrage*] shadow.
[40] *concernancy*] import, significance.
[41] *more rawer breath*] inadequate language.
[42] *another tongue*] i.e., simpler terms.
[43] *nomination*] mentioning.
[44] *approve*] commend.

OSR. You are not ignorant of what excellence Laertes is—

HAM. I dare not confess that, lest I should compare with him in excellence; but, to know a man well were to know himself.

OSR. I mean, sir, for his weapon; but in the imputation[45] laid on him by them in his meed,[46] he's unfellowed.

HAM. What's his weapon?

OSR. Rapier and dagger.

HAM. That's two of his weapons. But, well.

OSR. The King, sir, hath wagered with him six Barbary horses, against the which he has impawned,[47] as I take it, six French rapiers and poniards,[48] with their assigns,[49] as girdle, hanger,[50] and so. Three of the carriages, in faith, are very dear to fancy, very responsive[51] to the hilts, most delicate carriages, and of very liberal conceit.[52]

HAM. What call you the carriages?

HOR. I knew you must be edified by the margent[53] ere you had done.

OSR. The carriages, sir, are the hangers.

HAM. The phrase would be more german[54] to the matter if we could carry a cannon by our sides. I would it might be hangers till then. But, on. Six Barbary horses against six French swords, their assigns, and three liberal-conceited carriages—that's the French bet against the Danish. Why is this 'impawned,' as you call it?

OSR. The King, sir, hath laid, sir, that in a dozen passes[55] between yourself and him, he shall not exceed you three hits. He hath laid on twelve for nine. And it would come to immediate trial, if your lordship would vouchsafe the answer.

HAM. How if I answer no?

OSR. I mean, my lord, the opposition of your person in trial.

HAM. Sir, I will walk here in the hall. If it please his Majesty, it is the breathing time[56] of day with me. Let the foils be brought,

---

[45] *imputation*] reputation.
[46] *meed*] service.
[47] *impawned*] wagered.
[48] *poniards*] daggers.
[49] *assigns*] accessories.
[50] *hanger*] part of a belt to which the scabbard is attached.
[51] *responsive*] matching, suited.
[52] *liberal conceit*] (?) tasteful design.
[53] *margent*] margin (of a book, on which could be written explanatory notes).
[54] *german*] germane, appropriate.
[55] *passes*] bouts.
[56] *breathing time*] exercise period.

the gentleman willing, and the King hold his purpose, I will win for him an I can. If not, I will gain nothing but my shame and the odd hits.

OSR.   Shall I redeliver you e'en so?

HAM.   To this effect, sir, after what flourish your nature will.

OSR.   I commend my duty to your lordship.

HAM.   Yours, yours. [*Exit* OSRIC.] He does well to commend it himself; there are no tongues else for's turn.

HOR.   This lapwing runs away with the shell on his head.[57]

HAM.   He did comply with his dug[58] before he sucked it. Thus has he—and many more of the same breed that I know the drossy[59] age dotes on—only got the tune of the time and outward habit of encounter, a kind of yesty[60] collection, which carries them through and through the most fanned and winnowed[61] opinions; and do but blow them to their trial, the bubbles are out.[62]

Enter a Lord.

LORD.   My lord, his Majesty commended him to you by young Osric, who brings back to him that you attend him in the hall. He sends to know if your pleasure hold to play with Laertes or that you will take longer time.

HAM.   I am constant to my purposes; they follow the King's pleasure. If his fitness[63] speaks, mine is ready; now or whensoever, provided I be so able as now.

LORD.   The King and Queen and all are coming down.

HAM.   In happy time.

LORD.   The Queen desires you to use some gentle entertainment[64] to Laertes before you fall to play.

HAM.   She well instructs me.   [*Exit* Lord.

HOR.   You will lose this wager, my lord.

HAM.   I do not think so. Since he went into France, I have been in

---

[57] *This lapwing . . . head*] Horatio refers to the fact that Osric has put his hat back on. Lapwings were said to leave the nest shortly after hatching and therefore came to signify precocity and pretension.

[58] *did comply . . . dug*] was courteous to his mother's breast.

[59] *drossy*] frivolous.

[60] *yesty*] frothy.

[61] *fanned and winnowed*] tried and sifted.

[62] *do but blow . . . out*] i.e., when you put them to the test by conversing with them their expressions are found to be empty.

[63] *fitness*] convenience.

[64] *gentle entertainment*] courtesy.

	continual practice. I shall win at the odds. But thou wouldst not think how ill all's here about my heart; but it is no matter.
HOR.	Nay, good my lord—
HAM.	It is but foolery; but it is such a kind of gain-giving[65] as would perhaps trouble a woman.
HOR.	If your mind dislike anything, obey it. I will forestall their repair hither and say you are not fit.
HAM.	Not a whit. We defy augury. There is special providence in the fall of a sparrow. If it be now, 'tis not to come; if it be not to come, it will be now; if it be not now, yet it will come. The readiness is all. Since no man has aught of what he leaves, what is't to leave betimes? Let be.

Enter KING, QUEEN, LAERTES, *and* Lords, OSRIC *and other* Attendants
with foils and gauntlets; a table and flagons of wine on it.

KING.	Come, Hamlet, come, and take this hand from me.
	[*The* KING *puts* LAERTES' *hand into* HAMLET'S.
HAM.	Give me your pardon, sir. I've done you wrong;
	But pardon't as you are a gentleman.
	This presence[66] knows,
	And you must needs have heard, how I am punish'd
	With sore distraction. What I have done
	That might your nature, honour and exception[67]
	Roughly awake, I here proclaim was madness.
	Was't Hamlet wrong'd Laertes? Never Hamlet.
	If Hamlet from himself be ta'en away,
	And when he's not himself does wrong Laertes,
	Then Hamlet does it not, Hamlet denies it.
	Who does it then? His madness. If't be so,
	Hamlet is of the faction that is wrong'd;
	His madness is poor Hamlet's enemy.
	Sir, in this audience,
	Let my disclaiming from a purposed evil
	Free me so far in your most generous thoughts
	That I have shot mine arrow o'er the house
	And hurt my brother.
LAER.	I am satisfied in nature,
	Whose motive in this case should stir me most
	To my revenge; but in my terms of honour

---

[65] *gain-giving*] misgiving.
[66] *presence*] noble assembly.
[67] *exception*] disapproval.

I stand aloof, and will no reconcilement
Till by some elder masters of known honour
I have a voice[68] and precedent of peace
To keep my name ungored. But till that time
I do receive your offer'd love like love
And will not wrong it.

HAM.   I embrace it freely,
And will this brother's wager frankly play.—
Give us the foils. Come on.

LAER.   Come, one for me.

HAM.   I'll be your foil,[69] Laertes. In mine ignorance
Your skill shall, like a star i' the darkest night,
Stick fiery off[70] indeed.

LAER.   You mock me, sir.

HAM.   No, by this hand.

KING.   Give them the foils, young Osric. Cousin Hamlet,
You know the wager?

HAM.   Very well, my lord.
Your Grace has laid the odds o' the weaker side.

KING.   I do not fear it; I have seen you both,
But since he is better'd, we have therefore odds.

LAER.   This is too heavy; let me see another.

HAM.   This likes me well. These foils have all a length?

                                    [*They prepare to play.*

OSR.   Ay, my good lord.

KING.   Set me the stoups of wine upon that table.
If Hamlet give the first or second hit,
Or quit in answer of the third exchange,
Let all the battlements their ordnance fire:
The King shall drink to Hamlet's better breath,
And in the cup an union[71] shall he throw,
Richer than that which four successive kings
In Denmark's crown have worn. Give me the cups;
And let the kettle to the trumpet speak,
The trumpet to the cannoneer without,
The cannons to the heavens, the heaven to earth,
'Now the King drinks to Hamlet.' Come, begin.
And you, the judges, bear a wary eye.

[68] *voice*] authoritative judgment.
[69] *foil*] background on which a jewel is placed.
[70] *Stick fiery off*] stand out brightly.
[71] *union*] pearl.

Ham.	Come on, sir.	
Laer.	Come, my lord.	[*They play.*
Ham.	One.	
Laer.	No.	
Ham.	Judgement.	
Osr.	A hit, a very palpable hit.	
Laer.	Well, again.	
King.	Stay; give me drink. Hamlet, this pearl is thine.	

Here's to thy health.

                        [*Trumpets sound, and cannon shot off within.*
                               Give him the cup.

Ham.   I'll play this bout first. Set it by awhile.
          Come. [*They play.*] Another hit. What say you?

Laer.   A touch, a touch, I do confess.

King.   Our son shall win.

Queen.   He's fat[72] and scant of breath.
          Here, Hamlet, take my napkin, rub thy brows.
          The Queen carouses to thy fortune, Hamlet.

Ham.   Good madam.

King.   Gertrude, do not drink.

Queen. I will, my lord; I pray you, pardon me.

King.   [*Aside*] It is the poison'd cup; it is too late.

Ham.   I dare not drink yet, madam—by and by.

Queen. Come, let me wipe thy face.

Laer.   My lord, I'll hit him now.

King.   I do not think't.

Laer.   [*Aside*] And yet it is almost against my conscience.

Ham.   Come, for the third, Laertes. You but dally.
          I pray you, pass[73] with your best violence.
          I am afeard you make a wanton of me.[74]

Laer.   Say you so? Come on.   [*They play.*

Osr.   Nothing, neither way.

Laer.   Have at you now!

         [*Laertes wounds* Hamlet; *then, in scuffling, they change*
                 rapiers, and Hamlet *wounds* Laertes.

King.   Part them; they are incensed.

Ham.   Nay, come, again.   [*The* Queen *falls.*

Osr.   Look to the Queen there, ho!

Hor.   They bleed on both sides. How is it, my lord?

---

72 *fat*] unfit.
73 *pass*] thrust.
74 *make a wanton of me*] treat me like a spoiled child.

OSR.   How is't, Laertes?
LAER.   Why, as a woodcock to mine own springe,[75] Osric.
        I am justly kill'd with mine own treachery.
HAM.   How does the Queen?
KING.   She swoons to see them bleed.
QUEEN. No, no, the drink, the drink—O my dear Hamlet—
        The drink, the drink! I am poison'd.   [Dies.
HAM.   O villany! Ho! Let the door be lock'd.
        Treachery! Seek it out.   [Exit OSRIC; LAERTES falls.
LAER.   It is here, Hamlet. Hamlet, thou art slain.
        No medicine in the world can do thee good;
        In thee there is not half an hour of life.
        The treacherous instrument is in thy hand,
        Unbated and envenom'd. The foul practice[76]
        Hath turn'd itself on me. Lo, here I lie,
        Never to rise again. Thy mother's poison'd.
        I can no more. The King, the King's to blame.
HAM.   The point envenom'd too? Then, venom, to thy work.
                                            [Stabs the KING.
ALL.   Treason! treason!
KING.   O, yet defend me, friends. I am but hurt.
HAM.   Here, thou incestuous, murderous, damned Dane,
        Drink off this potion. Is thy union here?
        Follow my mother.   [KING dies.
LAER.   He is justly served.
        It is a poison temper'd[77] by himself.
        Exchange forgiveness with me, noble Hamlet.
        Mine and my father's death come not upon thee,
        Nor thine on me.   [Dies.
HAM.   Heaven make thee free of it. I follow thee.
        I am dead, Horatio. Wretched[78] Queen, adieu!
        You that look pale and tremble at this chance,
        That are but mutes or audience to this act,
        Had I but time—as this fell sergeant,[79] Death,
        Is strict in his arrest—O, I could tell you—
        But let it be. Horatio, I am dead,
        Thou livest. Report me and my cause aright

[75] *springe*] snare.
[76] *practice*] strategem, insidious device.
[77] *temper'd*] mixed.
[78] *Wretched*] unhappy.
[79] *sergeant*] sheriff's officer.

To the unsatisfied.

HOR.   Never believe it.
I am more an antique Roman[80] than a Dane.
Here's yet some liquor left.

HAM.   As thou'rt a man,
Give me the cup. Let go. By heaven, I'll have't.
O God, Horatio, what a wounded name,
Things standing thus unknown, shall live behind me!
If thou didst ever hold me in thy heart,
Absent thee from felicity awhile,
And in this harsh world draw thy breath in pain
To tell my story.   [*March afar off, and shot within.*

Enter OSRIC.

                 What warlike noise is this?

OSR.   Young Fortinbras, with conquest come from Poland,
To the ambassadors of England gives
This warlike volley.

HAM.   O, I die, Horatio.
The potent poison quite o'er-crows[81] my spirit.
I cannot live to hear the news from England;
But I do prophesy the election lights
On Fortinbras. He has my dying voice.
So tell him, with the occurrents,[82] more and less,
Which have solicited.[83] The rest is silence.   [*Dies.*

HOR.   Now cracks a noble heart. Good night, sweet prince,
And flights of angels sing thee to thy rest.   [*March within.*
Why does the drum come hither?

Enter FORTINBRAS, *and the* English Ambassadors, *with drum, colours, and* Attendants.

FORT.   Where is this sight?

HOR.   What is it you would see?
If aught of woe or wonder,[84] cease your search.

FORT.   This quarry cries on havoc.[85] O proud Death,
What feast is toward in thine eternal cell,
That thou so many princes at a shot

---

[80] *antique Roman*] i.e., one who chooses suicide rather than a dishonorable life.

[81] *o'er-crows*] triumphs over.

[82] *occurrents*] occurrences.

[83] *solicited*] moved (me to choose him).

[84] *wonder*] destruction, grief.

[85] *This quarry cries on havoc*] This heap of dead proclaims indiscriminate slaughter.

So bloodily hast struck?

FIRST AMB.   The sight is dismal;[86]
And our affairs from England come too late.
The ears are senseless that should give us hearing
To tell him his commandment is fulfill'd,
That Rosencrantz and Guildenstern are dead.
Where should we have our thanks?

HOR.   Not from his mouth,
Had it the ability of life to thank you.
He never gave commandment for their death.
But since so jump upon this bloody question[87]
You from the Polack wars, and you from England,
Are here arrived, give order that these bodies
High on a stage[88] be placed to the view;
And let me speak to the yet unknowing world
How these things came about. So shall you hear
Of carnal, bloody and unnatural acts,
Of accidental judgements, casual[89] slaughters,
Of deaths put on[90] by cunning and forced[91] cause,
And, in this upshot, purposes mistook
Fall'n on the inventors' heads. All this can I
Truly deliver.

FORT.   Let us haste to hear it,
And call the noblest to the audience.
For me, with sorrow I embrace my fortune.
I have some rights of memory[92] in this kingdom,
Which now to claim my vantage doth invite me.

HOR.   Of that I shall have also cause to speak,
And from his mouth whose voice will draw on more.[93]
But let this same[94] be presently perform'd,
Even while men's minds are wild, lest more mischance
On[95] plots and errors happen.

FORT.   Let four captains
Bear Hamlet like a soldier to the stage;

---

[86] *dismal*] horrifying.
[87] *jump . . . question*] immediately after this bloody business.
[88] *stage*] platform.
[89] *casual*] accidental.
[90] *put on*] instigated.
[91] *forced*] violent.
[92] *of memory*] traditional, remembered.
[93] *draw on more*] influence others (to vote for Fortinbras).
[94] *this same*] the aforementioned.
[95] *On*] in addition to; (?) as a result of.

For he was likely, had he been put on,
To have proved most royal; and, for his passage, [96]
The soldiers' music and the rites of war
Speak loudly for him.
Take up the bodies. Such a sight as this
Becomes the field, but here shows much amiss.
Go, bid the soldiers shoot.

> [*A dead march. Exeunt, bearing off the bodies;*
> *after which a peal of ordnance is shot off.*

[96] *passage*] passing, death.

Study Guide

Text by
Joanne K. Miller
(M.A., University of Northern Iowa)

Department of English
Harrison High School
West Lafayette, Indiana

Contents

> **Each scene includes List of Characters, Summary,
> Analysis, Study Questions and Answers, and
> Suggested Essay Topics.**

Introduction

The Life and Work of William Shakespeare

Details about William Shakespeare's life are sketchy, mostly mere surmise based upon court or other clerical records. His parents, John and Mary (Arden), were married about 1557; she was of the landed gentry, he a yeoman—a glover and commodities merchant. By 1568, John had risen through the ranks of town government and held the position of high bailiff, similar to mayor. William, the eldest son, was born in 1564, probably on April 23, several days before his baptism on April 26, 1564. That Shakespeare also died on April 23, 52 years later, may have resulted in the adoption of this birthdate.

William no doubt attended the local grammar school in Stratford where his parents lived, and would have studied primarily Latin rhetoric, logic, and literature [Barnet, viii]. At age 18 (1582), William married Anne Hathaway, a local farmer's daughter eight years his senior. Their first daughter (Susanna) was born six months later (1583), and twins Judith and Hamnet were born in 1585.

Shakespeare's life can be divided into three periods: the first 20 years in Stratford, which include his schooling, early marriage, and fatherhood; the next 25 years as an actor and playwright in London; and the last five in retirement back in Stratford where he enjoyed moderate wealth gained from his theatrical successes. The years linking the first two periods are marked by a lack of information about Shakespeare, and are often referred to as the "dark years";

the transition from active work into retirement was gradual and cannot be precisely dated [Boyce, 587].

John Shakespeare had suffered financial reverses from William's teen years until well into the height of the playwright's popularity and success. In 1596, John Shakespeare was granted a coat of arms, almost certainly purchased by William, who the next year bought a sizable house in Stratford. By the time of his death, William had substantial properties, both professional and personal, which he bestowed on his theatrical associates and his family (primarily his daughter Susanna, having rewritten his will one month before his death to protect his assets from Judith's new husband, Thomas Quiney, who ran afoul of church doctrine and public esteem before and after the marriage) [Boyce, 529].

Shakespeare probably left school at 15, which was the norm, and took some sort of job, especially since this was the period of his father's financial difficulty. Numerous references in his plays suggest that William may have in fact worked for his father, thereby gaining specialized knowledge [Boyce, 587].

At some point during the "dark years," Shakespeare began his career with a London theatrical company—perhaps in 1589—for he was already an actor and playwright of some note in 1592. Shakespeare apparently wrote and acted for Pembroke's Men, as well as numerous others, in particular Strange's Men, which later became the Chamberlain's Men, with whom he remained for the rest of his career.

When, in 1592, the Plague closed the theaters for about two years, Shakespeare turned to writing book-length narrative poetry. Most notable were "Venus and Adonis" and "The Rape of Lucrece," both of which were dedicated to the Earl of Southampton, whom scholars accept as Shakespeare's friend and benefactor despite a lack of documentation. During this same period, Shakespeare was writing his sonnets, which are more likely signs of the time's fashion rather than actual love poems detailing any particular relationship. He returned to play writing when theaters reopened in 1594, and published no more poetry. His sonnets were published without his consent in 1609, shortly before his retirement.

Amid all of his success, Shakespeare suffered the loss of his only son, Hamnet, who died in 1596 at the age of 11. But Shakespeare's career continued unabated, and in London in 1599, he became one of the partners in the new Globe Theater [Boyce, 589], built by the Chamberlain's Men. This group was a remarkable assemblage of "excellent actors who were also business partners and close personal friends . . . [including] Richard Burbage . . . [who] all worked together as equals . . . " [Chute, 131].

When Queen Elizabeth died in 1603 and was succeeded by her cousin King James of Scotland, the Chamberlain's Men was renamed the King's Men, and Shakespeare's productivity and popularity continued uninterrupted. He invested in London real estate and, one year away from retirement, purchased a second theater, the Blackfriars Gatehouse, in partnership with his fellow actors. His final play was *Henry VIII*, two years before his death in 1616.

Incredibly, most of Shakespeare's plays had never been published in anything except pamphlet form, and were simply extant as acting scripts stored at the Globe. Only the efforts of two of Shakespeare's company, John Heminges and Henry Condell, preserved his 36 plays (minus *Pericles*, the thirty-seventh) [Barnet, xvii] in the First Folio. Heminges and Condell published the plays, they said, "only to keep the memory of so worthy a friend and fellow alive as was our Shakespeare" [Chute, 133]. Theater scripts were not regarded as literary works of art, but only the basis for the performance. Plays were a popular form of entertainment for all layers of society in Shakespeare's time, which perhaps explains why Hamlet feels compelled to instruct the traveling Players on the fine points of acting, urging them not "to split the ears of the groundlings," nor "speak no more than is set down for them."

Present copies of Shakespeare's plays have, in some cases, been reconstructed in part from scripts written down by various members of an acting company who performed particular roles. Shakespeare's plays, like those of many of the actors who also were playwrights, belonged to the acting company. The performance, rather than the script, was what concerned the author, for that was how his play would become popular—and how the company, in which many actors were shareholders, would make money.

William Shakespeare died on April 23, 1616, and was buried two days later in the chancel of Holy Trinity Church where he had been baptized exactly 52 years earlier.

Historical Background

There is general agreement about the sources for Shakespeare's *Hamlet*. About 400 years prior to the Elizabethan version, Saxo Grammaticus told a similar tale in his *Historia Danica* (c. 1200). About 15 years before Shakespeare's version, Francois de Belleforest adopted the essential story in his *Histoires Tragiques* (1576), a popular collection of tales in French. Both of these sources survive as literary manuscripts.

However, most critics believe that another source, the so-called *Ur-Hamlet*, is the version most directly responsible for many of the elements which Shakespeare incorporated into his play. Although no written version of this precursor exists, and historians can only work backwards from documents which mention the *Ur-Hamlet*, it is believed that this play, probably written by Thomas Kyd, was acted in 1594 by the Lord Admiral's Men and the Lord Chamberlain's Men, the latter of which company Shakespeare belonged to.

While the earlier versions included similar elements to Shakespeare's Hamlet (the hero's love interest, fratricide, feigned madness, adultery, spies, and revenge), only Kyd's version includes the Ghost who seeks revenge. In fact, Kyd's famous play, *The Spanish Tragedy*, includes other elements which Shakespeare seems to have incorporated into *Hamlet*: "a procrastinating protagonist who berates himself for talking instead of acting and who dies as he achieves his revenge; . . . a play within a play, a heroine whose love is opposed by her family, and another woman who becomes insane and commits suicide" [Boyce, 238–239]. However, if Kyd did not author the *Ur-Hamlet*, both he and Shakespeare may have borrowed from this same "Ur-" source for their respective works.

There are other sources, both real and fictional, which may have contributed to Shakespeare's version, including women who killed themselves for love (1577), and a barber who confessed (in 1538) to murdering an Italian duke by putting lotion in his ears. In the second instance, Gonzago was the name of the plotter, rather than of the victim, as in Shakespeare's "mousetrap."

Hamlet was most likely performed in 1600, almost exactly at the midpoint of his writing career, which had begun as early as 1588 with *The Comedy of Errors*, and ended as late as 1613 with *Henry VIII*. Shakespeare's allusions to his *Julius Caesar* (1599) in *Hamlet*, and references by other playwrights in late 1600 (John Marston's *Antonio's Revenge*) place the performance of *Hamlet* fairly precisely. However, the Player's dialogue with Hamlet about the child actors is a direct reference to actual competition between rival theater companies in the spring of 1601; perhaps this scene was added later, or perhaps Shakespeare used Marston's play as a source rather than the other way around [Boyce, 239–240].

The first performance is held to be that of the Chamberlain's Men, in 1600 or 1601. Shakespeare's longtime theatrical associate, Richard Burbage, was the first Hamlet; tradition has it that Shakespeare himself played the Ghost in the original production.

The first publication of *Hamlet* was in 1603 in a quarto edition known as *Q1*, and generally regarded as reconstructed from actors' memories who had performed in the play. In 1604, *Q2* was published, most likely from Shakespeare's own manuscript; however, passages were edited out of *Q2* because they were politically sensitive or simply dated. Between 1611 and 1637, *Q3*, *Q4*, and *Q5* were published as reprints of each foregoing edition.

The first folio edition of Shakespeare's plays (1623), known as *F*, contained *Hamlet* and seems to have used *Q2* as its source. Significant differences include the restoration of the passages cut from *Q2*, the modernization of words thought by the editors to be out of date, and inclusion of some lines which seem to be actors' ad libs rather than Shakespeare's text. Modern editors usually use *Q2* because it is closest to Shakespeare's text, but also because it has the restored passages and other minor improvements [Boyce, 240].

Hamlet is regarded as one of Shakespeare's finest tragedies, along with *Othello*, *King Lear*, and *Macbeth*, all of which followed in the next five or six years (along with four other major plays). Over the years it has been the most often performed of Shakespeare's plays, and has been filmed at least 25 times and televised five times [Boyce, 241]. Most performances use an abridged text, since the original could take four to five hours. Beginning in 1775 with Sarah Siddons, women began playing the title role, including, in 1971, Judith Anderson at age 73 [Boyce, 240].

Master List of Characters

Barnardo, Francisco, Mercellus—*sentinels; officers in King of Denmark's army*

Horatio—*Prince Hamlet's friend and confidante; fellow-student at Wittenberg*

Ghost—*of dead King of Denmark, Prince Hamlet's father; brother of new King, husband of Gertrude*

Claudius—*brother of dead King of Denmark; now King, and new husband of Queen Gertrude, Prince Hamlet's mother*

Gertrude—*Prince Hamlet's mother, widow of former King, now wife to Claudius, new King.*

Polonius—*King Claudius' advisor; father to Laertes and Ophelia*

Reynaldo—*Polonius' servant, sent to Paris to spy on Laertes*

Laertes—*son to Polonius, brother to Ophelia; friend to Hamlet*

Prince Hamlet—*son of the late King, and of Queen Gertrude; nephew-stepson to King Claudius*

Voltemand and Cornelius—*messengers to King of Norway from Claudius*

Ophelia—*daughter to Polonius, sister to Laertes, beloved of Hamlet*

Rosencrantz and Guildenstern—*fellow students of Hamlet at Wittenberg; sent with Hamlet to England by Claudius to murder Hamlet*

Osric—*messenger who summons Hamlet to duel with Laertes*

The Players—*actors (adults) who formerly performed in the city, and who are now traveling because of the rising popularity of companies of child actors*

Grave diggers—*two clowns (rustics) who are disinterring an old grave in order to make way for a new burial, Ophelia*

Priest—*Doctor of Divinity (church official) presiding at Ophelia's funeral*

Fortinbras—*Prince of Norway whose father was killed by Hamlet's father; assumes throne of Denmark at play's end*

Ambassador—*from England, reporting to Claudius*

Summary of the Play

Prince Hamlet of Denmark is urged by his father's Ghost to avenge his murder at the hands of the dead king's brother, now King Claudius; to make matters worse, Claudius has married the widow, Hamlet's mother, Queen Gertrude. Denmark is under threat of invasion from young Fortinbras, who seeks to regain lands lost to Hamlet's father by Fortinbras' father. Claudius sends word to the King of Norway (Fortinbras' uncle) to curb Fortinbras' aggression. In the meantime, Hamlet feigns madness with his family and friends, including his beloved, Ophelia, sister to Laertes and daughter to Polonius. Both Polonius and Laertes warn Ophelia against Hamlet's amorous advances. Polonius believes Hamlet's "madness" to be love sickness. Laertes is given permission to return to his studies in Paris.

Claudius directs Gertrude to try to learn the cause of Hamlet's odd behavior; they suspect it is the old king's death and their own recent marriage. Meantime, Claudius and Polonius eavesdrop on Ophelia and Hamlet, who spurns her and appears mad. The King reveals to Polonius his plan to send Hamlet to England with Rosencrantz and Guildenstern.

Hamlet seizes the opportunity presented by a traveling troupe of players to expose the King's guilt with a "play within a play." Soon after, Hamlet delays killing Claudius because the King is at prayer, and Hamlet does not wish to send him to heaven instead of hell. When Gertrude meets with Hamlet as Claudius has directed, Polonius hides behind the arras in Gertrude's room to eavesdrop on the conversation. Hamlet, suspecting the interloper is Claudius, stabs and kills Polonius.

When Polonius' body is discovered, Claudius summons Hamlet and tells him he must sail to England for his own safety; Rosencrantz and Guildenstern accompany Hamlet, carrying letters to the English, threatening war unless they kill Hamlet. Hamlet eventually escapes, returns to Denmark, and is met by Horatio.

Ophelia has gone insane after Hamlet's departure and her father's death. Laertes returns and vows to avenge Polonius' death. Claudius contrives a fencing match between Hamlet and Laertes, during which Hamlet is to be injured with a poisoned sword tip and poisoned with a drink, thus assuring his death. When news arrives that Ophelia has drowned herself, Laertes is grief stricken. Hamlet and Horatio happen upon the burial site and funeral cortege; Hamlet tries to fight Laertes but is restrained.

Hamlet tells Horatio that he rewrote the papers carried by Rosencrantz and Guildenstern, and that the letters now call for their own deaths. Osric invites Hamlet to the duel with Laertes; Claudius has supposedly bet on Hamlet to win. Gertrude mistakenly drinks from the cup poisoned by Claudius for Hamlet, and dies; Laertes wounds Hamlet with the poisoned sword, and then Hamlet wounds Laertes when they accidentally exchange swords. When Laertes reveals the conspiracy, Hamlet wounds the King and forces the poisoned drink upon him. Laertes and Hamlet reconcile, and Laertes dies; Hamlet prevents Horatio from drinking the poison so that he can live to tell the truth. Hamlet names as his successor young Fortinbras, who arrives and orders Hamlet buried with all dignity.

Estimated Reading Time

Given a text with abundant and helpful footnotes, an average student should expect to spend at least an hour per act on the first read through; subsequent readings should take less time, as the language becomes more familiar. Certainly a five hour stretch is not advised; probably a few scenes at a time, or perhaps an entire act, would be a comfortable portion for an average reader. Since there are five acts with a total of 20 scenes, the student could expect to spend at least five hours in perhaps six to eight sessions.

Act I

Act I, Scene I (pages 1–6)

New Characters:

Barnardo, Francisco, and Marcellus: *sentinels*

Horatio: *Hamlet's close friend and confidante*

Ghost: *of Hamlet's father, the former King of Denmark*

Summary

Just after the striking of twelve, Francisco is relieved of his watch by Barnardo and Marcellus, who have entreated Horatio to stand with them this night to witness the reappearance of the dead king's apparition. The Ghost appears and disappears twice but does not speak to the four, who decide to tell Hamlet in the morning. They note that a Ghost often portends grave events, and believe the King's Ghost is related to the impending war with young Fortinbras of Norway, who seeks to regain the lands his late father lost in battle with the dead King of Denmark, Hamlet's father.

Analysis

The Ghost of Hamlet's father appears for the second time to Barnardo, Marcellus, and Francisco, who are this time accompanied by Horatio, Hamlet's trusted friend and fellow student—perhaps his scholarly title lending credence to the apparition. When they persuade Hamlet to witness the sight, the third time is the charm; the heretofore silent Ghost speaks—but only to Hamlet, whom it has drawn apart, not to the others.

Thus begins one of the play's recurrent motifs: indirection and deception. The various witnesses have different interpretations of the events. The officers assume "that this portentous figure / Comes armed through our watch so like the King / That was and is the question of these wars" with young Fortinbras. Hamlet, however, learns that his father's Ghost wants him, "If thou didst ever thy dear father love—…[to] / Revenge his foul and most unnatural murder."

Act I, Scene II (pages 7–14)

New Characters:

Claudius, King of Denmark: *Prince Hamlet's uncle and stepfather*

Gertrude, the Queen: *Hamlet's mother*

Polonius: *the King's advisor*

Laertes: *son to Polonius*

Prince Hamlet: *son of the late King and Queen Gertrude*

Voltemand and Cornelius: *messengers to King of Norway*

Summary

King Claudius announces that, despite his grief over his brother's recent death, he has taken Gertrude to wife. He also informs the court of young Fortinbras' aggression, and assigns Voltemand and Cornelius to deliver a dispatch to the King of Norway (Fortinbras' uncle) urging that he restrain his nephew. Laertes asks the King's permission to return to France, which he left to attend the coronation. The King grants the request, being assured that Polonius also assents. The King and Queen then urge Hamlet to cease his mourning, and to abandon his plan to return to his studies in Wittenberg; Hamlet agrees.

Everyone departs, leaving Hamlet alone to lament his mother's hasty remarriage to a man less worthy than her first husband, Hamlet's father. Horatio, Marcellus, and Barnardo enter and tell Hamlet of the Ghostly apparition; he vows to watch with them that night and speak to it.

Analysis

King Claudius and his new bride worry over Hamlet's odd behavior; Gertrude correctly guesses that he is upset over his father's death and their "o'erhasty" marriage, a surmise which suggests that the queen feels some twinge of guilt over her recent actions. The royal couple press Hamlet to stay in Denmark at court, and not return to his studies in Wittenberg.

Claudius' motives are, of course, ulterior: to spy on Hamlet in order to learn the true cause of his madness, again suggesting that Claudius has some cause to fear retribution from his nephew/son. Perhaps incredibly, Hamlet agrees to their request to remain, even before he vows to avenge his father's death. Why he would stay in an environment he finds uncomfortable and distasteful is a puzzle, unless we assume filial obedience as his overriding motive. More likely, however, this turn of events is another instance of the inexorable workings of fate, bringing together all the "actors" in some cosmic drama, as later scenes will bear witness.

Act I, Scene III (pages 15–19)

New Character:

Ophelia: *daughter to Polonius; sister to Laertes*

Summary

Laertes meets Ophelia to say his farewells before returning to France. He warns her to beware of Hamlet's trifling with her, and urges her to remain chaste. Ophelia agrees to heed his advice, while urging him to obey it as well. Polonius enters and counsels Laertes, who departs. Polonius also warns Ophelia of Hamlet's amorous intentions, and finally instructs her to avoid him altogether. She assents.

Analysis

This scene presents tender, if somewhat humorous, dialogue between sister and brother, father and son, and father and daughter. Buried in the conversation, however, is the undercurrent of honesty vs. deceit, love vs. betrayal, reality vs. appearances—all themes which recur throughout the play. Both Laertes and Polonius show great solicitude for Ophelia's welfare, and she exhibits demure obedience to their advice, born of wider experience of the world than her own.

Act I, Scene IV (pages 19–22)

Summary

Hamlet, Horatio, and Marcellus wait just after midnight to see the Ghost. It appears, and beckons to Hamlet, who follows it. Horatio and Marcellus go after them.

Analysis

First Horatio, and now Hamlet, have been brought to verify the appearance and identity of the Ghost. Hamlet appears resolute as he follows the beckoning apparition, though the others advise against it. His courage and resolution in this short scene are in sharp contrast to his apparent attitude in later scenes as he struggles with the issue of revenge.

Act I, Scene V (pages 23–28)

Summary

The Ghost of his father tells Hamlet that he was murdered by poison poured into his ear by Claudius. The Ghost urges Hamlet to avenge him, but to leave judgment of his mother to heaven. As the Ghost leaves, Hamlet swears to remember his father. Hamlet refuses to divulge the conversation to Horatio and Marcellus when they appear, and the Ghost reappears, repeatedly crying for them to "Swear" not to tell what they have seen. Hamlet also instructs them not to reveal the truth if he appears to be acting "odd" later on, and they finally so swear. Hamlet laments his appointed role as avenger of so great a wrong.

Analysis

That the Ghost swears the soldiers to secrecy puts an extra burden on Hamlet. His mission to avenge his father may require him to do things which will appear odd or, as it turns out, insane, to onlookers. But the men who could explain his behavior are sworn not to reveal its cause. Further, Hamlet is sworn to leave his mother's judgment to heaven. Thus, Hamlet is admonished against releasing anger at his mother, yet obliged to pursue revenge against Claudius in ways that may seem illogical and unwarranted. His resulting mental anguish seems inevitable.

Study Questions

1. Why does the Ghost of Hamlet's father appear but not speak to the officers on sentinel duty?

2. What do Ghostly apparitions usually portend, according to these witnesses?

3. What is the content of the dispatches Claudius has sent with Voltemand and Cornelius to the King of Norway?

4. In his soliloquy, what are Hamlet's reasons for objecting to his mother's remarriage?

5. What advice does Laertes give to Ophelia as he says farewell to her prior to his departure for Paris?

6. What advice does she give Laertes in return?

7. What is the thrust of the advice Polonius gives Laertes as his son prepares to leave?

8. What does Polonius instruct Ophelia to do regarding Hamlet?

9. What does the apparition tell Hamlet?

10. What two-part oath does Hamlet extract from his companions following the encounter with the Ghost?

Answers

1. Horatio believes he has offended it by demanding that it speak, and Marcellus believes his threat of violence was ill-conceived on a spirit, which is "as the air, invulnerable." Horatio and Marcellus also recall the folk wisdom that the cock's crowing sends spirits to their "confine." Additionally, in the season just before Christmas, the cock crows all night, and "no spirit dare stir abroad...So hallowed and so gracious is that time."

2. Horatio remembers similar Ghostly appearances were reported shortly before Julius Caesar's fall, and believes the Ghost to be a "precurse of feared events" to Denmark. "Or if thou hast uphoarded in thy life / Extorted treasure in the womb of earth, / For which, they say, you spirits oft walk in death," suggests that Horatio acknowledges that the apparition may not have any particular relevance to the current political situation.

3. Claudius wants Norway, uncle to Fortinbras, "to suppress [Fortinbras'] further gait herein, in that the levies, / The lists, and full proportions are all made / Out of [Norway's] subject...."

4. Hamlet feels the marriage was too soon after his father's death; he can't see how his mother could have so soon forgotten her love and devotion to her husband. Furthermore, he feels his uncle is "no more like my father / Than I to Hercules." He believes his mother has violated English canon law, which held that marriage with a deceased brother's widow was incestuous [Hubler, 45].

5. Laertes tells his sister to regard Hamlet's attentions as trifling, toying, temporary diversions of youthful fancy. Also, he reminds her that Hamlet, as heir apparent, is subject to the will of Denmark; he may say he loves her now, but if the state requires it, he would have to marry otherwise. If in the meantime she loses her virtue to him, it will be for nothing. "Be wary then; best safety lies in fear...."

6. She urges him to take his own advice, and not be like a pastor who instructs his flock how to achieve heaven but who "Himself the primrose path of dalliance treads..."

7. It is wide ranging, but urges moderation, integrity, thrift, and "above all, to thine own self be true...Thou canst not then be false to any man."

8. Polonius says Ophelia is a "baby" to have believed Hamlet's "tenders of affection," which are "mere implorators [solicitors] ... [meant] to beguile." He commands her to "Be something scanter of your maiden presence.... [nor] slander any moment leisure / As to give words or talk with the Lord Hamlet."

9. The Ghost reveals the circumstances of his murder and charges Hamlet to avenge his death, but to "Leave [thy mother] to heaven" and to her own conscience.

10. Hamlet makes them swear never to tell what they have seen that night, and never, "How strange or odd some'er I bear myself (As I perchance hereafter shall think meet To put an antic disposition on), / That you, at such times seeing me, never shall...note / That you know aught of me...." In other words, he makes them swear not to reveal that his madness is merely put on.

Suggested Essay Topics

1. Contrast the attitudes towards the death of the old King as expressed by Claudius and Hamlet.

2. Compare the advice given to Ophelia by Laertes and that given by Polonius.

Act II

Act II, Scene I (pages 29–33)

New Character:

Reynaldo: *Polonius' servant*

Summary

Polonius sends Reynaldo to Paris to spy on Laertes, instruct-ing him to use delicate indirection to learn of Laertes' behavior from "other Danskers [who] are in Paris." After Reynaldo leaves, Ophelia enters, distressed, and tells her father that Hamlet has just approached her with "his doublet all unbraced, / No hat upon his head, his stockings fouled, / Ungartered, and down-gyved to his ankle." She says he "held [her] hard" by the wrist, studied her silently for several moments, sighed "piteous and profound," and then left her. Polonius believes Hamlet is lovesick because Ophelia has shunned him, and modifies his earlier suspicion that Hamlet meant only to trifle with Ophelia. Polonius and Ophelia depart to inform Claudius of this news.

Analysis

Scene I shows Ophelia to be a naive young girl who trusts her father's judgment and is obedient to his will. Polonius' tedious in-structions to Reynaldo echo his earlier advice to both Ophelia and Laertes, and foreshadow his behavior in Scene II. When Reynaldo asks why he is being sent to spy on Laertes, Polonius' justification is so circuitous even he loses track of what he was saying: "What was I about to say? By the mass, I was about to say something! Where did I leave?"

Act II, Scene II (pages 33–50)

New Characters:

Rosencrantz and Guildenstern: *longtime friends and former schoolmates of Hamlet*

Voltemand and Cornelius: *sent by Claudius as ambassadors to King of Norway*

The Players: *traveling actors hired to perform at the castle*

Summary

King Claudius and Queen Gertrude receive Rosencrantz and Guildenstern, childhood friends of Hamlet, who agree to visit him and seek the cause of Hamlet's "transformation." Polonius enters to announce the arrival of Voltemand and Cornelius from Norway, and to say that he believes he has found the "very cause of Hamlet's lunacy." However, he delays revealing the information until the ambassadors have been heard, although Claudius does "long to hear" of it. Voltemand and Cornelius report that the ailing King of Norway, having discovered that young Fortinbras intended to attack Denmark rather than Poland, has redirected Fortinbras' aggression against Poland and now asks safe passage through Denmark for Norway's armies. Claudius agrees to consider the request.

Finally, when Polonius begins his story, he is so discursive that Gertrude pleads, "More matter, with less art." He then begins to read them the letter he took from Ophelia. Impatient, Gertrude interrupts with "Came this from Hamlet to her?" But Polonius controls the pacing with, "Good madam, stay awhile. I will be faithful." When Claudius asks how Ophelia has received Hamlet's love, Polonius takes the opportunity to cite his own virtues as a watchful father, who prudently checked and advised his daughter. To Claudius' query, "Do you think 'tis [love sickness]?", Polonius confidently answers, "Hath there been such a time…That I have positively said, ''Tis so,' When it proved otherwise?…I will find /

Where truth is hid, though it were hid indeed Within the center." He even stakes his career as advisor on it if he is wrong: "Let me be no assistant for a state / But keep a farm and carters."

Having given a very dramatic account of Hamlet's love sickness, Polonius arranges that Claudius and he will eavesdrop on a contrived conversation between Ophelia and Hamlet to prove his suspicions. The royal pair exit quickly as Hamlet enters, reading a book.

Polonius and Hamlet have a brief conversation full of non sequiturs and punned insults, which confirms Polonius' opinion regarding the prince's madness. The old man leaves when Rosencrantz and Guildenstern enter. Hamlet suggests that in coming to Denmark they have come to a prison, and finally gets them to admit that they have been "sent for." He even guesses their assignment: to discover why he has "of late ... lost all [his] mirth ... " so that "Man delights [him not], nor woman neither." The pair tell Hamlet that they have persuaded a traveling company of tragedians to perform for the court. As the players enter, Hamlet confides to his friends that he is only feigning his madness, despite what his "uncle-father and aunt-mother" believe: "I am but mad north-northwest: when the wind is southerly I know a hawk from a handsaw."

Polonius enters to announce the arrival of the players, whom Hamlet warmly welcomes. After he has one of the players recite a section from Aeneas' tale to Dido detailing Pyrrhus' murder of Priam, Hamlet secretly asks the actor if the players could present *The Murder of Gonzago* the next night, including a short insert "of some dozen or sixteen lines" which Hamlet will provide. The actor agrees.

When all have left, Hamlet contrasts his own seeming lack of passion in avenging his father's death to the actor's impassioned performance for imaginary characters the player does not even know. Hamlet resolves to test whether his father's Ghost is a devil sent to damn him by staging a play which presents a murder similar to his father's. Claudius' reaction to the scenes will reveal whether or not he is guilty.

Analysis

The lengthy second scene slows the lively pace which was characteristic of Act I, which had five fairly brief scenes, followed by the brisk first scene of Act II. This slowdown allows Shakespeare to establish beyond doubt that Claudius is guilty of the King's murder, and to begin to explore Hamlet's tortured mental state, caught between love, grief, and vengeance. The loyalty of Hamlet's friends, Rosencrantz and Guildenstern, is turned against him by his parents; yet, when Hamlet presses them, they give up the charade and admit their mission. They have even arranged the theatrical interlude because they know Hamlet was "wont to take...delight in" their performances. Their obvious affection for Hamlet creates a problem for the reader when, in Act V, Scene II, Hamlet reveals that he has forged the letters which will result in their deaths. He will justify his actions, saying essentially that his friends got caught in the middle, between him and Claudius; that their "own insinuation" (meddling) has brought about their defeat.

The conversation about the established adult acting companies versus the increasingly popular child actors was not only topical for Shakespeare's audiences, but is also dramatically integral to the intergenerational motif of the play: the youth rising up to supplant their elders. Furthermore, the motif of illusion vs. reality which pervades the play is reinforced here with the several mentions of young boys playing the parts of women, also a timely reference. In addition, the suggestion that women are weaker or otherwise inferior is a recurrent motif: "frailty, thy name is woman—"; "O most pernicious woman!"; "...it is such a kind of gaingiving as would perhaps trouble a woman."

Voltemand and Cornelius bring news of Norway's curbing of Fortinbras' revenge aimed at Denmark, reinforcing another of the recurring motifs in this play: parents vs. children, and its flipside, children (sons, in this case) seeking to avenge their fathers' deaths. Fortinbras' father had lost his lands to Hamlet's father in the recent war, and young Fortinbras plans to regain them by attack. His uncle, now King of Norway, intercedes and sets him against Poland. Hamlet and Fortinbras are both dispossessed heirs to the throne; in Act V, Scene II, Hamlet will give his "dying voice" to Fortinbras' accession to the throne of Denmark, and Fortinbras will eulogize

Hamlet as "a soldier" and "most royal." Thus, out of the chaos, we are assured order will be restored, and power passed into capable and worthy hands.

Hamlet's inane conversations with both Polonius and with Rosencrantz and Guildenstern are riddled with vulgar innuendoes, which foreshadows his scenes with Ophelia and Gertrude. The discrepancy between outer appearances and inner qualities is thus manifested once again; Hamlet even states this theme directly in his conversation with Gertrude, when he tells her that her trespass "will but skin and film the ulcerous place / Whiles rank corruption, mining all within, / Infects unseen." That Hamlet's madness is merely pretense in this scene is suggested by his remark as Polonius departs ("These tedious old fools!") and by his disclosure that his parents are "deceived" about his madness.

When Polonius announces the arrival of the players, Hamlet remarks to Guildenstern and Rosencrantz "That great baby you see there is not yet out of his swaddling clouts;" to which Rosencrantz counters, "... they say an old man is twice a child." Clearly Hamlet does not respect Polonius, despite his politically important posi-tion. Throughout the play, Polonius appears as arrogant, foolish, self-important, and unaware that others find him amusing, if not tedious. In proclaiming his own skills as an advisor and father, he has apparently forgotten that he was earlier forced to admit his change of mind, abandoning his assumption that Hamlet meant to trifle with Ophelia: "I am sorry that with better heed and judg-ment I had not quoted him.... By heaven, it is as proper to our age / To cast beyond ourselves in our opinions / As it is common for the younger sort / To lack discretion."

Hamlet continues to bait the king's advisor with allusions to Jeptha, a Biblical king who sacrificed his daughter, implying a parallel to Polonius' "loosing" Ophelia to Hamlet to verify his mad-ness. That Hamlet understands the motives of those around him to be duplicitous is becoming increasingly clear, and that Hamlet's madness is merely pretense, increasingly certain. If he is not mad, we may perhaps assume that his actions—and his inaction—are conscious and calculated.

Many critics have argued the issue of Hamlet's inaction—that is, his delay in avenging his father's death. The prince frequently laments his procrastination, contrasting himself to Fortinbras (who must be restrained from his planned vengeance for his father's death) and to Pyrrhus (who takes sporting delight in "mincing" Priam—merely the father of Paris, the actual murderer of Pyrrhus' father, Achilles). What is it that holds Hamlet back? Probably no one theory will encompass the body of evidence to be found in the entire work, but several major interpretations have been supported over the centuries by critics.

It is possible that Hamlet really had no opportunity to kill Claudius, with the exception of the time he found him at prayer. Not wishing to kill Claudius when the king's soul and conscience were clear, Hamlet delays. Ironically, Claudius reveals that although he has prayed, "Words without thoughts never to heaven go"; Hamlet could have damned Claudius, had the prince only carried out his impulse.

Hamlet himself suggests another of the popular theories: his "native hue of resolution / Is sicklied o'er with the pale cast of thought." In other words, he is not able to carry out the deeds which he has resolved to do, mired in his own "analysis paralysis." In Act II, Scene II, Hamlet suggests that Denmark is a prison, and compares it to his mind: "...there is nothing either good or bad but thinking makes it so." This passage also supports the theory of action arrested by intellect.

The question of Hamlet's inaction is further complicated by the attitudes evidenced by several characters. The Player King tells the Player Queen that when her passions (i.e., her grief and loyalty) have cooled, her actions will be governed by other concerns and she will remarry. Hamlet chides Gertrude about her hasty remarriage, saying because of her age, she cannot have been ruled by her passions (i.e., lust), and must have been ruled by "judgment" (i.e., reason). The Ghost restrains Hamlet's rebuke of Gertrude, urging him to channel his anger at Claudius; in other words, to control his passions as he seeks vengeance. And when Hamlet pays tribute to his loyal friend Horatio, he remarks that Horatio is not "passion's slave," and whose "blood [passion] and judgment" is so well blended that he is not vulnerable to Fortune's "buffets and rewards." For Hamlet, the dilemma is the proper yoking of passion, which would spur him to immediate vengeance, with reason, which is God-given, and which would temper Hamlet's actions with prudent judgment. Hamlet seems unable to strike the balance, and is forever trying to weigh the emotional against the rational. The result is his inaction.

Hamlet has been dubbed the Melancholy Dane because of the many expressions of his sense of loss and grief at his father's death. Elizabethans were familiar with the concept of *melancholia*, believed to be caused by an excess of the humour (bodily fluid), black bile. The sufferer's moods would swing from deep depression and self-deprecation, to highly emotional outbursts. Certainly Hamlet's puzzling behavior, which appears insane to others, could be a manifestation of this supposed disorder.

More modern critics note the Oedipal pattern in Hamlet's relationship with his mother. To the extent that Claudius has done that which Hamlet himself desired to do (kill his father and marry his mother), the personae of Claudius and Hamlet merge. To avenge the murder-marriage is to commit suicide; indeed, Hamlet contemplates that very thing in his famous "To be or not to be" speech. Perhaps Hamlet hesitates to kill Claudius because of religious strictures against suicide, rather than against murder.

Other critics believe that Hamlet fears the apparition of his father is not an "honest Ghost," and that his uncertainty restrains his vengeance. If the Ghost is "a devil . . . [in] a pleasing shape" who "abuses [Hamlet] to damn [him]," then to take matters into his own hands would go against Hamlet's religious beliefs. Beliefs of the time held that royalty ruled by divine right, so the murder of Hamlet's father would therefore call for divine justice. If Hamlet is merely God's tool, the murder is divinely ordained and sanctioned. However, if the Ghost is not heaven sent, if Hamlet seeks revenge for his own purposes, the murder is not holy and Hamlet's revenge against Claudius would be a sin. As he says, "I'll have grounds / More relative than this;" he will let Claudius' reaction to the "mousetrap" guide him, rather than depending solely on the Ghost's injunction.

A very generous critical reading credits Hamlet with an awareness of his own selfish motives; murdering Claudius would clear the path to his own kingship. Hamlet suggests this thinking as he explains his cause to Horatio, noting that Claudius "Popped in between th' election and my hopes. . . . " He delays throughout the play, these critics say, because he wants to make sure that he is truly avenging his father, not merely seeking his own advancement.

Each of these major theories can be supported with textual evidence, some more strongly than others. Hamlet's obvious intellect and education might persuade the reader that he is less a victim of circumstances and more a creature tormented by his ability to see the situation from many angles, fraught with consequences political and spiritual, public and personal.

Hamlet's plan to have the players enact *The Murder of Gonzago* with the addition of "some dozen or sixteen lines which [he] would set down" is another example of the use of indirection to learn the truth. Of course, the players themselves embody this principle of "acting" or pretending, engaging in "seeming" rather than in "being." Hamlet alludes to this ironic duplicity when he notes the actor's ability to "drown the stage with [real] tears And cleave the general ear with horrid speech" over an imagined murder, while he himself, "the son of a dear father murdered," can only manage to curse his own inaction "like John-a-dreams."

If we think of the players as actors—those who do, who perform, who carry out resolve—Hamlet's invidious comparison of the player's performance to his own, further reinforces his disgust at his own delay and inaction in carrying out the Ghost's charge to avenge his father's death. For instance, at Ophelia's graveside, Hamlet insists that he loved her more than "forty thousand brothers," but later tells Horatio that "the bravery of [Laertes'] grief" made him forget himself, "For by the image of my cause I see / The portraiture of his."

Study Questions

1. What task does Polonius assign Reynaldo in Paris?

2. Why is Ophelia so upset when she speaks with her father?

3. In what respect does Polonius change his mind about Hamlet and the prince's relationship to Ophelia?

4. What task does Claudius assign to Rosencrantz and Guildenstern?

5. What news do Voltemand and Cornelius bring back from Norway?

6. What do Claudius and Gertrude conclude after hearing Polonius read the letter from Hamlet to Ophelia?

7. What does Polonius mean in an aside, as he speaks with Hamlet, "Though this be madness, yet there is method in't"?

8. What does Hamlet make Rosencrantz and Guildenstern confess?

9. Why have Hamlet's two friends arranged for the theatrical troupe to perform at the palace?

10. What is the significance of the speech which Hamlet requests from the actor, taken from the story of the Trojan War?

Answers

1. Polonius gives Reynaldo "money and…notes" to give to Laertes; and instructs him "to make [indirect] inquire / Of his behavior." Polonius wants to know what Laertes is doing in Paris, and intends "By indirections [to] find directions out."

2. "Affrighted," she reports that Hamlet came to her private room, his clothing undone and dirty, and his expression looking "As if he had been loosed out of hell / To speak of horrors—…." He held her by the wrist and stared and sighed, and then went out the door, his eyes still on her "with his head over his shoulder turned."

3. Polonius diagnoses Hamlet's behavior as "the very ecstasy of love, / Whose violent property fordoes itself / And leads the will to desperate undertakings.…" He apologizes that he had earlier misjudged Hamlet, fearing "he did but trifle / And meant to wrack thee.…" He excuses his error by noting that it is as common for elders to be overcalculating as it is for youth to "lack discretion."

4. Claudius entreats the pair to remain at court for "Some little time" and "draw [Hamlet] on to pleasures" in an attempt to learn what has caused his "transformation." Claudius says his motive is a desire to help Hamlet recover: "…Whether

aught to us unknown afflicts him thus, That opened lies within our remedy."

5. Voltemand reports that the old King, uncle to young Fortinbras, had at first thought his nephew's preparations were for war against Poland. But, discovering they were "against your Highness," he stopped Fortinbras and rebuked him. Fortinbras promised never to wage war against Denmark, whereupon Norway rewarded his nephew with an annual allowance of "threescore thousand crowns" and sent him "against the Polack." Norway now asks for Fortinbras' "quiet pass Through [Claudius'] dominions for this enterprise...."

6. Polonius states that since he instructed Ophelia to shun Hamlet, the prince's behavior has deteriorated from "a sadness, then into a fast, Thence to a watch, thence into a weakness, / Thence to a lightness, ... Into the madness wherein now he raves...." The Queen agrees: "It may be, very like." This is a shift from Gertrude's earlier assumption that "it is no other but the main, His father's death and our o'erhasty marriage."

7. Polonius realizes that although Hamlet's conversation with him seems irrational, it makes a certain kind of sense. The particular line reference has to do with the book which Hamlet purports to be reading, which is critical of old men and their infirmities and flaws. Hamlet points out that if Polonius "could go backward" like a crab, the old man would be the same age as Hamlet; therefore, Hamlet says, although he "most powerfully and potently" believes old men to be as the writer describes, he sees that he and Polonius are basically the same—that Polonius is just an older version of himself, or that he is just a younger version of Polonius. This reinforces what Polonius says: "'A is far gone, far gone. / And truly in my youth I suffered much extremity for love, very near this."

8. Hamlet urges them to reveal "whether you were sent for or no." After brief consultation, Guildenstern admits, "My lord, we were sent for." Hamlet then proceeds to explain

why they have been sent for, detailing his own symptoms
of depression and malaise.

9. Rosencrantz identifies the traveling company as "Even those
    you were wont to take such delight in, the tragedians of
    the city." The performance has been arranged for Hamlet's
    pleasure, apparently.

10. Hamlet praises the artistic quality of the play from which
    the scene is taken, noting that the play did not appeal to
    the masses. He asks particularly for " ... Aeneas' tale to
    Dido, ... especially when he speaks of Priam's slaughter."
    The allusion is to a play based on Virgil's *Aeneid*, the passage
    which tells how Pyrrhus, son of Achilles, extracts revenge
    upon the father (Priam) of Achilles' murderer (Paris). The
    intensity of the violence is horrifyingly graphic. This scene
    of revenge acts as a foil to Hamlet's own delay in avenging
    his father's murder.

Suggested Essay Topics

1. Draw a character profile of Polonius from his interactions in
    this act with Reynaldo (Scene I), Ophelia (Scene I), Gertrude
    and Claudius (Scene II), Hamlet (Scene II), and the Players
    (Scene II).

2. Compare/contrast the relationship which the King and
    Queen have with Rosencrantz and Guildenstern, to the re-
    lationship which Hamlet has with Rosencrantz and Guilden-
    stern, as defined in Scene II.

Act III

Act III, Scene I (pages 51–56)

Summary

In the presence of Polonius and Ophelia, King Claudius and Queen Gertrude question Rosencrantz and Guildenstern about their recent conversation with Hamlet; the pair report that although Hamlet confessed to being "distracted," he would not reveal the cause, evading questioning with "a crafty madness."

Hamlet's friends also report that Hamlet was pleased to learn of the visit of the traveling players, and that he has arranged a performance for that night, to which he has invited the King and Queen. The two men leave, and Claudius instructs Gertrude to leave also so as not to encounter Hamlet, for whom he has secretly sent, "That he, as 'twere by accident, may here / Affront Ophelia." Gertrude obeys, confiding to Ophelia her hope that Hamlet's love for Ophelia is the cause of his "wildness," and that her "virtues / Will bring him to his wonted way again...." Claudius and Polonius instruct Ophelia to pretend to be reading a book of devotions so that Hamlet will find her solitude plausible. They depart just as Hamlet enters.

The Prince speaks to himself regarding the relative merits of life and death, "To be, or not to be." He weighs the troubles of living against the unknown nature of death and the afterlife. He compares death to sleep, sleep which is full of dreams which "must give us pause." When he notices Ophelia at her devotions, he asks her to pray for his sins. She tells Hamlet that she wishes to return some "remembrances" of his, but he denies that he gave her anything.

She protests that he did give them, along with "words of sweet breath," which he also denies.

Hamlet then urges Ophelia to "Get thee to a nunnery," that all men are "arrant knaves," not to be believed. He then decries marriage in general, and says that "Those that are married already—all but one—shall live. The rest shall keep as they are." He exits, leaving Ophelia to lament his apparent insanity.

Polonius and Claudius emerge from their concealment. Claudius notes that Hamlet's words did not sound either like love or like madness, and announces that he will send Hamlet to England to collect overdue tribute. He hopes the change of scenery and the ocean voyage will get rid of the "something in his soul" which is bothering Hamlet. Polonius agrees to the King's plan, but urges one more attempt to discover the cause of Hamlet's "grief." after the play, Gertrude is to sound him out, and Polonius plans to eavesdrop. If this plan does not work, Polonius tells Claudius to send Hamlet to England, "or confine him where / Your wisdom best shall think." Claudius agrees, and says the "Madness in great ones must not unwatched go." They exit.

Analysis

This act begins with a stage crowded with those characters most closely associated with Hamlet, with the exception of Horatio and Laertes: Claudius, Gertrude, Polonius, Ophelia, Rosencrantz and Guildenstern. As each one is assigned his task in the discovery of Hamlet's malaise, that character departs. When at last the stage is empty but for Ophelia, Hamlet enters.

Every character is involved in duplicity at this point: Rosencrantz and Guildenstern are not being completely honest with Claudius, as they were not completely honest with Hamlet; Gertrude disappears so Hamlet does not suspect that he is being set up; Claudius and Polonius conceal themselves so they can eavesdrop; and Ophelia pretends to be in maidenly devotions in order to engage Hamlet in conversation.

Hamlet, meantime, has conceived of the Mousetrap in order to trick Claudius into exposing his guilt. The Prince then proceeds to lie to Ophelia, denying that he gave her "remembrances" or that he spoke lovingly to her; she is convinced he is insane. At Polonius' suggestion, Claudius continues his deceit with the plot to ship Hamlet to England with Rosencrantz and Guildenstern, supposedly to collect overdue tribute.

Even after overhearing Hamlet's interlude with Ophelia, Polonius urges one final attempt to discern the cause of Hamlet's mental state: the scene in Gertrude's closet which, ironically, causes his own death. Polonius is not only overbearing and pompous, self-important and self-righteous; he is bent on orchestrating every step of every dance. It is his job to give counsel to the King; but he insists on giving advice to everyone: his son, his daughter, Hamlet, the Queen, Reynaldo; he even admits to having played Julius Caesar in the university, "and was accounted a good actor"—presumably he would advise the Players, if called upon.

Hamlet's remarks to Ophelia about marriage are worth noting. He says that all men are "arrant knaves," which is certainly the case in Claudius' court, as we have seen. But he also decrees that everyone who is presently married shall live, but one; and the rest "shall keep as they are," presumably unwed. Remember that Claudius and Polonius are eavesdropping; Claudius hears this "all but one." Surely he senses Hamlet's intent, for a few moments later, Claudius announces his plan to send Hamlet to England. As Claudius later reveals to the pair, this move is more for his own protection than for Hamlet's well-being.

Once again Polonius lays his heavy hand on the details, urging the King to either send Hamlet to England "or confine him where / Your wisdom best shall think." Polonius seems unconcerned whether Hamlet is a threat to his daughter's virtue or to Claudius' reign; Polonius sees an opportunity to exercise control and influence, and takes it—again and again.

Act III, Scene II (pages 57–68)

Summary

Hamlet enters, giving instructions to several of the Players on the appropriate and most effective delivery of the "speech" which he has prepared for insertion into the evening's performance. As the Players exit, Polonius enters with Rosencrantz and Guildenstern, who inform Hamlet that Claudius and Gertrude have agreed to attend the play. Hamlet urges the trio to go help hasten the Players, then summons Horatio. Hamlet expresses his love and respect for Horatio, then asks Horatio to scrutinize Claud-ius during the one scene which "comes near the circumstance...of my father's death." Horatio agrees.

Gertrude invites her son to sit beside her, but he refuses in favor of a seat with Ophelia, whom he engages in risque banter. The dumb show (pantomime) begins, enacting the murder of a King by one who pours poison in his ears; the widowed Queen at first appears disconsolate, but eventually accepts the love of the man who murdered her husband. Hamlet assures Ophelia that the actors will explain the meaning of the dumb show.

Following a brief Prologue, the Player King and Player Queen speak of love, death, and remarriage. The Player King and Queen discuss the likelihood of her remarriage after his impending death; she vows she will not, but he argues that when we make decisions in the heat of the moment, we fail to carry them out when the emotion fades: "What to ourselves in passion we propose, The passion ending, doth the purpose lose." The Player King also notes that fortune does not follow our desires; so "'tis not strange That even our loves should with our fortunes change."

The Player Queen declares that she would rather starve, be imprisoned, be without trust, hope, and joy, and have "lasting strife, If, once a widow, ever I be wife!", especially if the second husband had murdered the first. She says such a marriage would be for reasons of "thrift, but none of love," but the Player King argues that "So think thou wilt no second husband wed, / But die thy thoughts when thy first lord is dead."

When Claudius asks if this play is meant to give offense, Hamlet assures him "they do but jest, poison in jest; no offense i' th' world...we that have free souls, it touches us not." But as the play progresses and the actor portraying Lucianus (the king's nephew) pours poison in the sleeping king's ear, Hamlet comments, "You shall see anon how the murderer gets the love of Gonzago's wife." Claudius bolts from his seat, Polonius ends the performance and calls for lights, and everyone leaves except Hamlet and Horatio. They believe they have exposed Claudius, proving the Ghost's validity.

Rosencrantz and Guilden-stern enter, and urge Hamlet to obey his mother's request that he come to her before he goes to bed. The pair attempt to persuade Hamlet to reveal the "cause of distemper," but he evades their questions and accuses them of trying to play upon him like the recorders the Players have just entered with: "Call me what instrument you will, though you can fret me, you cannot play upon me." Polonius enters and repeats Gertrude's request, which Hamlet says he will heed. When all others have departed, Hamlet resolves to hold his anger in check, rebuking his mother but not harming her.

Analysis

The second scene also opens with a full stage as Hamlet addresses the Players about dramatic delivery; as the Players depart to make ready, Polonius enters with Rosencrantz and Guildenstern. Hamlet quickly moves that trio offstage to "hasten" the Players. Then Horatio enters, and he and Hamlet speak as dear and close friends. Horatio, who had earlier been enlisted by Claudius and Gertrude to sound out Hamlet, now sides with his long time friend and school mate—more duplicity.

This technique repeated from Scene I, of many becoming few, stresses the increasing intensity of the machinations of the opposing forces: Claudius' in the first, and Hamlet's in the second. They mirror each other, but are inverse images: evil for good. But now the stage again fills to overflowing with the Players, the members of the royal court, the lords and ladies attendant thereon, and Guards with torches. Hamlet refuses his mother's invitation to sit beside her, going instead to Ophelia and engaging in bawdy innuendoes.

Shakespeare has crowded the stage and placed Ophelia and Hamlet front and center with seemingly inappropriate and confusing dialogue. When Hamlet comments that his mother has remarried not "*two hours*" after his father's death, Ophelia remarks that it is "*twice two months*." But when he restates the matter, he makes it only "*two months*." Likewise, the Players were originally scheduled to perform "tomorrow night;" but moments later, they are hurrying to make ready for the performance "presently" that very night. This seeming confusion over chronology is really Shakespeare's way of telescoping time, lending urgency to the matter at hand—Hamlet's revenge on the murderer of his father.

As the dumb show concludes, Ophelia asks Hamlet what it means; he answers "mischief," referring to his plan to expose Claudius. The Prologue does not satisfy Ophelia's curiosity, and she notes that "'Tis brief, my lord." Hamlet answers, "As woman's love," returning to his theme of his mother's infidelity to her dead husband's memory. Hamlet, pursuing his "mischief," asks his mother, "how like you this play?" Gertrude answers, "The lady doth protest too much, methinks," suggesting that from her perspective, remarriage would not be an impossibility for a widow. Hamlet replies, "O, but she'll keep her word," implying that the Player Queen, at least, is faithful to her vows—an invidious comparison that surely is not lost on Gertrude.

Guildenstern and Rosencrantz, sent to summon Hamlet to his mother's room, reveal that Claudius is "in . . . marvelous [distemper]," not from drink, as Hamlet suggests, but from "choler" (anger). Hamlet's suggestion that they should rather be summoning a doctor to purge the king and make him well is a foreshadowing of the imagery he will use when he finds Claudius at prayer: "This physic but prolongs thy sickly days." When Rosencrantz and Guildenstern report back to Claudius a few moments later, they speak of the necessity of protecting the king's health against any harm that may be intended by Hamlet. Their remarks make clear that the life of "majesty," upon whom so many other lives depend, is of far greater importance than an ordinary man's life.

This conversation helps to justify Hamlet's later action of sealing their death warrant; they have tried to "play upon [him]", taking Claudius' part against him. Hamlet explains to Horatio that he does not feel guilty for their fates; the pair simply got caught between the thrustings "of mighty opposites." His pragmatic view ironically echoes their own attitude, that the life of the king is more important than any other's; since Hamlet had hoped to become king (by election) at his father's death, he is the "majesty" this time around, not Claudius.

Act III, Scene III (pages 68–71)

Summary

Claudius enters with Rosencrantz and Guildenstern; Claudius is convinced that Hamlet, in his "madness," means to harm him in some way. He proposes to send Hamlet to England, along with Rosencrantz and Guildenstern, for safety's sake. They agree, noting that the fortunes of "Majesty" always affect the lives of many others besides itself. This voyage is to commence at once.

Polonius enters to inform Claudius that Hamlet is on his way to Gertrude's private room; Polonius announces that he will hide "behind the arras," in order to "o'erhear" their conversation. Polonius says he expects Gertrude to severely scold Hamlet, but notes that, as Hamlet's mother, she will be biased toward anything he may say to her. Thus, "'Tis meet that some more audience than a mother" should hear Hamlet's remarks. Polonius promises Claudius that he will return with a full report before the king goes to bed.

Claudius then soliloquizes about his guilt over the murder of his own brother, which he compares to the murder of Abel by Cain. Claudius laments the fact that he is unable to pray and thus receive mercy, which would cleanse him of this sin. He suspects that his offense would not be forgiven, since he retains all the benefits deriving from the murder: "My crown, mine own ambition, and my queen." Perhaps on earth one can "[Buy] out the law. But 'tis not so above." At last, the king manages to kneel in a final attempt at repentance.

Hamlet enters, sees Claudius apparently at prayer, and reasons that to murder Claudius now would "send [this same villain] To heaven" rather than to hell. He vows to wait and kill Claudius—as Claudius had killed Hamlet's father—"full of bread, / With all his crimes broad blown, as flush as May," while the king is "about some act / That has no relish of salvation in't—...." Hamlet notes that Claudius' prayer has only postponed his eventual death.

Ironically, as Hamlet exits, Claudius rises, and discloses that he has still been unable to pray and receive the spiritual peace he seeks: "My words fly up, my thoughts remain below. Words without thoughts never to heaven go."

Analysis

Prominently foregrounded in this scene is Claudius' guilt and the fear which attends it. He imagines—rightly so—that Hamlet means to harm him. And he feels the need to repent before heaven in order to escape eternal damnation. Thus Claudius fears both earthly and divine retribution, and in this scene both are postponed. Hamlet waits until a more suitable time to kill the king, and Claudius finds himself unable to pray with satisfactory results.

The importance given to Claudius' life, as "majesty," is ironic; for Claudius has murdered his brother—also "majesty"—and Hamlet, likely to be elected "majesty," is on Claudius' trail. The question of whose life is most important in the grand scheme of things is therefore moot, since the former King, Claudius, and Hamlet all have a claim to that coveted seat.

Act III, Scene IV (pages 72–78)

Summary

Polonius urges the Queen to be sharply critical of Hamlet's actions, and to tell him that she has had to intercede on his behalf, standing "between / Much heat and him." Polonius then hides behind the wall tapestry as Hamlet enters. Hamlet speaks very directly to his mother, telling her that she has offended his father, and proposes revealing her "innermost part" to her. Gertrude cries out in fear that Hamlet means to murder her, prompting Polonius to call out from behind the curtain. Hamlet, supposing the eavesdropper to be Claudius, thrusts his sword through the curtain, killing Polonius, over whom Hamlet says, "Thou wretched, rash, intruding fool, farewell! I took thee for thy better." Hamlet scolds the old man for being "too busy," thus endangering his own life. Hamlet then insists that his mother sit down and hear him out; she continues to berate him for his rudeness and claims not to know what act or deed of hers he speaks of "that roars so loud and thunders...."

Hamlet produces two images, one of his father, the other of his uncle. He contrasts them for Gertrude, expressing his disbelief that she could have so soon forgotten her first husband, on whom "every god did seem to set his seal / To give the world assurance of a man." He reasons that she cannot have been driven by passion, "for at [her] age / The heyday in the blood is tame,...And waits upon the judgment, and what judgment / Would step from this to this?" He finally declares that virtue melts and all shame disappears when passion rules over reason.

Gertrude begs Hamlet to stop, for she now sees her guilt; but he continues to recount her sin of incest with "A murderer and a villain, / A slave that is not twentieth part the tithe / Of your precedent lord, a vice of kings, / A cutpurse of the empire and the rule,..." Then the Ghost enters, visible only to Hamlet, who asks if his father has come to scold him for not yet carrying out his revenge. The Ghost directs Hamlet to comfort his mother, who is very disturbed by Hamlet's words and by his speaking to "th' incorporal air."

Gertrude is certain that Hamlet is mad, but he urges her to realize that it is not his madness but "[her] trespass" that speaks. He begs her to "Confess [herself] to heaven, / Repent what's past, avoid what is to come...." He asks her to refrain from sleeping with Claudius that night, "And that shall lend a kind of easiness / To the next abstinence...." Further, Hamlet tells her not to reveal to Claudius that he is not really mad, and she agrees. He reminds her that he is scheduled to sail to England with Rosencrantz and Guildenstern, whom he does not trust anymore than "adders fanged." But he tells his mother that he plans to outsmart them.

Hamlet then drags Polonius out of the room, calling his body "the guts." He notes that while alive, Polonius was "a foolish, prating knave," but that he is now "most still, most secret, and most grave...."

Analysis

Hamlet continues with imagery of health and disease in his conversation with Gertrude. He insists that he is healthy, not mad. He pleads with her to recognize that her "trespass" "will but skin and film the ulcerous place Whiles rank corruption, [under]mining all within, Infects unseen." This image also echoes the play's persistent motif of appearance vs. reality, seeming vs. being, deception vs. honesty.

Study Questions

1. What do Rosencrantz and Guildenstern report to Claudius regarding their conversation with Hamlet?

2. What do the pair fail to reveal to Claudius?

3. What favor does Hamlet ask of Horatio?

4. What is the plot of the Dumb Show the Players present?

5. What is the significance of the play's title, "The Mousetrap"?

6. What does Hamlet mean, as he prepares to visit his mother, when he says, "O heart, lose not thy nature"?

7. What rationale do Rosencrantz and Guildenstern give for accepting Claudius' commission to take Hamlet to England forthwith?

8. What is ironic about Hamlet's failure to kill Claudius while the King is kneeling in prayer?

9. What is Hamlet's reaction when he realizes he has killed Polonius rather than Claudius, whom he had presumed to be the one hiding behind the curtain?

10. What is the apparent purpose of the Ghost's appearance in the Queen's bedroom while Hamlet speaks with his mother?

Answers

1. They say Hamlet was polite but not very inclined to talk about what was bothering him. They report that Hamlet seemed pleased that the Players had been engaged for a performance.

2. They do not disclose that Hamlet made them admit that they had been sent by Claudius, nor that Hamlet revealed that Claudius and Gertrude are deceived about his seeming madness.

3. He wants Horatio to carefully observe Claudius during the play, to watch his reactions, to help to determine whether the Ghost which named Claudius murderer was heaven sent or from "Vulcan's stithy."

4. A queen and king make affectionate show; he lies down and falls asleep, she leaves. Another man enters and pours poison in the king's ear, and leaves. The queen returns, is distraught, but is eventually comforted and ultimately seduced by the poisoner himself.

5. The play "is the image of a murder done in Vienna," and is, in fact, entitled, "The Murder of Gonzago," which Hamlet specifically requests the Players to perform with the addition of the lines which he inserts. That he tells Claudius it is called, "The Mousetrap," suggests his ulterior motive, especially since he continues, "Your Majesty, and we that have free souls, it touches us not." The clear implication is that Claudius does not have a clear conscience, and will, therefore, be "touched" by the play—as he obviously is.

6. He does not wish to forget that she is his mother, whom he does not mean to harm; on the other hand, he wants to rebuke her for her actions. He remarks on this inconsistency: "My tongue and soul in this be hypocrites."

7. They say that because so many lives depend upon a king's life, he must be protected. A king's death acts like a "gulf" (whirlpool) and sucks whoever is nearby down with it. Whatever affects the king, affects the populace as a whole: "Never alone Did the King sigh, but with a general groan."

8. Claudius kneels but is unable to pray. Had Hamlet killed him then, as he first intended, Claudius' soul would have been damned.

9. Hamlet is disrespectful to Polonius, and not in the least remorseful about his error. In essence he says Polonius was a busy body who deserved what he got. He "[lugs] the guts" into the next room without respect or ceremony. He does say that he repents Polonius' death, but says he was only acting as heaven's "scourge and minister," and knows that he "will answer well / The death [he] gave him."

10. The Ghost says, "This visitation Is but to whet thy almost blunted purpose." Hamlet has been carried away in scolding his mother for her marriage to his father's brother, a man

much inferior to her husband. Gertrude has repeatedly cried for Hamlet to "speak no more," but he has been unrelenting. The Ghost now reminds Hamlet of his task of revenge, and bids him give comfort now to his mother, on whom "amazement...sits." Because she can neither hear nor see the Ghost, she concludes that Hamlet is truly insane; the Ghost asks Hamlet to "step between her and her fighting soul!"

Suggested Essay Topics

1. Discuss the thematic connection between Hamlet's scene with Ophelia where he speaks of *honesty*, his speech to the Players on *acting*, and his speech to Horatio on *flattery*.

2. Compare Claudius' thoughts on his own guilt as he tries to pray to Gertrude's recognition of her guilt when confronted by Hamlet.

3. Discuss the grouping of characters from scene to scene in Act III, beginning with a crowded stage in Scene I and ending with Gertrude alone in Scene IV. What does Shakespeare achieve with the rapidly changing cast on stage as the action in this act unfolds?

SECTION FIVE

Act IV

Act IV, Scene I (pages 79–80)

Summary

Claudius, Gertrude, Rosencrantz and Guildenstern enter; Claudius remarks on Gertrude's sighing, which he asks her to explain. She dismisses the two young men, and then relates to Claudius the recent events in her closet; she says Hamlet, "in his lawless fit," has killed Polonius. Claudius notes that he himself would have been killed, had he been the one hiding behind the curtain. He regrets that, out of love for Hamlet, he neglected to do what was best; that is, he "Should have kept short, restrained, and out of haunt / This mad young man," but instead "let [him] feed / Even on the pith of life" like a disease kept unacknowledged.

Gertrude reveals that Hamlet, who has gone to remove Polonius' body, "weeps for what is done," which she says proves his madness is genuine. Claudius reminds Gertrude that he is shipping Hamlet out at daybreak, which must be made acceptable to the court. He summons Rosencrantz and Guildenstern and bids them hasten to find Hamlet, "speak fair," and bring Polonius' body into the chapel. They leave, and Claudius advises Gertrude that they must tell their "wisest friends" what has happened to Polonius, and that they are sending Hamlet away. The King hopes, by coupling these two events, to throw all ill will toward Hamlet, avoiding any taint of slander himself. They exit, with Claudius "full of discord and dismay."

Analysis

Act IV begins with four relatively short scenes, presenting the King and Queen; then Hamlet with Rosencrantz and Guildenstern; then Rosencrantz, Guildenstern, Hamlet, and the King; then Hamlet, Rosencrantz and Guildenstern with the Captain of Fortinbras' army. Shakespeare is speeding up the action in these brief scenes, quickening the pace as Claudius moves swiftly to protect himself from Hamlet, even as Hamlet baits him by playing hide-and-seek with Polonius' body. When Hamlet and the others encounter Fortinbras, Hamlet desires to get on with his appointed task of avenging his father. Shakespeare thus continues the sense of building urgency in this act.

Act IV, Scene II (page 81)

Summary

Hamlet enters, having "Safely stowed" the body of Polonius. Rosencrantz and Guildenstern enter, seeking the corpse, but Hamlet won't tell where it is hidden, saying only he has "Compounded it with dust, whereto 'tis kin." Then Hamlet calls Rosencrantz a "sponge...that soaks up the King's countenance, his rewards, his authorities." But that when the King needs what they "have gleaned, it is but squeezing you and, sponge, you shall be dry again." When they ask again of the body's whereabouts, Hamlet again refuses to say, but agrees to go with them to the King, whom Hamlet says is "a thing...Of nothing." Hamlet dashes offstage as if they are pursuing him in a game of hide-and-seek: "Hide fox, and all after."

Analysis

True to her word to Hamlet, Gertrude is at great pains to assure Claudius that Hamlet's madness is genuine. She even stretches the truth by saying Hamlet "weeps for what is done"—Hamlet repents, but says "heaven hath pleased it so,...That I must be their scourge and minister." Claudius is at equally great pains to convince Gertrude that he is acting in Hamlet's best interest in shipping him off to England. Claudius plans to manipulate the public disclosure of information to his best advantage. Similarly he will attempt to manipulate England's allegiance in arranging Hamlet's murder (Scene III), and to manipulate Laertes' anger by excusing his own inaction out of love for Gertrude and public sentiment for Hamlet (Scene VII).

Act IV, Scene III (pages 82–84)

Summary

Claudius enters with several men, whom he has told of Hamlet's murder of Polonius, and that he has "sent to seek him and to find the body." He tells them it is dangerous to allow Hamlet to remain at large, but that because of Hamlet's popularity among the "distracted multitude," his punishment must not seem too heavy; the public only judge what they can see, and weigh only the punishment, "But never the offense." Claudius says Hamlet's sudden leaving must seem to be part of a careful plan in order to keep things "all smooth and even."

Rosencrantz and Guildenstern enter and report that Hamlet will not reveal the location of Polonius' body, and that Hamlet is waiting outside. Claudius summons him, but Hamlet will only tell the King, first, that Polonius is "At supper," where he is being eaten by worms; and second, that Polonius is in heaven, or perhaps in hell. But finally he reveals that Polonius can be found "as you go up the stairs into the lobby" where he "will stay till you come."

The King tells Hamlet that, for his own safety, he is being sent to England at once. Hamlet then bids the King farewell, calling him "dear Mother," since "father and mother is man and wife, man and wife is one flesh, and so, my mother." Hamlet exits, and Claudius orders the others to follow him and get him on board ship without delay, since everything that depends on this aspect of his plan is all "sealed and done."

Left alone, Claudius expresses his hope that England will obey the letters that Rosencrantz and Guildenstern carry which call for Hamlet's "present death." He notes that England is still in awe of Denmark because of past defeats, and he hopes that this fear will insure their cooperation. He says that Hamlet is like a fever in his blood which must be cured, or Claudius can not have happiness, no matter what else may befall him.

Analysis

Although Claudius is trying desperately to orchestrate the events to Hamlet's disadvantage, Hamlet remains in control despite his seeming madness. All Claudius and the others can do is react to Hamlet's inane remarks and puzzling actions. Claudius is struggling both at home and abroad—in England—to rally public opinion and political power into his own camp.

Act IV, Scene IV (pages 84–86)

New Characters:

Young Fortinbras: *nephew to the aged king of Norway*

Captain: *officer in Fortinbras' army*

Summary

Fortinbras sends his Captain to Claudius, seeking escort for his army's safe march through Denmark. He says if the King wishes, he will meet personally with him. Fortinbras exits with his army. Hamlet and Rosencrantz enter and learn from the Captain that the army, headed for "some part of Poland," means to attack a "little patch of ground that hath in it no profit but the name," not worth "five ducats." Hamlet doubts the Poles will defend such a worthless area, but the Captain tells him "it is already garrisoned." Hamlet comments that "Two thousand souls and twenty thousand ducats" is a high price to pay for something so worthless, and notes that this sort of behavior results from "much wealth and peace," destroying from within like an abscess.

Left alone, having sent his companions on ahead, Hamlet notes that events are conspiring to spur his revenge. He says a man who only eats and sleeps is but a beast; surely God gave us *reason*. He wonders why he does not act on his thoughts, since he has "cause, and will, and strength, and means To do't." Hamlet says that even young Fortinbras, "a delicate and tender prince," takes great risk for little gain, "When honor's at the stake." Hamlet notes his own great motivations ("a father killed, a mother stained") do not move him to action, while Fortinbras' army is about to engage in a battle in which more men will be killed than the worthless land they fight for can hold in burial. He vows to have only "bloody" thoughts from now on.

Analysis

In Scene IV, Hamlet is moved to note his own delay and in-action in seeking revenge, as contrasted with the willingness of Fortinbras' and the Polish armies to fight and die for nothing more than honor. Their battlefield is nearly worthless, but he has great motive: "a father killed, a mother stained."

Act IV, Scene V (pages 86–93)

Summary

Horatio, Gertrude, and a Gentleman enter. At Horatio's urging, the Queen finally agrees to speak with Ophelia, who the Gentle-man reports to be in a distracted, pitiable state, babbling nonsense about her dead father. Ophelia enters singing of a dead man, and a maid deflowered. Claudius enters, and seeing her state, orders Horatio to "Follow her close; give her good watch." Alone with Gertrude, Claudius relays all the bad news from court: Polonius' murder and hasty burial, Hamlet's "remove" to England, public unrest at Polonius' death, Ophelia's madness, and Laertes' secret return from France and his suspicions that Claudius is somehow responsible for Polonius' death. Claudius says all these events are killing him, like shrapnel from a cannon, "in many places."

A Messenger enters with news that Laertes has overtaken the King's officers, and is now being hailed as the "rabble's" choice for king. Gertrude laments that the "false Danish dogs" are on the wrong trail. Laertes bursts in upon the King and Queen, insists that those accompanying him wait outside, and angrily demands to know the whereabouts of his father. Gertrude attempts to restrain Laertes from accusing or harming Claudius, but Claudius declares that, as King, he is divinely protected from treason, and humors Laertes' wrath. Claudius assures Laertes that he had nothing to do with Polonius' death, and that he grieves deeply for his demise.

Ophelia enters, singing of her father's death and distribut-ing imaginary flowers, apparently quite mad and unresponsive to Laertes' comments to her. Laertes is touched by her state and moved to revenge. When Ophelia leaves, Claudius implores Laertes to hear him out in the presence of whichever of Laertes' friends the young man would select, "to judge 'twixt you and me." Claudius vows to relinquish everything, including his life, to Laertes if he is found responsible for Polonius' death. They depart to discuss Polonius' "means of death" and his improper, unceremonious burial.

Analysis

Scene V presents yet another contrast to Hamlet's delay; Laertes bursts in upon the King and Queen and demands to know about his father's death. Gertrude, in her accustomed role as peacemaker and restrainer-of-violent-men, tries to soothe Laertes' wrath over his father's death and his sister's madness; and Claudius, in his usual self-serving half-truth declaration, swears to forfeit everything if he is directly or indirectly responsible for Polonius' death. That the "rabble" have proclaimed Laertes their choice for King makes it doubly important that Claudius keep Laertes from harboring any animosity toward him. To have murdered the king, only to be impeached by the fickle populace, would make Claudius' sins weigh heavily indeed.

Ophelia presents perhaps the furthest end of a spectrum on which sit also Hamlet, Laertes, and young Fortinbras. In the face of her father's death, she goes crazy. Perhaps Shakespeare makes a gender distinction here, as Laertes (Scene VII) forbids his tears on hearing of Ophelia's death, but says when he is alone, "The woman will be out." Woman, as weaker or gentler, cannot bear the heavy burden as well as man; Ophelia loses that capacity (reason) which Hamlet notes several times in the play is what separates us from beasts. Hamlet's madness is, while convincing to many who witness it, completely feigned. He is admittedly tormented by his conflicting desires and fears, but he is not crazy. He needs constant prompting in his vengeance, and continually berates himself for his weak resolve.

On the other hand, Laertes acts promptly at the news of his slain father, seeking the villain even in the King's chambers; but he is easily turned aside and manipulated by Claudius, who turns him into a tool against Hamlet—Laertes' friend and Claudius' enemy.

And Fortinbras, after a false start to attack Denmark, whose former king slew his father, is redirected against Poland in a battle over land not worth dying for, purely for principle and honor. Not one of these children really achieves a satisfactory resolution in the search for vengeance.

Act IV, Scene VI (pages 93–94)

New Characters:

Sailors: *seafaring men who bring news from Hamlet*

Summary

Horatio and a few others are accosted by Sailors with a letter from Hamlet to Horatio, detailing his capture at sea by pirates, who, he says, treated him well. The letter instructs Horatio to deliver the "letters I have sent" to the King, and then come at once to him, guided by "these good fellows." Hamlet adds that Rosencrantz and Guildenstern still sail toward England, and says "Of them I have much to tell thee."

Horatio promises to reward the Sailors for delivering the messages.

Analysis

The unlikely capture-rescue of Hamlet by the pirates is, of course, dramatically necessary to effect Hamlet's return to Denmark, but it strains plausibility even more than the turn of events in the final sword fight (Act V, Scene II). The interface between possibility and plausibility is stretched taut. This unlikely series of events, however, does reinforce Hamlet's frequent remarks about the role of fate in men's lives.

Hamlet's use of the phrase, "compelled valor," echoes his rebuke to his mother in Act III, Scene IV: "Assume a virtue, if you have it not." As Hamlet feigned bravery in boarding the pirate ship, Gertrude was urged to feign virtue in absenting herself from Claudius' bed. The motif of illusion versus reality, seeming versus being, play acting versus genuine, is again foregrounded.

Act IV, Scene VII (pages 94–100)

Summary

Laertes asks Claudius why, as King, he did not act against Hamlet, whom Claudius accuses of "[pursuing] my life." Claudius cites two reasons. First, his own love for Gertrude, whose love for Hamlet is so great that he cannot counteract it. Second, the love the general public has for Hamlet makes it impossible for them to see Hamlet's faults; they would tend to turn Claudius' accusations back upon himself. Claudius tries to assure Laertes that they are united in their love of Polonius and in their desire for revenge against Hamlet for his plottings.

A Messenger enters with letters from Hamlet, for Claudius and for Gertrude. Hamlet tells the King that he has landed "naked [without any means or provisions] on your kingdom," and asks to see Claudius the next day, at which time he will "recount the occasion of my sudden and more strange return." The postscript adds, "alone." Claudius enlists Laertes in a plot to kill Hamlet which is so foolproof that even Gertrude will "call it accident." The King flatters Laertes' skills as a fencer, and says Hamlet is so envious of Laertes' reputation that he will accept a challenge to duel Laertes, especially if he believes that Claudius has wagered on the outcome. Laertes vows to poison his sword tip to insure Hamlet's death if he be "but scratched withal." As double insurance, Claudius promises to poison a drink, which Hamlet will call for "When in your motion you are hot and dry" toward the end of the bout.

Gertrude enters with news that Ophelia has drowned in the stream as she tried to hang flower garlands on the willow branches. Laertes withholds his tears as too womanly, and leaves in an agitated state. Claudius tells Gertrude that he had to work hard to calm Laertes, and now fears that "this will give it start again," so they follow Laertes.

Analysis

Claudius is again—or still—struggling to maintain control of the situation, but now it is Laertes who threatens to upset the King's plans. Claudius puts on a show of bravado in the face of Laertes' demands, and insinuates Laertes into his plot against Hamlet. Now Claudius openly intends to deceive Gertrude as he murders her son; previously he had deceived her covertly in the murder of her husband. That Claudius is ruthless as well as resolute becomes apparent when, at news of Ophelia's death, the King says they need to watch Laertes to keep him calm. His true motive, of course, is to protect his own position against Laertes, whom the people have proclaimed as their choice for king.

Study Questions

1. What is Claudius' response when Gertrude tells him that Hamlet has murdered Polonius?

2. What does Claudius direct Rosencrantz and Guildenstern to do?

3. Why does Hamlet hide Polonius' corpse and then dash away when Rosencrantz and Guildenstern question him about it?

4. Why does Hamlet call Claudius "dear Mother"?

5. Why does Fortinbras send word to the Danish king (Claudius)?

6. How does Hamlet contrast himself (all men) to beasts?

7. How does Claudius propose to satisfy Laertes' suspicions?

8. What reasons does Claudius give Laertes for not taking action against Hamlet, who, Claudius says, "Pursued [his] life"?

9. Why does Claudius plan to poison the drink, in addition to poisoning the rapier tip which Laertes will wield?

10. How does Ophelia drown?

Answers

1. He says he himself would have been killed, had he been behind the curtain; that Hamlet's continued freedom threatens him, the Queen herself, and everyone. He fears he will be blamed for not keeping Hamlet restrained, but that love often prevents us from seeing the best course. Claudius tells

her that Hamlet must be sent away (by ship), and that they must make people understand and approve their actions.

2. He directs them to get help and find Hamlet, "speak fair" to him, and bring Polonius' body into the chapel; "I pray you haste in this."

3. Hamlet is continuing in his "madness," behaving in ways which seem irrational to his family and friends. His seeming insanity will also act as a kind of shield for him; how can Claudius order his punishment for Polonius' murder if he was mad? Madmen are not responsible for their actions. Finally, Hamlet is taking delight in tormenting those who are obviously humoring him, while at the same time plotting against him.

4. Because "father and mother" equal "man and wife," and "man and wife" is one flesh, Claudius and Gertrude are one and the same. Hence, Claudius can be called "mother" and, presumably, Gertrude could be called "father."

5. He wants Claudius to provide safe escort for his (Norwegian) army as they march across Denmark, as Claudius had earlier promised.

6. He says a man who spends his time merely sleeping and feeding is only a beast; God gave man reason, to see both ahead and behind, not to become moldy from disuse. He can't decide if "thinking too precisely on th' event" is "bestial oblivion [forgetfulness]" or "some craven scruple." He believes such thoughts are one part wisdom and three parts cowardice; since he has "cause, and will, and strength, and means to do't," he doesn't see why he hesitates.

7. He tells Laertes to gather his choice of his wisest friends to hear Claudius' version of the events; he promises to give up everything, including his life, if he be shown to have caused—directly or indirectly—Polonius' death. Otherwise, he asks Laertes to join with him to give Laertes' soul "content." Laertes specifies that he wants the answers to a number of

issues surrounding his father's death, and Claudius agrees, adding, "where th' offense is, let the great ax fall."

8. Claudius says that Hamlet's mother "Lives almost by [Hamlet's] looks, and...She is so conjunctive to [Claudius'] life and soul," that the King cannot do anything which would hurt her. Secondly, he says that public sentiment is so solidly behind Hamlet that his sins would be transformed "to graces," and Claudius' charges would fall on himself rather than "where [he] had aimed them."

9. If the sword point does not work properly, and their true purpose be discovered, the tainted cup, offered to Hamlet when he is "hot and dry," will insure his death. Claudius, having bet on Hamlet to win, will be above suspicion in his death.

10. She is trying to hang flower garlands on the branches of a weeping willow which overhangs a brook; the branch breaks, spilling her into the water. Her clothes puff out and buoy her up for awhile, but eventually become saturated and pull her "to muddy death."

Suggested Essay Topics

1. Trace the way Claudius tries to manipulate the following characters in this act in order to achieve his own ends: Gertrude, Rosencrantz and Guildenstern, Hamlet, and Laertes.

2. Discuss the implications of Ophelia's song lyrics. What do they suggest about her relationship with Hamlet, and her grief for her father, especially as causes for her apparent madness?

SECTION SIX

Act V

Act V, Scene I (pages 101–109)

New Characters:

Two Clowns: *rustics who are digging Ophelia's grave*

Doctor of Divinity: *priest who presides at Ophelia's burial*

Summary

The two rustics discuss the particulars of Ophelia's death and burial. The coroner has ruled that she shall have a Christian burial, which would mean that her death was accidental. But the men believe that Ophelia must have drowned herself, and suicide would prevent her from having a Christian burial. They decide that because she is a gentlewoman, she—like her class—is more privileged to drown or hang herself than are her fellow Christians. They make grisly jokes as they continue digging; then one sends the other to fetch him a tankard of beer. The one left digging sings about love and the brevity of life, as Hamlet and Horatio come upon him.

Horatio reasons that the man's exposure to these matters has hardened him to death. The Clown roughly throws out a number of skulls, to which Horatio and Hamlet assign identities such as politician, courtier, a Lord or Lady, lawyer, and buyer of land. When they inquire whose grave the Clown digs, he replies it is for a woman. The Clown reveals that he has been a gravedigger since Hamlet's father overcame old Fortinbras, the very day that young Hamlet was born. He answers Hamlet's further inquiries by noting that young Hamlet was sent to England because he was mad, and will return when he is better: "or, if 'a do not, 'tis no great matter there...There the men are as mad as he." The Clown identifies one skull as Yorick's, the King's jester, whom Hamlet says "hath borne me on his back a thousand times." They continue discussing mortality and the return of man, no matter how noble, to the dust from whence he came.

From some distance, Horatio and Hamlet see the King, Queen, Laertes, a Doctor of Divinity, and various Lords entering with a coffin. The priest tells Laertes that because of her "doubtful" death, Ophelia cannot have complete rites, such as "To sing a requiem," and must lie "in ground unsanctified...Till the last trumpet." Gertrude strews flowers over the body, saying she had hoped "[Ophelia's] bride bed to have decked," not her grave. Laertes leaps into the grave to hold his sister one last time before they cover her, and then asks that they bury him too.

At that, Hamlet comes forward to protest Laertes' actions: "I loved Ophelia. Forty thousand brothers / Could not with all their quantity of love / Make up my sum." The two men struggle, and are finally parted by Horatio and the attendants. Gertrude and Claudius assure Laertes that Hamlet's words and actions are "mere madness" which will soon pass. Horatio ushers Hamlet out, and Claudius urges Laertes to patiently await the working out of the plot of which they spoke earlier.

Analysis

Just as Act I began and ended with the appearance of the Ghost, Act V begins with the graveyard scene and ends with the multiple murders and imminent funeral rites. Throughout this final act are numerous references to death, as well as discussions of man's mortality. The rustics believe Ophelia, as a member of the gentility, to have special privilege in regard to her burial; but Hamlet and Horatio note that the unearthed skulls might belong to a person from any social class. Even Hamlet's once-beloved jester, Yorick, is sickening in his inevitable decomposition. That death and decay is the common end of all mankind underlies Hamlet's remarks to Horatio, where he notes that Alexander and Caesar could, in death, "stop a beer barrel" or "patch a wall."

This scene echoes Act IV in which Hamlet tells Claudius that Polonius is "At supper," meaning that he is now being eaten by maggots, and describes the food chain that enables "a king [to] go a progress through the guts of a beggar." Even the gravedigger sings of his youthful days of sweet love making, which have fallen victim to "age with his stealing steps," which "hath shipped me into the land, / As if I had never been such."

When the Clown reveals that he has been digging graves since the day of Hamlet's birth, the juxtaposition of death and birth cannot be ignored. Furthermore, the coincidence of the former King's victory over old Fortinbras on that same day lends a nobility to Hamlet by right of his royal birth. Yorick's skull, while part of the comic business, is another juxtaposition of youth (Hamlet's) with death (the jester's). This blending of the personal with the political is a motif upon which the revenge theme relies heavily throughout the play.

The hand of Fate is heavy, especially in this last act. Hamlet voices his belief that "There's a divinity that shapes our ends, Rough-hew them how we will." The series of coincidences which began with the accidental murder of Polonius in Act III continues with the incredibly easy exchange of death warrants for Guildenstern and Rosencrantz in place of his own, Hamlet's capture/rescue by the pirates, his unwillingness to postpone the fencing match with Laertes, his refusal of the poisoned cup until he finishes the bout, and the subsequent mistaken poisonings of Gertrude and Laertes. All of these events feed into the sense of inevitability and injustice, qualities which heighten the tragedy in this play, as they do in classical tragedy. That Hamlet's own weaknesses compound the external circumstances help define the play as Elizabethan, in which the protagonist's flawed nature conspires to bring the universe down upon him.

Act V, Scene II (pages 109–122)

Summary

Hamlet explains to Horatio how he managed to switch the letter which Rosencrantz and Guildenstern carried, ordering Hamlet's
death, for one which ordered their own upon their arrival in England. Because of how smoothly this "changling" occurred, Hamlet
expresses his belief that fate, or some "divinity," works out the
details of our lives even when we have only a rough plan. Hamlet
says that he feels no guilt for ordering the deaths of Rosencrantz
and Guildenstern, since they so eagerly pursued his under Claudius' direction. And is it not now incumbent upon him, Hamlet
continues, to also pay back the King for his evil deeds? Hamlet
expresses his regret that he lost his temper with Laertes, whose
grief and cause mirrors his own; he vows to "court his favors," and
adds that Laertes' bravado has spurred his own resolve.

Osric enters with an invitation from Claudius to engage in a
fencing match with Laertes, whose excellent qualities and skills
are discussed at some length and agreed upon by Hamlet, Horatio,
and Osric. Osric says Claudius has wagered substantial goods that
Hamlet can beat Laertes, the duel to begin immediately if Hamlet is willing. Hamlet sends Osric to Claudius with his consent; a
Lord returns at once, asking if Hamlet will engage Laertes now or
later.

The duel is immediately arranged, with the King and Queen
set to attend; Gertrude sends word to Hamlet to be courteous to
Laertes before they begin duelling. Horatio predicts that Hamlet will
lose, but Hamlet says he has been practicing and feels confident,
despite a sense of misgiving "as would perhaps trouble a woman.".
Horatio says if Hamlet has any misgivings at all, he will postpone
the match and say Hamlet is "not fit." But Hamlet again expresses
his belief in fate, and says "readiness is all;" whatever is meant to
be will come sooner or later.

Claudius and Gertrude enter with the entourage attendant
upon the fencing match, including Laertes, whom Claudius takes
by the hand to Hamlet, urging reconciliation. Hamlet asks Laertes'
pardon, attributing any offensive acts to his well-published madness. Laertes accepts the apology "in nature," but withholds total

reconciliation until the opinions of his elders can verify that he will not diminish or relinquish his honor by making peace with Hamlet.

Claudius ascertains that Hamlet understands the wager, and Hamlet replies that Claudius has "laid the odds o' th' weaker side." Claudius admits this, but says it is only because Hamlet has improved. The pair take up foils; Laertes puts back the one Osric provides as "too heavy," and takes another. Claudius drops a pearl into a cup as added incentive for Hamlet, and says if Hamlet scores the first, second, or repays the third hit, the King will drink to him, which will signal the cannoneer to fire so that all will know of Hamlet's success.

After Hamlet's first "palpable hit," Claudius drinks, the cannons fire, and he urges Hamlet to drink; Hamlet, however, wishes to "play this bout first; set it by awhile." After the second hit, Gertrude drinks to Hamlet's success—from the poisoned cup, despite Claudius' attempts to stop her. As Laertes and Hamlet resume, they somehow exchange rapiers and are both wounded. Gertrude realizes she has been poisoned and dies; Hamlet orders the doors locked and the treachery sought out.

Laertes admits that the villainy "is here," and tells him they are both doomed, having been poisoned by the rapier, and that "the King's to blame." Hamlet then wounds Claudius with the "envenomed" point, and forces him to drink the rest of the poisoned cup and "Follow my mother." The King dies, Laertes and Hamlet forgive one another, and Laertes dies. Horatio intends to drink the rest of the cup, but Hamlet takes it from him and urges him "to tell [his] story."

Osric enters with news that Fortinbras has returned victorious from Poland. Hamlet endorses him as the next King of Denmark and then dies. Fortinbras and his retinue enter, and the Ambassador from England notes that it is too late for Claudius to thank them, that his commandment has been carried out, "That Rosencrantz and Guildenstern are dead." Horatio corrects the Ambassador: "He never gave commandment for their death." Horatio then orders the bodies placed "High on a stage" for public view, and vows to "Truly deliver" all the bloody and unnatural acts which have transpired to cause these deaths.

Fortinbras with sorrow sees that he now has the opportunity to assume the Danish throne; Horatio hints that Hamlet spoke favorably to that issue, but urges the public ceremonies commence "lest more mischance [on top of] plots and errors happen." Fortinbras orders Hamlet's body carried "like a soldier" to the stage, and says if Hamlet had had the chance, he would "have proved most royal." He orders appropriate funeral rites for Hamlet, including the firing of ordnance, which ends the play.

Analysis

For four acts, Hamlet and Laertes have not met on stage, yet their lives have been closely intertwined. Hamlet's confusing and truncated relationship with Ophelia and his inadvertent murder of Polonius have made the two young men virtual enemies. Claudius has fanned the flame of Laertes' vengeance, even setting up the sword fight in which Hamlet is to be murdered. They finally meet in Act V, Scene I, at Ophelia's graveside, where they struggle and proclaim their respective loves for the young maiden. But their reconciliation is foreshadowed several times. Hamlet asks Laertes, "What is the reason that you use me thus? I loved you ever"; and shortly thereafter he tells Horatio that he is "very sorry...That to Laertes I forgot myself," and that he plans to "court his favors." Later, Hamlet receives Gertrude's message to "use some gentle entertainment to Laertes before you fall to play," and Hamlet responds, "She well instructs me."

As they prepare to fence, Claudius takes Laertes' hand and puts it into Hamlet's, urging peace; Hamlet asks Laertes to pardon him, pleading madness. Of course, at this point, Laertes still intends to kill Hamlet, so the reconciliation is feigned. But as Laertes tells Claudius that this time he will score a hit against Hamlet, Laertes adds in an aside, "And yet it is almost against my conscience." And Gertrude's death evokes Laertes' confession to Hamlet: "Hamlet, thou art slain;...The foul practice Hath turned itself on me...Thy mother's poisoned...The King, the King's to blame." As he dies, Laertes asks Hamlet to "Exchange forgiveness with me,...Mine and my father's death come not upon thee, Nor thine on me!" Hamlet answers, "Heaven make thee free of it!"

There are several instances of irony in this act. For instance, Ophelia, almost certainly an innocent in this story fraught with betrayal and deceit, is denied a Christian burial because of the suspicious nature of her death. If her death were accidental, as it appears to be, she should have been given full holy rites. Everyone seems to love and want to protect Ophelia: Polonius, Laertes, Gertrude, Claudius—even Hamlet, though he denies it. His "get thee to a nunnery" speech suggests his desire to protect her from men, who are "arrant knaves all," not to be believed; no doubt he thinks primarily of Claudius, but also of himself, as he feigns his madness throughout the play.

At any rate, the pure maid must spend eternity "in ground unsanctified," presumably the fate shared by Polonius, Claudius, and Gertrude for their plottings. Perhaps Laertes and Hamlet will also lie in unsanctified ground for their deeds, unless their acts are done in the name of divine justice, a fine point which troubles Hamlet throughout the play. That she is killed by the "natural" world rather than by the political, which otherwise dominates the play, is further irony; she is done in by the world she claims as her own, shown most clearly by the flowers in her "mad scene."

Compounding her ultimate fate is Hamlet's admission at her funeral that he did love her more than "forty thousand brothers," despite his earlier protestations to the contrary. If Hamlet had not denied his love, perhaps she would not have gone mad, even at Polonius' death.

Laertes exhibits irony in his reluctance to fully accept Hamlet's apology, reconciling "in nature" only, "Till by some elder masters of known honor / I have a voice and precedent of peace / To keep my name ungored." Earlier, Laertes was bound to stop at nothing in seeking revenge against Claudius, whom he believed to have killed Polonius. At that time, Claudius urged Laertes to assemble his "wisest friends" to "hear and judge" whether Claudius bore any guilt. The irony is that Claudius, who urged delay and wise counsel, is guilty in principle; while Hamlet, who seeks forgiveness, is ultimately innocent—Polonius' death was accidental. In neither case is an impaneled "jury" likely to know the difference.

A final irony stems from the firing of the cannons in this act. Claudius sets up an elaborate system of signals, beginning with a toast to Hamlet's "hits," which will result in the firing of the cannons. But at the very end of the play, Fortinbras orders "soldiers' music and the rite of war" for Hamlet's passage, and orders, "Go, bid the soldiers shoot," and the stage directions indicate "a peal of ordnance" are to be shot off. What Claudius intended, in a perverse way as signals of Hamlet's success, serve at last as indication of Hamlet's death.

Just as the important events surrounding the Players' preparation and presentation of "The Mousetrap" are telescoped into a very short time frame (see Analysis for Act II), the events leading up to the sword fight are compressed. Claudius first suggests the duel to Laertes in Act IV, Scene VII. He counsels patience at Ophelia's funeral, indicating that their "last night's speech" will soon be put into action. In the next scene, Osric informs Hamlet of the King's wager , set for "immediate trial" if Hamlet agrees. He sends Osric back with his affirmative response, and a Lord returns to double check, and Hamlet again agrees to fight at once and sends the messenger back to Claudius. The royal party enters to witness the duel on page 116, and between pages 117 and 118, everyone has been mortally wounded; by the middle of page 120, Gertrude, the King, Laertes, and Hamlet are all dead. The sense of urgency is created by the increasingly brief interludes between events relevant to the duel.

When Laertes reveals to Hamlet that the treachery "is here" and that "No med'cine in the world" can save him, another motif is brought full circle: physical disease as manifestation of spiritual corruption. Evil has finally claimed everyone except Horatio (whom Hamlet barely prevents from committing suicide with the poisoned cup) and Fortinbras. The chain began with Claudius' murder of his brother in order to achieve the kingship, a political goal; and continued with Claudius' marriage to Gertrude, a personal prize.

In tandem, these two events precipitate those that follow: Polonius' death, Ophelia's madness and death, and the deaths of Rosencrantz and Guildenstern, Gertrude, Claudius, Laertes, and Hamlet. The Ghost's directive in Act I has finally been achieved.

But for all of Hamlet's hesitation, the actual revenge on Claudius is almost incidental, certainly not a premeditated part of the duel.

That Fortinbras succeeds to the Danish throne is significant: like Hamlet, he was seeking to avenge his dead father, a king; but unlike Hamlet, he did not delay and sought to act almost at once. Only the wise counsel and constructive interference of his uncle prevented war with Denmark. As it happened, Fortinbras' entrance at the finale of the sword fight is perfectly timed, and he has both revenge and royalty at the play's conclusion.

Study Questions

1. Why is there debate surrounding the nature of Ophelia's funeral?

2. How long has the gravedigger been sexton, and when did he first become employed?

3. What joking insult to the English does Shakespeare put into the gravedigger's dialogue, regarding Hamlet's madness?

4. What cause does Laertes ascribe to Ophelia's madness, which led to her death?

5. What prompts Hamlet's outburst at Ophelia's graveside?

6. What order did Claudius' letter, carried by Guildenstern and Rosencrantz, convey to the English regarding Hamlet's fate?

7. How does Hamlet justify his counterfeit command that Rosencrantz and Guildenstern are to be murdered by the English?

8. In his apology to Laertes, what does Hamlet mean when he says, "I have shot my arrow o'er the house and hurt my brother"?

9. Why does Hamlet forbid Horatio to drink the rest of the poisoned cup?

10. Who will ascend to power as the new King of Denmark?

Answers

1. The issue is whether her drowning was accidental, in which case she may have a Christian burial—which the coroner has ruled, the gravedigger says; or whether it was intentional, in which case she may not have a Christian burial. Later, the Doctor of Divinity confirms that though "Her death was doubtful," the King has ruled that her burial be Christian. Thus, the gravedigger's supposition that nobility carries special privilege is probably true in this case.

2. The gravedigger has served as sexton for thirty years; he came the "day that our last king Hamlet overcame Fortinbras. . . . that very day that young Hamlet was born."

3. The gravedigger notes that Hamlet has been sent to England to "recover his wits," but adds that if he doesn't, it will not matter because "There the men are as mad as he."

4. Laertes blames Ophelia's madness on the "wicked deed," presumably her father's murder; he calls down a "ten times treble" curse on the killer, Hamlet.

5. He feels that Laertes is trying to outdo his own grief for Ophelia with all Laertes' rantings and his leaping into the grave. He leaps in as well, and says he'll "rant as well as [Laertes]."

6. For the good of both Denmark and England, they were to cut off Hamlet's head as soon as they had read the letter.

7. He tells Horatio that "they did make love to this employment." Their "baser natures" got caught in the sword play of "mighty opposites."

8. He means that his murder of Polonius was not "a purposed evil" and that he did not intentionally harm Laertes by his action, which Hamlet attributes to his own madness.

9. He wants Horatio to tell his (Hamlet's) story so that his name will be cleared rather than "wounded."

10. Fortinbras, whom Hamlet predicts will win the election; and Fortinbras himself remarks that he has some "rights of memory in this kingdom" which he plans to take advantage of, though he "with sorrow…[embraces his] fortune."

Suggested Essay Topics

1. Compare Claudius' use of the "arranged" fencing match between Laertes and Hamlet to Hamlet's use of "The Mousetrap," and his rewriting of the letters carried by Rosencrantz and Guildenstern.

2. Discuss the professions of love and grief expressed at Ophelia's funeral by Laertes and Hamlet, as compared to similar scenes featuring Claudius, in terms of their implications for the play's outcome: who is honest, deserving, and just, among the play's key players?

SECTION SEVEN

Bibliography

Barnet, Sylvan, "Shakespeare: Prefatory Remarks," in William Shakespeare, *The Tragedy of Hamlet, Prince of Denmark*. Edward Hubler, ed. New York: Signet Classic, 1963 (viixx).

Boyce, Charles, *Shakespeare A to Z*, New York: Roundtable Press, 1990. "Hamlet," (231–234); "*Hamlet*," (234–241); "Quiney, Thomas," (529); "Shakespeare, William," (586–591).

Chute, Marchette, "Shakespeare, William," in *The New Book of Knowledge*, vol. 5 (17); Grolier, Inc., 1980. (130b–134).

DOVER · THRIFT · EDITIONS

FICTION

ADVENTURES OF HUCKLEBERRY FINN, Mark Twain. (0-486-28061-6)

THE AWAKENING, Kate Chopin. (0-486-27786-0)

A CHRISTMAS CAROL, Charles Dickens. (0-486-26865-9)

FRANKENSTEIN, Mary Shelley. (0-486-28211-2)

HEART OF DARKNESS, Joseph Conrad. (0-486-26464-5)

PRIDE AND PREJUDICE, Jane Austen. (0-486-28473-5)

THE SCARLET LETTER, Nathaniel Hawthorne. (0-486-28048-9)

THE ADVENTURES OF TOM SAWYER, Mark Twain. (0-486-40077-8)

ALICE'S ADVENTURES IN WONDERLAND, Lewis Carroll. (0-486-27543-4)

THE CALL OF THE WILD, Jack London. (0-486-26472-6)

CRIME AND PUNISHMENT, Fyodor Dostoyevsky. Translated by Constance Garnett. (0-486-41587-2)

DRACULA, Bram Stoker. (0-486-41109-5)

ETHAN FROME, Edith Wharton. (0-486-26690-7)

FLATLAND, Edwin A. Abbott. (0-486-27263-X)

GREAT AMERICAN SHORT STORIES, Edited by Paul Negri. (0-486-42119-8)

GREAT EXPECTATIONS, Charles Dickens. (0-486-41586-4)

JANE EYRE, Charlotte Brontë. (0-486-42449-9)

THE JUNGLE, Upton Sinclair. (0-486-41923-1)

THE METAMORPHOSIS AND OTHER STORIES, Franz Kafka. (0-486-29030-1)

THE ODYSSEY, Homer. (0-486-40654-7)

THE PICTURE OF DORIAN GRAY, Oscar Wilde. (0-486-27807-7)

SIDDHARTHA, Hermann Hesse. (0-486-40653-9)

THE STRANGE CASE OF DR. JEKYLL AND MR. HYDE, Robert Louis Stevenson. (0-486-26688-5)

A TALE OF TWO CITIES, Charles Dickens. (0-486-40651-2)

WUTHERING HEIGHTS, Emily Brontë. (0-486-29256-8)

ANNA KARENINA, Leo Tolstoy. Translated by Louise and Aylmer Maude. (0-486-43796-5)

AROUND THE WORLD IN EIGHTY DAYS, Jules Verne. (0-486-41111-7)

THE BROTHERS KARAMAZOV, Fyodor Dostoyevsky. Translated by Constance Garnett. (0-486-43791-4)

CANDIDE, Voltaire. Edited by Francois-Marie Arouet. (0-486-26689-3)

DOVER · THRIFT · EDITIONS

FICTION

DAISY MILLER, Henry James. (0-486-28773-4)

DAVID COPPERFIELD, Charles Dickens. (0-486-43665-9)

DUBLINERS, James Joyce. (0-486-26870-5)

EMMA, Jane Austen. (0-486-40648-2)

THE GIFT OF THE MAGI AND OTHER SHORT STORIES, O. Henry. (0-486-27061-0)

THE GOLD-BUG AND OTHER TALES, Edgar Allan Poe. (0-486-26875-6)

GREAT SHORT SHORT STORIES, Edited by Paul Negri. (0-486-44098-2)

GULLIVER'S TRAVELS, Jonathan Swift. (0-486-29273-8)

HARD TIMES, Charles Dickens. (0-486-41920-7)

THE HOUND OF THE BASKERVILLES, Arthur Conan Doyle. (0-486-28214-7)

THE ILIAD, Homer. (0-486-40883-3)

MOBY-DICK, Herman Melville. (0-486-43215-7)

MY ÁNTONIA, Willa Cather. (0-486-28240-6)

NORTHANGER ABBEY, Jane Austen. (0-486-41412-4)

NOT WITHOUT LAUGHTER, Langston Hughes. (0-486-45448-7)

OLIVER TWIST, Charles Dickens. (0-486-42453-7)

PERSUASION, Jane Austen. (0-486-29555-9)

THE PHANTOM OF THE OPERA, Gaston Leroux. (0-486-43458-3)

A PORTRAIT OF THE ARTIST AS A YOUNG MAN, James Joyce. (0-486-28050-0)

PUDD'NHEAD WILSON, Mark Twain. (0-486-40885-X)

THE RED BADGE OF COURAGE, Stephen Crane. (0-486-26465-3)

THE SCARLET PIMPERNEL, Baroness Orczy. (0-486-42122-8)

SENSE AND SENSIBILITY, Jane Austen. (0-486-29049-2)

SILAS MARNER, George Eliot. (0-486-29246-0)

TESS OF THE D'URBERVILLES, Thomas Hardy. (0-486-41589-9)

THE TIME MACHINE, H. G. Wells. (0-486-28472-7)

TREASURE ISLAND, Robert Louis Stevenson. (0-486-27559-0)

THE TURN OF THE SCREW, Henry James. (0-486-26684-2)

UNCLE TOM'S CABIN, Harriet Beecher Stowe. (0-486-44028-1)

THE WAR OF THE WORLDS, H. G. Wells. (0-486-29506-0)

THE WORLD'S GREATEST SHORT STORIES, Edited by James Daley. (0-486-44716-2)

THE AGE OF INNOCENCE, Edith Wharton. (0-486-29803-5)

FICTION

AGNES GREY, Anne Brontë. (0-486-45121-6)

AT FAULT, Kate Chopin. (0-486-46133-5)

THE AUTOBIOGRAPHY OF AN EX-COLORED MAN, James Weldon Johnson. (0-486-28512-X)

BARTLEBY AND BENITO CERENO, Herman Melville. (0-486-26473-4)

BEOWULF, Translated by R. K. Gordon. (0-486-27264-8)

CIVIL WAR STORIES, Ambrose Bierce. (0-486-28038-1)

A CONNECTICUT YANKEE IN KING ARTHUR'S COURT, Mark Twain. (0-486-41591-0)

THE DEERSLAYER, James Fenimore Cooper. (0-486-46136-X)

DEMIAN, Hermann Hesse. (0-486-41413-2)

FAR FROM THE MADDING CROWD, Thomas Hardy. (0-486-45684-6)

FAVORITE FATHER BROWN STORIES, G. K. Chesterton. (0-486-27545-0)

GREAT HORROR STORIES, Edited by John Grafton. Introduction by Mike Ashley. (0-486-46143-2)

GREAT RUSSIAN SHORT STORIES, Edited by Paul Negri. (0-486-42992-X)

GREAT SHORT STORIES BY AMERICAN WOMEN, Edited by Candace Ward. (0-486-28776-9)

GRIMM'S FAIRY TALES, Jacob and Wilhelm Grimm. (0-486-45656-0)

HUMOROUS STORIES AND SKETCHES, Mark Twain. (0-486-29279-7)

THE HUNCHBACK OF NOTRE DAME, Victor Hugo. Translated by A. L. Alger. (0-486-45242-5)

THE INVISIBLE MAN, H. G. Wells. (0-486-27071-8)

THE ISLAND OF DR. MOREAU, H. G. Wells. (0-486-29027-1)

A JOURNAL OF THE PLAGUE YEAR, Daniel Defoe. (0-486-41919-3)

JOURNEY TO THE CENTER OF THE EARTH, Jules Verne. (0-486-44088-5)

KIM, Rudyard Kipling. (0-486-44508-9)

THE LAST OF THE MOHICANS, James Fenimore Cooper. (0-486-42678-5)

THE LEGEND OF SLEEPY HOLLOW AND OTHER STORIES, Washington Irving. (0-486-46658-2)

LILACS AND OTHER STORIES, Kate Chopin. (0-486-44095-8)

MANSFIELD PARK, Jane Austen. (0-486-41585-6)

THE MAYOR OF CASTERBRIDGE, Thomas Hardy. (0-486-43749-3)

THE MYSTERIOUS STRANGER AND OTHER STORIES, Mark Twain. (0-486-27069-6)

NOTES FROM THE UNDERGROUND, Fyodor Dostoyevsky. (0-486-27053-X)

DOVER·THRIFT·EDITIONS

FICTION

O PIONEERS!, Willa Cather. (0-486-27785-2)

AN OCCURRENCE AT OWL CREEK BRIDGE AND OTHER STORIES, Ambrose Bierce. (0-486-46657-4)

THE OLD CURIOSITY SHOP, Charles Dickens. (0-486-42679-3)

THE OPEN BOAT AND OTHER STORIES, Stephen Crane. (0-486-27547-7)

ROBINSON CRUSOE, Daniel Defoe. (0-486-40427-7)

THIS SIDE OF PARADISE, F. Scott Fitzgerald. (0-486-28999-0)

THE THREE MUSKETEERS, Alexandre Dumas. (0-486-45681-1)

TWENTY THOUSAND LEAGUES UNDER THE SEA, Jules Verne. (0-486-44849-5)

WHITE FANG, Jack London. (0-486-26968-X)

WHITE NIGHTS AND OTHER STORIES, Fyodor Dostoyevsky. (0-486-46948-4)

NONFICTION

GREAT SPEECHES, Abraham Lincoln. (0-486-26872-1)

WISDOM OF THE BUDDHA, Edited by F. Max Müller. (0-486-41120-6)

NARRATIVE OF SOJOURNER TRUTH, Sojourner Truth. (0-486-29899-X)

THE TRIAL AND DEATH OF SOCRATES, Plato. (0-486-27066-1)

WIT AND WISDOM OF THE AMERICAN PRESIDENTS, Edited by Joslyn Pine. (0-486-41427-2)

GREAT SPEECHES BY AFRICAN AMERICANS, Edited by James Daley. (0-486-44761-8)

INTERIOR CASTLE, St. Teresa of Avila. Edited and Translated by E. Allison Peers. (0-486-46145-9)

GREAT SPEECHES BY AMERICAN WOMEN, Edited by James Daley. (0-486-46141-6)

ON LIBERTY, John Stuart Mill. (0-486-42130-9)

MEDITATIONS, Marcus Aurelius. (0-486-29823-X)

THE SOULS OF BLACK FOLK, W.E.B. DuBois. (0-486-28041-1)

GREAT SPEECHES BY NATIVE AMERICANS, Edited by Bob Blaisdell. (0-486-41122-2)

WIT AND WISDOM FROM POOR RICHARD'S ALMANACK, Benjamin Franklin. (0-486-40891-4)

THE AUTOBIOGRAPHY OF BENJAMIN FRANKLIN, Benjamin Franklin. (0-486-29073-5)

OSCAR WILDE'S WIT AND WISDOM, Oscar Wilde. (0-486-40146-4)

THE WIT AND WISDOM OF ABRAHAM LINCOLN, Abraham Lincoln. Edited by Bob Blaisdell. (0-486-44097-4)

DOVER · THRIFT · EDITIONS

NONFICTION

ON THE ORIGIN OF SPECIES, Charles Darwin. (0-486-45006-6)

SIX GREAT DIALOGUES, Plato. Translated by Benjamin Jowett. (0-486-45465-7)

NATURE AND OTHER ESSAYS, Ralph Waldo Emerson. (0-486-46947-6)

THE COMMUNIST MANIFESTO AND OTHER REVOLUTIONARY WRITINGS, Edited by Bob Blaisdell. (0-486-42465-0)

THE CONFESSIONS OF ST. AUGUSTINE, St. Augustine. (0-486-42466-9)

THE WIT AND WISDOM OF MARK TWAIN, Mark Twain. (0-486-40664-4)

LIFE ON THE MISSISSIPPI, Mark Twain. (0-486-41426-4)

BEYOND GOOD AND EVIL, Friedrich Nietzsche. (0-486-29868-X)

CIVIL DISOBEDIENCE AND OTHER ESSAYS, Henry David Thoreau. (0-486-27563-9)

A MODEST PROPOSAL AND OTHER SATIRICAL WORKS, Jonathan Swift. (0-486-28759-9)

UTOPIA, Sir Thomas More. (0-486-29583-4)

GREAT SPEECHES, Franklin Delano Roosevelt. (0-486-40894-9)

WALDEN; OR, LIFE IN THE WOODS, Henry David Thoreau. (0-486-28495-6)

UP FROM SLAVERY, Booker T. Washington. (0-486-28738-6)

DARK NIGHT OF THE SOUL, St. John of the Cross. (0-486-42693-9)

GREEK AND ROMAN LIVES, Plutarch. Translated by John Dryden. Revised and Edited by Arthur Hugh Clough. (0-486-44576-3)

WOMEN'S WIT AND WISDOM, Edited by Susan L. Rattiner. (0-486-41123-0)

MUSIC, Edited by Herb Galewitz. (0-486-41596-1)

INCIDENTS IN THE LIFE OF A SLAVE GIRL, Harriet Jacobs. (0-486-41931-2)

THE LIFE OF OLAUDAH EQUIANO, Olaudah Equiano. (0-486-40661-X)

THE DECLARATION OF INDEPENDENCE AND OTHER GREAT DOCUMENTS OF AMERICAN HISTORY, Edited by John Grafton. (0-486-41124-9)

THE PRINCE, Niccolò Machiavelli. (0-486-27274-5)

WOMAN IN THE NINETEENTH CENTURY, Margaret Fuller. (0-486-40662-8)

SELF-RELIANCE AND OTHER ESSAYS, Ralph Waldo Emerson. (0-486-27790-9)

COMMON SENSE, Thomas Paine. (0-486-29602-4)

THE REPUBLIC, Plato. (0-486-41121-4)

POETICS, Aristotle. (0-486-29577-X)

THE DEVIL'S DICTIONARY, Ambrose Bierce. (0-486-27542-6)

NARRATIVE OF THE LIFE OF FREDERICK DOUGLASS, Frederick Douglass. (0-486-28499-9)

DOVER · THRIFT · EDITIONS

NONFICTION

GREAT ENGLISH ESSAYS, Edited by Bob Blaisdell. (0-486-44082-6)

THE KORAN, Translated by J. M. Rodwell. (0-486-44569-0)

28 GREAT INAUGURAL ADDRESSES, Edited by John Grafton and James Daley. (0-486-44621-2)

WHEN I WAS A SLAVE, Edited by Norman R. Yetman. (0-486-42070-1)

THE IMITATION OF CHRIST, Thomas à Kempis. Translated by Aloysius Croft and Harold Bolton. (0-486-43185-1)

PLAYS

ANTIGONE, Sophocles. (0-486-27804-2)

AS YOU LIKE IT, William Shakespeare. (0-486-40432-3)

CYRANO DE BERGERAC, Edmond Rostand. (0-486-41119-2)

A DOLL'S HOUSE, Henrik Ibsen. (0-486-27062-9)

DR. FAUSTUS, Christopher Marlowe. (0-486-28208-2)

FIVE COMIC ONE-ACT PLAYS, Anton Chekhov. (0-486-40887-6)

FIVE GREAT COMEDIES, William Shakespeare. (0-486-44086-9)

FIVE GREAT GREEK TRAGEDIES, Sophocles, Euripides and Aeschylus. (0-486-43620-9)

FOUR GREAT HISTORIES, William Shakespeare. (0-486-44629-8)

FOUR GREAT RUSSIAN PLAYS, Anton Chekhov, Nikolai Gogol, Maxim Gorky, and Ivan Turgenev. (0-486-43472-9)

FOUR GREAT TRAGEDIES, William Shakespeare. (0-486-44083-4)

GHOSTS, Henrik Ibsen. (0-486-29852-3)

HAMLET, William Shakespeare. (0-486-27278-8)

HENRY V, William Shakespeare. (0-486-42887-7)

AN IDEAL HUSBAND, Oscar Wilde. (0-486-41423-X)

THE IMPORTANCE OF BEING EARNEST, Oscar Wilde. (0-486-26478-5)

JULIUS CAESAR, William Shakespeare. (0-486-26876-4)

KING LEAR, William Shakespeare. (0-486-28058-6)

LOVE'S LABOUR'S LOST, William Shakespeare. (0-486-41929-0)

LYSISTRATA, Aristophanes. (0-486-28225-2)

MACBETH, William Shakespeare. (0-486-27802-6)

MAJOR BARBARA, George Bernard Shaw. (0-486-42126-0)

MEDEA, Euripides. (0-486-27548-5)

PLAYS

THE MERCHANT OF VENICE, William Shakespeare. (0-486-28492-1)

A MIDSUMMER NIGHT'S DREAM, William Shakespeare. (0-486-27067-X)

MUCH ADO ABOUT NOTHING, William Shakespeare. (0-486-28272-4)

OEDIPUS REX, Sophocles. (0-486-26877-2)

THE ORESTEIA TRILOGY, Aeschylus. (0-486-29242-8)

OTHELLO, William Shakespeare. (0-486-29097-2)

THE PLAYBOY OF THE WESTERN WORLD AND RIDERS TO THE SEA, J. M. Synge. (0-486-27562-0)

PYGMALION, George Bernard Shaw. (0-486-28222-8)

ROMEO AND JULIET, William Shakespeare. (0-486-27557-4)

THE TAMING OF THE SHREW, William Shakespeare. (0-486-29765-9)

TARTUFFE, Molière. (0-486-41117-6)

THE TEMPEST, William Shakespeare. (0-486-40658-X)

TWELFTH NIGHT; OR, WHAT YOU WILL, William Shakespeare. (0-486-29290-8)

RICHARD III, William Shakespeare. (0-486-28747-5)

HEDDA GABLER, Henrik Ibsen. (0-486-26469-6)

THE COMEDY OF ERRORS, William Shakespeare. (0-486-42461-8)

THE CHERRY ORCHARD, Anton Chekhov. (0-486-26682-6)

SHE STOOPS TO CONQUER, Oliver Goldsmith. (0-486-26867-5)

THE WILD DUCK, Henrik Ibsen. (0-486-41116-8)

THE WINTER'S TALE, William Shakespeare. (0-486-41118-4)

ARMS AND THE MAN, George Bernard Shaw. (0-486-26476-9)

EVERYMAN, Anonymous. (0-486-28726-2)

THE FATHER, August Strindberg. (0-486-43217-3)

R.U.R., Karel Capek. (0-486-41926-6)

THE BEGGAR'S OPERA, John Gay. (0-486-40888-4)

3 BY SHAKESPEARE, William Shakespeare. (0-486-44721-9)

PROMETHEUS BOUND, Aeschylus. (0-486-28762-9)